God give them a place of
"refreshment, light, and peace."

Thomas Slatcoff

Atrocity in the Nave

A Novel

SLATCOFF
AND **COMPANY** LLC

Atrocity in the Nave   2017-6-F2.1
CS - 6908261

"Oh, my dear child, your innocence. You did nothing wrong. You didn't deserve to suffer. They stole your innocence."

Aunt Llona
Atrocity in the Nave

Description

Mozes Olah was plagued by visions of three, faceless, hallowed, figures dressed in the vestments of Roman Catholic priest. The images caused pain in his head, dreams of murders, and awkwardness with females, since his childhood in *'40'*, a coal mine patch neighborhood on the outskirts of Windber, Pennsylvania. His profession became his solace: *Criminal Investigator II, Office of Inspector General* for the modern-day City of Pittsburgh. Because of his investigative prowess, the *'Burgh* scofflaws gave Mozes the moniker *Hotshot MO*. Detailed to the *Pittsburgh Bureau of Police, Homicide Squad*, Mozes collaborated with a lone homicide detective to investigate the alleged involvement of the Mayor with the cover-up of select murders. Exposed were the deep, dark, secrets of Mozes' past.

About the Author

 Thomas Slatcoff returned to private business after he served twenty-three years in federal law enforcement and retired as a Senior Criminal Investigator. He served The People of the United States of America from the Executive Branch -

U.S. Department of Justice
Drug Enforcement Administration - Diversion Control *and*
INTERPOL - U.S. National Central Bureau

U.S. Department of Agriculture
Office of Inspector General - Office of Investigations

U.S. Department of Homeland Security
Federal Law Enforcement Training Center - Counterterrorism Division

U.S. Department of Energy
Office of Special Operations *and*
Washington Regional Counterintelligence Office

As a Federal Law Enforcement Officer, Thomas was enriched through:

> The diversity of assignments and tasks to execute and manage the day-to-day operations of fighting crime. Focus areas included employee integrity, government program fraud, public safety, national security, continuity of government operations, and Protective Service Operations – the security, safety, and continuity for members of the Presidential Cabinet.

> The diversity of co-workers, associates, and people from around the world who he had the good fortune to meet. Daily the personalities and cultures provided knowledge, experiences, and friendships to facilitate a global understanding of people and events.

Thomas used his diverse experiences, knowledge, and observations gained from private business, global government service, law enforcement, and life to create literary works to *Entertain, Inform, and Inspire*. For more about Thomas, please visit Slatcoff.com.

Other Literary Works by Thomas Slatcoff

Operation Red X, SLATCOFF AND COMPANY LLC, 2016

Atrocity in the Nave is a work of fiction.

The names, characters, and events in the book are the product of the author's imagination, or are used fictitiously and not intended as accurate representations of real incidents or people, living or dead.

The places, cities, towns, organizations, and entities are used fictitiously and not intended as accurate representations of real places, cities, towns, organizations, and entities or anyone, in any manner, associated with the same.

Published by:

Florida, USA
Contact@Slatcoff.com
www.Slatcoff.com

First Print Edition: June 2017

ISBN – 13-978-0-9971506-2-9

18

IN MEMORY

Mother,
Mary Elizabeth Sklodowski Slatcoff

and

Father,
Peter Slatcoff, Jr.

Angels then. Angels now.

Your example, continued patience, and unconditional love
built my foundation.

It supports me well. It is unshakable. It is timeless.

Thank you.

Love you.
See you when I get there.

Mary, Samantha, Lauren, Bethany

I am flattered by your belief I have something to offer others.

I am motivated by your support and enthusiasm for me.

I am inspired by your love for me.

Love you.

Jacob

I wonder …

Will you be a reader like your mother and father?

Will you read my literary works?

Will I make your list of best authors?

Love you.

You may not know how much you contributed to my literary journey.

Lauren Slatcoff

Your literary insight motivates me.
Your sharing inspires me.
I will forever cherish our coffeehouse conversations.

Thank you.

Samantha Slatcoff

Your spirited discussion made this work better.

Thank you.

Julie Cook Slatcoff
Tony Battiste

Thank you for continued motivation, insight, and discernment.

Pray for the victims of the atrocity

Prayer After an Experience of Violence...

I say to you, love your enemies and pray for those
who persecute you. (Matt 5:43)

Lord, I come to You wounded and in pain; violence has been done to me. I am in need of healing; of Your gentle touch, Your tender voice and compassionate heart, help me to transform my pain into new life.

Give me the strength and courage to live life vigorously, again and to not be afraid of stranger or friend. Turn my despair into hope, my hate into love and my anger into joy.

Let me seek to be reconciled with those who have caused me harm. Help me to forgive, as You forgave. Help me to love my enemies and pray for those who have persecuted me. Bring justice and peace to the lives of those who have done me harm. Let them see Your face and feel the warmth of Your love so that they may never injure another.

Lord, we pray for Your mercy and compassion, we live in troubled times, and the answers to our problems are not simple or easy. Send Your Spirit upon us to strengthen our resolve to root out the violence, hate, and fear in our lives. Replace it with Your forbearance and love. Create in us hearts of courage, grace us with the ability to stand against the violence of our day: the violence in ourselves, our homes, streets, and communities.

In Your name, we pray, Amen.

1   **The Point**

Mo hung his head low as he talked to himself.

"Friday morning. Again, I find it difficult. Why me God? The visions. The three figures. They create an intense religious obligation in me. An extreme religious duty compels me to do it."

Mo looked down at his hands which were larger, thicker, and stronger than the hands of his late father. One of the few memories he had of him.

He slowly said to himself in a somber tone, "Did I do it again? No. Oh, Dear God! No!"

Mo sat near the edge of the river as the thick, dense, fog rose from the Monongahela. He sat at the point of three rivers, in an old city; once the envy of the world that desired its industrial might. The world that envied the resolve of the blue-collar immigrant labor force. A workforce of proud people comprised of generations of European descendants with strong minds and stronger backs.

He was part of the ancestry, but he did not feel so proud. Unlike his ancestors, he felt he had a weak mind which forced his strong back to labor for a disingenuous cause.

The three, faceless, hallowed, figures of his dreams continued to direct *Mo*. Out of religious obligation, *Mo* followed their directions.

Mo drew his weak, tired, body to his knees. On his hands and knees, he slowly crawled to the river. At the water's edge, *Mo* dipped his dark red toned hands into the cold river. He positioned the warm, naked, body face up in the water and placed the deceased's hands, left over right, atop the body. Steam rose from the body when it met the cold river water. *Mo* nudged it into the river current. He watched it float away as he cleaned his hands of last night's labor.

The city came to life for another day while *Mo* took care of business. Aromas from the restaurants' breakfast fare started to waft through the air. The hum of commuter traffic escalated all around him. Sadly, the morning smells and sounds of the *'Burgh* did not push the dastardly, hallowed, figures out of his mind.

Mo rose from the water edge. When he turned, his mind displayed the three, faceless, hallowed, figures dressed in the vestments of Roman Catholic priest. He briefly paused in thought.

Mo continued to walk toward his bicycle and mounted it for his trek across town. Straddled over his bicycle, he paused again, longer this time. He pondered disturbing thoughts and finished with, "Oh, God, help me. I implore You, God. Help me."

With a puzzled expression on his face, *Mo* peddled off from Point State Park. He was on his way to his boring nine dollars and twenty-seven cents an hour food service job in the Strip District. He often pondered the point of his work.

Mo followed his usual route from the park and crossed over Commonwealth Place to Liberty Avenue. As usual, on the southeast corner, Officer Jo started her day shift on beat patrol.

Mo, in his usual manner, shouted, "Good morning, Officer Jo!"

Officer Jo warmly and enthusiastically responded, "Good morning *Mo*."

They exchanged warm smiles.

Office Jo pointed and shook her right index figure at him and said, "No helmet again *Mo*?"

Mo smiled mostly with contentment from the attention of a female. He continued his long stare to admire the busty, curvy, female in a tailor fitted police uniform.

"Oh, what a sight," he thought to himself.

Mo was too focused on Officer Jo and not the motoring traffic. There was a sharp blast of a car horn which interrupted his stare. The blare of the horn broke his focus, and he fixed his attention back to the roadway and the early morning commuter traffic.

As *Mo* navigated the route, one of the hallowed figures appeared. It was the *Teacher*. The apparition hovered alongside *Mo*. Its vestments gently rose and fell from the wind encapsulation. *Mo* was speechless as he continued to peddle along.

"*Mo*, forget about her. We don't go after law enforcement officers," said the *Teacher*. "Do you hear me *Mo*? No law enforcement officers. Too much attention will come our way. We don't want that."

Mo did not respond. In a groove, he began to rapidly pedal down the bike lane on Liberty Avenue on his way to the *Strip*. He was amused, all the green lights gave him the right of way to the early morning commuter, cross, traffic. He was on time for his 7 a.m. start at the coffee shop.

2   The Morning Routine

It was a typical cold January day in western Pennsylvania. December was mild, with no snow for the traditional Catholic Christmas. January introduced old man winter to the *'Burgh*. For the Orthodox Christmas, the weather forecast predicted seven to ten inches of snow from a massive winter storm brought on by the lake-effect snows from Lake Erie.

Mozes took his right hand out from under the warm covers, reached over to the bedside table, and picked up his cellphone. He pressed the control button once to display the *Enter passcode* screen and tapped in the seven-digit code to unlock the phone. He tapped the alarm clock app, found the button next to 5 a.m., and silenced the annoying alarm. He fumbled more and turned off three other alarms. He returned his hands under the warm covers, cellphone still in hand. Mozes snuggled into the comfort and pulled the blankets tight. He wanted to remain in the warm, comfortable, bed.

It was now 5:15 a.m., Mozes threw the covers back and swung his legs to the side of the bed. He sat at the edge, and his warm feet hit the cold, wood, floor. He paused for a minute as he recalled the dream from which he woke. He wondered what caused him to dream of murders. Dreams he had since his youth. And throughout the day, with no rhyme or reason, visions continued to appear to Mozes. In the moony interludes, both the dreams and visions cast him as *Mo*. He struggled unsuccessfully since his youth to bar the dreams and visions from his attention.

The visions first appeared to Mozes when he was a child and lived in *Mine 40*, a coal mine patch neighborhood, some eighty miles east of Pittsburgh. It was a model, nineteenth century, coal mine patch neighborhood, critical to the industrial might of the United States of America, on the outskirts of Windber, a company coal town, in the then bustling bituminous coalfields of rural northeast Somerset County, southwest Pennsylvania. Locals called the neighborhood '*40*'.

Mozes, in his mind, replayed his first vision of the three, faceless, hallowed, figures. The replay had the clarity and freshness of the apparitions first appearance when Mozes, at six years, played in the shadow of the boney pile, on the '*40*' playground. Mozes was alone at the playground, next to the company store, and dusk gave way to a cover of darkness.

Mozes swung on an old, wooden seat, swing attached by two rusty, thick, link, chains. It squeaked with every leg pump from exposure to the year-round four-season weather. As he gained momentum and height, the three, faceless, hallowed, figures first appeared to Mozes. The three figures appeared in the air and hovered. Startled, Mozes stopped pumping to slow the swing to jump off and flee to the top of Third Street, to his home and the safety of his mother and father. Mozes seemed to lack self-control and became subject to the command of the vision, the hallowed figures.

The hallowed figures descended to the ground as the swing slowed. Mozes became calm and immediately named them all. One, *All-Seeing*. Another *Teacher*. The third, *Guiding*. He never knew the reason for the enforced monikers; he just knew they fit. In turn, the hallowed figures called him *Mo*. From when they first appeared, Mozes and the hallowed figures started to run together. Mozes was never in control of the visions or the dreams.

What troubled Mozes was the memory when he tried to explain the dreams and visions to the company doctor. His mother arranged the doctor visit to identify the cause of the phenomenon. He tried to put into words the vivid dreams of murders and what the faceless, hallowed, figures told him to do. It was difficult for him. The company doctor was dismissive.

Within, Mozes rolled a memory.

"The characters of the visions in my head were very, very, very bad people. Sick people. Terrible people. I knew, but the doctor didn't. He didn't understand how the visions compelled me to do what they told me to do. The doctor said the dreams and visions were a figment of my imagination and I was a child with a keen imagination. The doctor at the company hospital didn't help me. Even at a young age, I sensed the company doctor knew more than what he diagnosed. It seemed the lack of a diagnosis also troubled mother."

Mozes stood up and moved off to the bathroom for his morning grooming. A shower, shave, blow dry and sculpture that left not a hair out of place. He finished the grooming with a liberal spray of cologne.

In the oversized walk-in closet, Mozes selected his attire for the day. He retrieved a finely tailored, solid dark blue, one hundred percent, pure wool, suit; a well starched and pressed long-sleeved white shirt with French cuffs and a stylish blue tie, with red stripes, to bring the ensemble together. He accented the French cuffs with a pair of artistic cuff links depicting a Baltimore and Ohio Railroad red and black steam locomotive on a white background. These he acquired on one of his many trips in search of antiques.

Mozes paused with memory after he had suited.

"I fashioned myself after the manikins in the windows of the locally owned iconic department store in the downtown business area of Johnstown, a steel mill town near Windber. One of the few memories from my childhood in *'40'* was when the family shopped 'downtown' for Christmas. At that time, the family finances only afforded me to window shop. A situation that then, caused me to look jealously at all who were well-dressed and appeared to mimic the manikins. It was then, as a youth, I committed to myself I would change my social station."

Mozes continued in thought.

"Those days are gone now. I no longer have to window shop. I am financially affluent; an economic level that provides me the opportunity to imitate the current fashion styles displayed in prominent men's magazines or designer clothing from branded manufacturers of men's clothing. Private haberdasheries in New York City, Miami, London, and Hong Kong are now my norm. What I avoid are the Pittsburgh men's shops. I detest being out and about the *'Burgh* and dressed the same as someone else."

Back from his thoughts, Mozes moved through the bedroom. He first stopped at the nightstand, retrieved his cellphone, and clipped it to his belt on his left side.

Mozes next moved to his dresser and picked up his Rolex watch and clasped the heavy jewelry onto his right wrist. He took the keys, loaded them into the right front pants pocket and arranged them so not to create a bulge. He took his small wallet, unclipped the paper bills and counted them. Mozes wanted to avoid pecuniary embarrassment in the event of a romantic interlude with a fair lady of European descent during his day. Something the *'Burgh* served up well even after years of inter-ethnic marriages. He clipped the money back to the small wallet and placed it into his left front pants pocket and adjusted it to avoid the bulge.

He paused and stared at himself in the dresser mirror. He shook his head because he did not understand himself.

Within, he wondered an obtuse thought of himself.

"Why is it so difficult for me? I desire female companionship, but it's so awkward with them. Ever since my high school days, I've had pain, excruciating pain, in my head, every time I think about female companionship."

Mozes opened the top right dresser drawer, moved some underwear around and retrieved a 9 mm, semi-automatic, Beretta Model 92 FS, pistol and a plastic belt clip-on holster. This was his duty weapon. He snugged it up on his right-hand side hip careful not to wrinkle the heavy starched and sharply pressed lines of his white shirt. He reached back into the underwear drawer and retrieved a pair of cased handcuffs. He clipped the cuffs to his left side, to the rear of his telephone. He went back into the drawer a third time and retrieved a two-magazine ammo pouch and snugged it to the front of his phone. Finally, Mozes took a gold color shield affixed to a leather holder and clipped it to his right side, in front of his duty weapon. The symbol provided visible identification to those who saw his concealed carry duty weapon by accident or in the course of his duties.

Next, Mozes retrieved a leather credential case, a protective carrying case for his law enforcement credential and opened it. On the left was another gold, law enforcement shield and on the right, was an identification card. The top centered, three, gold, embossed, lines displayed *City of Pittsburgh, Pennsylvania, Office of Inspector General, Investigations*. Mozes' photograph, name, title, statutory authority, and signature, and the name and signature of the Inspector General were all displayed. The ID card was used to identify himself during his official duties and conveyed law enforcement powers to Mozes within the city limits of the *'Burgh*. In the dim light, he read the inscription to himself, then slowly closed the case and gingerly placed it into his left rear pocket of his suit pants. Mozes was almost ready for duty.

Last, but not least, from his dresser drawer, with his left-hand, Mozes took a primly folded, ironed, handkerchief monogrammed **MO** and placed it in the right, inside, suit jacket, pocket. He strategically placed it there, so he had to retrieve it with his left-hand. He used this handkerchief when he found himself in the company of a fair Pittsburgh lady in need of his emotional support. This freed his right hand, his dominant hand, to comfort the lady in need with a soft, gentle, touch, strategically placed as necessary. Mozes was perpetually poised.

He declared to himself, "Despite the awkwardness, I'll be ready."

Mozes also used this handkerchief during the performance of his official duties; as he interrogated suspects, male or female, young or old, and diverse ethnic backgrounds, all suspected of wrongdoing. Mozes fashioned his own interview and interrogations tactics and methods from a time-honored human relations course. It was common for Mozes to swirl the suspect's emotions to the point of crying when he used the self-developed tactics. The suspect's crying signaled their desire to confess their wrongdoing. At that moment, he moved closer to the suspect, retrieved the handkerchief with his left hand, and offered it to the crying suspect. He used his right hand to touch the suspect's shoulder or arm, to draw the suspect into his comfort. From the position of support, he encouraged the suspects to tell the truth to someone who would listen and understand why they committed the crime for which they were suspect. He was sincere when he consoled them. He held the office record for the number of signed, written, confessions obtained from suspects and used to prevail at trials. His success suggested the operation of supernatural influences.

Colleagues of Mozes said he overdressed for his duties as Investigator II with the OIG where his primary responsibility was the investigation of personnel misconduct cases. Mozes admirably shrugged off their unsolicited critique with a smirk. He knew his colleagues did not get it. He was okay with that.

Mozes took one final look in the dresser mirror and noticed a little lint on his suit jacket near the top button. As he picked the lint, he saw a couple of his fingernails were dirty about the cuticles and nail beds. He immediately went to the bathroom sink and washed his hands but the soap and warm water, with hand-to-hand agitation, did not remove the dark red color. Bewildered, he picked up a fingernail brush, made a substantial lather on the brush, then vigorously scrubbed the dark red stains and removed them. He rinsed the nailbrush and set it aside to dry. He thoroughly dried his hands and returned the wet hand towel to the towel rack to dry. He carefully inspected his hands; they were void of any red color. He turned the light out and walked out of the bathroom.

Mozes moved through the bedroom. He paused to reminisce in silence as he stared at the bed. He pulled himself out of the silent pause and continued. He turned the lights out, and the rhythmic sound of the ceiling fan started to slow. He walked out of the bedroom.

Mozes pulled his solid black, pure wool, winter topcoat off the antique, wooden, hall tree by the front door. He flung the custom fitted, wool, overcoat around him, floated into it, and adjusted the fit. Mozes did not button the coat. Tactical readiness required it to be open so he could access his duty sidearm when necessary. The open coat was also jaunty. He crushed the pockets to check for his supple, black, sheepskin leather, gloves and nodded to himself in the affirmative. He retrieved his blue, silk, scarf; a custom-tailored scarf made to match the blue color of his eyes. The tailors who worked for the private Haberdashers often designed fashion accessories to highlight his sexy, blue, eyes. He adjusted the silk scarf about his neck.

Mozes took a final look at himself in the decorative, full-length, mirror by the front door. He was content with his appearance. His morning routine made him visually suitable to engage the day."

This routine was another youthful commitment Mozes made to himself. At an early age, Mozes told himself he would never do work that made him dirty like the coal miners who walked the streets and allies of *'40'* on their way home from their work at the mine.

Mozes was not stuck-up, his humble beginnings prohibited such a selfish attitude. Rather, his youthful commitment was to fulfill the desire of his father, as said to him by his mother, which was her passion too. Mozes' father wanted Mozes to do better than he did. Mozes' father worked hard to give Mozes the opportunity to have a profession in which he wore a suit. Both his mother and father believed the suit signified a white collar professional job, void of the dirt they associated with a blue color coal miner profession.

Mozes closed his apartment door, double-checked it locked, and turned into the hallway.

3   Mental Preparation

Mozes sauntered down the hallway to the elevator. He pressed the down arrow button and waited for the elevator to arrive on the third floor.

As he waited, Mozes studied his reflection in the wall of mirrors that decorated the elevator alcove. He did not notice the female tenant from apartment 3C joined him until a sexy, Bulgarian-accented, voice sounded.

"Good morning Mozes. How are you today?"

Mozes immediately stopped looking at himself and turned to the direction of the sexy voice.

"Good morning Viktorija. I'm fine. Thank you. How are you?"

Viktorija drew out her sexy, Bulgarian, accent.

"I'm doing okay."

Mozes studied her beauty. He slowly looked up from her designer, leather, high-heeled, short boots; her bare shins and her thick, wool, coat that struggled to hold her curvaceous torso. He briefly paused at her breast, then moved up to her lips and stopped at her eyes. He laid his blue eyes on her blue eyes and the seductiveness of her blue eyes held him.

"You look stunning today as usual."

Again, the sexy, Bulgarian-accented, voice sounded.

"Oh, come on Mozes. You're too kind to me. Thank you."

In a rare show of boldness, in the company of a female, Mozes said, "No. Look in the mirror at yourself. If you weren't with the Doctor, I'd ask you out."

"Well, Mozes, the doctor left me. He stopped coming around. He didn't call for about three months, and he didn't return my calls." She paused a moment and continued. "I don't know. I'm not dating him anymore. That I know."

The elevator arrived, and the bell sounded as the doors opened. Mozes stepped aside and motioned for Viktorija to enter first. His hand slid into the door pocket to hold it open.

"Thank you, Mozes. You're such a gentleman."

Viktorija stepped into the elevator, turned, and positioned herself on the rear wall. She looked up to Mozes.

"Mozes, you blushed. How sweet."

Mozes, with a broad grin and flushed cheeks, moved into the elevator. He reached in front of her to the control panel, pushed the first-floor button, and the doors closed. The elevator started to descend with a jerk. The bump caused Viktorija to fall into Mozes. Mozes caught her with a soft, gentle, touch of his large, strong, hands. He slid his hands down her back and around her petite waist. He steadied her with a tug of his hands and then held her.

The moment had Viktorija unrestrained. She felt aloft.

"Oh. Oh. Excuse me," Viktorija said in an uncontrolled mumble.

Slowly, Viktorija started to move out of Mozes' large, strong, hands. Mozes intensified his sexy, blue-eyed, gaze into her large, dazzling, blue eyes lightly accented with makeup that complemented her big blues and her naturally bronzed complexion. Mozes' hot blues threw a spell over Viktorija. With their eyes locked, she stopped, and they looked longingly into each other's eyes.

The sound of the elevator bell announced its arrival at the first floor. The sound broke the spell and Mozes forced Viktorija to stand erect. She wobbled as Mozes continued to support her until she snapped back from his spell.

Slowly Viktorija said, "You're strong."

All the while, Mozes savored the aroma of Viktorija's perfume. The sweet scent caused a passionate encounter for the start of his day. He delighted in her attention which he believed he created by his spell.

Mozes motioned for Viktorija to exit first when the doors opened. A bit exhausted from the encounter she slowly walked out. Mozes followed, and they walked to the front door of the apartment building.

"Let me get that."

Mozes controlled the door for Viktorija to exit the apartment building. He followed behind her.

Viktorija turned to Mozes. Her soft, sexy, Bulgarian accent sounded.

"Thank you, Mozes. You have a good day. I know I will now."

Her plump lips, accented by a light application of a conservative, red, lipstick, created a seductive smile.

"You have a good day Viktorija," Mozes slowly said.

Viktorija slowly turned and walked toward the bus stop.

Mozes continued to stare at her. Her thick, winter, coat struggled to conceal her curvaceous shell, and her derriere aristocratically moved side to side. A near perfect posture accentuated her confidence. She appeared perfectly poised and sure of herself.

A gust of cold, winter, wind shivered Mozes and broke his hypnotic stare of Viktorija's covered beauty. He turned and walked to the apartment building parking lot. There he entered his vehicle, a black over black, Porsche Cajun GTS Turbo. He started the SUV and allowed it to warm up before he gently placed the leather wrapped, console, gear selector in drive, and eased out of the parking lot.

Mozes slowly moved along in the surface street morning rush hour traffic. He used the time to prepare himself mentally for the day. First, he cleared his mind of the early morning, dreamy, interlude with Viktorija. Then he inhaled deeply and held it. In a controlled manner, he exhaled. He continued with every inhale and exhale longer than the one before. He continued his deep breathing and visualized his day to mentally organized his schedule and prioritized his tasks.

Mozes turned right onto Grant Street, and the three, faceless, hallowed, figures filled his Porsche, the *All-Seeing* in the front and the *Teacher* and the *Guiding* in the rear. They said nothing, only chanted. They too seemed to prepare themselves for the day.

Mozes stopped for a red light on Grant Street, one block from the United States Federal Courthouse building, for the Western District of Pennsylvania. He broke the silence, "What is it today?"

Before the figures answered Mozes, he jack-rabbited from the traffic light; his reaction to the automobile horns which sounded from behind. He turned his attention back to the vision and listened to the *Teacher*.

"*Mo*, we all saw how you looked at her. You thought it might work with her. It didn't work in the past."

Mozes focused his eyes on the congested morning rush hour traffic.

"Why not? Help me work it out."

There was no reply. Mozes looked about the car; the faceless, hallowed, figures were gone. He rubbed and massaged the nape of his neck in an attempt to ease the tension brought on by the sharp pain that moved through his head.

Mozes continued to operate his SUV on Liberty Avenue and into the Strip District to a nondescript warehouse. There he maneuvered his personal vehicle into a parking spot and turned it off. Mozes rubbed and massaged the nape of his neck, exited the SUV, closed the door, and locked it. He walked to the employee entrance of the OIG office building and unlocked the door with his city government key card and entered.

4   "Thank God it's Friday."

Mozes walked down the stark hallway. It quickly gave way to a bullpen-designed office setting with cubicles. Ten cubicles positioned in the middle of the office space, two rows of five each. These were the offices for an Investigator I. Along the inner wall were three private offices. These were the offices for an Investigator II. To the front were two large offices. The larger of the two was the Inspector General (IG). The other was the Deputy Inspector General (DIG). From the cubicles to the front offices, space increased in size. The size dictated by an archaic City of Pittsburgh personnel rule that required a certain amount of square footage per office per position title.

The office staff included the IG, the DIG, two Investigator IIs and eight Investigator Is. This was short of the budgeted staff ceiling by one Investigator II and two Investigator I positions. Office scuttlebutt was the IG used the Investigator II vacancy as an advantage over the Investigator I staff as an empty promise of promotion. Office rumor labeled this the IG's crude management technique to retain staff. The two Investigator I positions were open because the IG could not find competent, responsible, productive applicants to fill the position. He continued to interview prospective candidates, but prospects were unable to stand up to the IG's grueling interview questions.

The City of Pittsburgh electorate, through a referendum, overwhelming voted to create a statutory OIG due to blatant corruption by the Pittsburgh political machine.

Criminologists from a famed Department of Criminology, of a nearby state college, believed the political corruption was due in part to the economic recession that began in late 2006 and the subsequent real estate bubble of the same period. The Federal government spouted statistics to show the recession was over. The government's position was in direct conflict with people from outside Washington D.C., who, from all walks of life, demonstrated hard cold personal life challenges as evidence of the opposite.

Some criminologists believed the political corruption started in the late 1950s or early 1960s and simply went underground when government watchdog groups called attention to it at the end of the 1970s.

Still, other criminologists believed the political corruption dated back to the end of the 1800s when key immigrant entrepreneurs forged industrial empires and monopolies up and down the three rivers. They believed the political corruption continued for over one hundred and fifty years. These criminologists surmised, from then to modern times, the political corruption continued unabated as an ongoing way to manage the day-to-day operations of government. For the most part, it was kept undercover and only surfaced during difficult economic times.

The criminologists, who believed the political corruption was a cancer to the City of Pittsburgh for over one hundred and fifty years, gave these examples:

In the 1970s, political corruption surfaced due to an economic collapse caused by the decline in demand for steel made in the United States of America. Cheaper production costs, particularly from Japan and China, were the primary cause of the decrease in demand. Though the long-standing Pittsburgh steel giants blamed the decline in orders for the increased labor costs the various unions continually demanded at every labor contract renewal.

Regardless of the cause, the economic collapse placed the City of Pittsburgh's big business and political machine into disarray and conflict. The political machine continued to demand extortion payments from the big companies. The big companies refused to pay the extortion payments. They did not have the money due to the decline in orders. Also, they did not need to sway politicians to perform favors to 'ease the wrath' of city regulators who inhibited their bottom line. The failure to *pay to play* caused the political machine to level the wrath of government regulators on the large enterprises. The regulators imposed repetitive fines that progressively increased with every violation. The fines resulted in enormous sums. The enormous sums depleted the cash reserves of the big businesses.

When challenged for only having two examples these criminologists noted the study of political crime in the United States of America was a relatively new discipline. This was due in large part to the political pressure not to study political crime or political corruption.

Finally, in the 1970s, from the leadership of the Federal government and the Jimmy Carter Administration, the study of political crime started. President Carter established Office of Inspectors General throughout the Federal government to fight fraud, waste, and abuse within the departments of the Executive Branch. This practice eased political pressure on the state, county, and local governments to study political crime and to combat political crime or corruption at all levels of government.

Even so, throughout the United States of America, areas remained where the political machine and its corrupt practices still existed. The City of Pittsburgh was one of those areas. The City of Pittsburgh's corrupt political machine continued business as usual.

In modern day Pittsburgh, the political machine continued to shake down big business. The modern day political machine, descendants of the former political machine, did not understand why big companies did not pay as they pressured their *pay to play* policy.

Failure to pay produced a lack of cash flow for the political machine. The political machine concocted a tedious procedure to skim money from the city treasury. It too failed to produce a cash flow of *'other people's money.'*

As such, the political machine turned to small businesses for the lucrative *pay to play* cash flow. Small businesses were unable to pay the exorbitant sums as demanded by the political machine. Their businesses simply did not have the cash flow to sustain the payments. The extortion demands forced a large percentage of small businesses out of business. Like their predecessors, the current political machine was without business savvy. They did not understand how business cash flow worked. They were too accustomed to the access and use of *'other people's money.'*

To abate the shrinking profits, the cocky, avaricious members of the political machine launched a scheme against small businesses. First, the political machine directed regulators to levy fictitious violations against the small business owners. When the fines went unpaid, the City Attorney filed civil charges to litigate for payments. When the fines continued to go unpaid, the City Attorney levied a lien against whatever assets the small business owner had, both business and personal assets, including their individual homes. Still unable to pay, the City Attorney turned the debt over to a collection agency for seventy cents of every dollar the collection agency collected. Once this money was in the city treasury, the political machine systematically skimmed it from the treasury.

The debt collectors maintained a steady and relentless assault on the small business owners to collect the monies. This stripped the small business owners of all their assets and many of the small business owners, both males and females, went into the government social, financial, *public assistance program subculture* to survive. Once productive citizens became recipients of the top five government welfare programs – section 8 housing, welfare, food stamps, Medicaid and the Lifeline Program, a discounted cellular telephone.

Today was Friday. Only two staff members were in the office, the DIG and an Investigator I, the minimal staff the IG maintained on Fridays. The other ten Investigators were off from work, their compressed workweek day off. The IG's policy for a compressed workweek allowed staff to work 4 ten hour days for their 40-hour workweek. It established Friday as the compressed workweek day off.

The Mayor's policy for a compressed workweek required all city entities and organizations to have two staff members in their respective offices during regular business hours, 8 a.m. to 5 p.m., Monday through Friday. At least one of the two had to be at the management level and the compressed day off had to be the same day of the week, every week, for all the employees.

To adhere to the Mayor's policy, all Investigator I and II staff rotated the coverage for Fridays. The DIG, a management level employee, always worked the compressed day off because the IG did not place himself in the rotation.

Mozes stopped by the office to drop off a case file. He wanted to return it to the office, so it was not out of the office any longer than overnight just in case someone needed it.

Management did not hesitate to summon investigators back to the office to return files even on their day off. This happened to Mozes once when he was enjoying his compressed day off at the casino, 30 miles south of the *'Burgh*. He was winning at a quarter machine when the IG management summoned him to return a file he signed out. He left the hot machine and contended with lunch hour traffic on a Friday afternoon, from the casino to his apartment on Fifth Avenue, then across town to the Strip District office. He wanted no risk of this type of inconvenience ever again.

As Mozes walked by the DIG's office, he observed the closed door. This struck Mozes as odd. He continued through the bullpen, to the file room. The motion sensor light switch caused the lights to come on as he entered. He went directly to the file cabinet to return the file to the proper holder and position, closed the drawer and quickly exited the room.

Mozes retraced his path into the office. In the bullpen area, he noticed there was no one present for coverage.

Mozes thought, "She's probably in the restroom."

He continued to walk through the front office area. He passed the DIG's office, and the office door was still closed. Again, this struck Mozes as odd.

Mozes thought, "Maybe he stepped out to get coffee."

Mozes continued to walk out of the office to his vehicle. He wondered, "Are the office rumors about those two true. Are they in a romantic relationship? The DIG should know better.

OIG supervisors cannot have a romantic relationship with their subordinates. I won't want to be in his shoes. Right there in the office. Is that why I didn't see them in the office? Is that why his office door was closed? It's my day off. I'm out of here. It's not my concern why no one is in the office or if something is going on behind the DIG's closed door. Thank God it's Friday."

The expression *"Thank God it's Friday"* caused Mozes to chuckle to himself. He remembered his fraud investigator training days at the Federal Law Enforcement Training Center (FLETC) in Glynco, Georgia. Mozes attended the Inspector General Criminal Investigator Training Program through the sponsorship of the FLETC State, Local and Tribunal Division. There he heard the expression from the blind man who tended the small convenience store in the classroom building. The blind man loudly exclaimed, in a thick southern drawl, *"Thank God it's Friday"* numerous times throughout the morning class breaks. The blind man's signature expression used to amuse all the students and instructors.

Mozes entered his vehicle, started it and sat for a minute to let it warm up. He gently slid the center, console, shifter to reverse, checked his backup camera and eased out of the parking space. There was a loud thump on the passenger side door as he was about to shift into drive. He looked in the direction of the noise and did not see anything but a familiar scent permeated his Porsche. The smell was sweet and light, not overpowering. He knew he had experienced this smell before. He took a short inhale.

"Mm, that's so sweet."

Spellbound, he heard a faint knocking on the front passenger window. The knocking, persisted and got louder, brought Mozes out of his spell. He looked disoriented as the scent dissipated. Finally, Mozes looked over to the front passenger window and saw a uniformed police officer. He electronically lowered the window.

"Hi there. How are you?"

"How am I? How are you? Are you feeling okay? Did you pass out there?"

"No. I'm okay. I may need a little coffee. Would you like to join me?"

"Are you sure? It looks like you passed out."

"No. I'm good. I'm on my way to Gheorghi's Joe's for some coffee."

"Okay. Have a nice day."

"Thank you. You too."

The Police Officer walked away, and Mozes touched the one-touch, electronic window control to close the passenger side window. He slid the console-mounted, gear selector to drive and eased out of the parking lot onto Smallman Street to make his way to Gheorghi's Joe and some coffee. At Smallman and 27th, stopped at the stop sign, he rubbed and massaged the nape of his neck in an attempt to ease the tension brought on by the sharp pain moving through his head.

5   Coffee on the *Strip*

Mozes turned left onto Penn Avenue from 27th Street. He continued to Gheorghi's Joe, a long established coffee shop on the *Strip*. There was always congestion on the *Strip*, more so on Fridays when Penn Avenue street parking filled in early. A block away from Gheorghi's Joe, Mozes glided into a street parking space. After he had adjusted his Porsche Cayenne, he turned it off, exited, and locked it.

He walked by the parking kiosk and smiled and thought to himself, "I'll only be a few minutes. I just want to get a cup of coffee and go. I'm not going to register with the *'Burgh*."

The new city street parking kiosks required drivers to register with the city. To street park, drivers first had to enter the vehicle's license plate number. The method of payment was a credit or debit card or quarters. Most users did not realize the city parking procedures documented their movement around the *'Burgh* for the government. This at the suggestion of an obscure Federal agency within the U.S. Department of Homeland Security.

He shook his head and continued to Gheorghi's Joe.

Mozes entered the coffee shop and walked directly to the front counter. He greeted the clerk behind the counter.

"Hello. Good morning. How are you?"

In an uneven tone, the clerk replied, "Fine. What can I get you?"

"I'll have a large coffee. Plain. Please."

"Okay."

"Where's Ronda?"

"Don't know."

"Is she off today? Usually, she works on Fridays."

"Don't know."

"What's your name?"

The clerk walked back to Mozes with a cup of coffee in her hand and extended it to him.

"Here's your coffee."

She ignored his question.

"Thank you. You're not very talkative."

"Can I get you anything else sir?"

Again, she avoided Mozes attempt to converse.

"Not today."

"Next," the clerk summoned.

Mozes moved out of the way of the next customer, turned and walked to the cash register to pay.

"Good morning sir. What did you get?"

"Good morning. A large coffee."

"Okay. Anything else for you?"

"No. Nothing else, thanks."

"That'll be $2.57."

"There you go."

Mozes handed the cashier a five-dollar bill. The cashier handed back the change and said, "Thank you. You have a beautiful day."

"You as well."

Mozes started to walk away from the register and then jerked back.

"Where's Ronda today? Doesn't she work on Fridays?"

"Have a nice day sir. Thank you. Next."

The cashier also ignored the questions from Mozes.

Mozes was taken aback and put off by the unusual crass behavior of the store employees. Their attitudes and shortness were not the usual demeanor for employees at Gheorghi's Joe. It was not how Ronda talked to him. He walked outside.

Off to the left of the front door, Gheorghi, the owner, stood on the street. Gheorghi saw Mozes and greeted him in a somber tone.

"Hello, Mozes. How are you today?"

Mozes was puzzled as to why Gheorghi was not his usual enthusiastic self.

"Hello, Gheorghi. I'm fine. Thank you. How are you today?"

"Okay."

"Gheorghi, you don't seem yourself. Your clerks, they have somewhat of an attitude today. Where's Ronda?"

"You don't know? You work with the city police and you don't know?"

"Know what Gheorghi?"

"Ronda was found dead today. Murdered. The Police were here early this morning and interviewed all the employees. I opened an hour late. They told all of us, all the staff, not to talk to anyone about their questions or Ronda."

"Well, your employees aren't talking. They aren't saying anything to me. I guess they aren't rude now that I know."

"Yeah. We were all shaken up about this. The Police Detective said this wasn't the only murder he was investigating. He alluded to multiple, brutal, murders in the city over the last six or seven months. All appeared to be related."

"What? There wasn't anything on the local news about a murder spree, about brutal murders."

"Don't you talk to the other officers? Don't you people have briefings? Roll call? What the hell goes on in the police bureau?"

"Gheorghi, I don't work with the police. I'm employed with the Office of Inspector General. I don't know what goes on in the Bureau of Police."

Gheorghi was surprised and confused.

"What? Where? What is the Office of Inspector General? What is that?"

"Yes, the Office of Inspector General. Our mission is to combat the fraud, waste, and abuse within all city departments and organizations. We police the employees of the city, to give you a thumbnail sketch."

"Is that right. Well, I'll be. I bet you keep busy. Oh, I bet you keep real busy."

"When you talk about these murders, Gheorghi I don't know any more than what I hear from the news outlets. So, Ronda?"

"She was found floating in the Ohio River. The police officer gave up no more details than that. We all asked, but he said nothing more."

"She was a pleasant person, a friendly person."

"How do you know her, Mozes?"

"From coming here."

"Mozes, please excuse me. I must go back in. You have a good day."

Gheorghi mumbled to himself as he walked away from Mozes and toward the front door to the store.

"You work for the Inspector General. The city has an Office of Inspector General. How did I miss that?"

"We have a page on the city's website. Go check us out. You have a good day Gheorghi."

"Okay. I'll have to check."

Gheorghi entered his store.

6   Ringing Church Bells

Mozes walked down Penn Avenue to his vehicle. In the distance was the muffled sound of ringing church bells. These were the church bells from the Saint Stanislaus Kostka Church; a historic church built from 1891 – 1892. It was one of the city's oldest churches and listed on the National Registry of Historic Places. It was a prime example of the so-called "Polish Cathedral" style of churches. Today, the ringing church bells sounded to notify the community the time of day as the bells had since 1892.

Mozes dropped his coffee cup and clutched his ears when he heard the faint church bells. He pressed his hands hard against his ears to avoid the noise, no matter how faint and his gait slowed as he focused on suppressing the noise. He began to stagger about the sidewalk and pedestrians moved out of his way, so they did not collide. It appeared Mozes was out of control, unable to manipulate his muscles from the excruciating pain caused by the ringing church bells. He finally came to an abrupt stop in the middle of the sidewalk and started to buckle over.

At that moment, the ringing bells stopped. Cautiously, Mozes began to stand up straight. In a guarded fashion, he slowly released the pressure of his hands on his ears. He slowly moved his hands to be able to reapply pressure if the ringing church bells started again.

Mozes said to himself, "Will this ever stop?"

This continued to happen since Mozes' childhood in his birth town. There it was much, more excruciating because of the intensity of the sound from the number of churches. All twelve churches struck their bells at the same time; on the half hours, once. On the hour, they rang the number of times for the hour.

"Will this ever stop? Oh, the pain, the pain," Mozes said.

Mozes saw numerous doctors in attempts to alleviate or at least reduce the pain. His doctor visits started in his childhood when his mother saw him buckle over with pain and discovered it happened every time he heard ringing church bells. Mozes' description of the pain, the length of time he was troubled by the suffering, and the fact ringing church bells brought on the torment, befuddled all the doctors he visited. Furthermore, when the ringing church bells silenced, the pain ceased. Over time, the best the collection of physicians diagnosed was a conditioned response to pain brought on by the ringing church bells. Some of the doctors even referred to it as a Pavlovian conditioning. None of the doctors pinpointed the stimulus. They were at a loss for any deeper explanation of this mysterious ailment that afflicted Mozes.

When Mozes heard ringing church bells while in church, the bells did not bother him. This was unusual to Mozes and at times spooked Mozes. The fact remained; when he was in a church, he had no pain when he heard ringing church bells. It was almost as if the sanctity of the church protected him or the Trinity protected him within the sanctity of the church. Mozes was at a loss to explain it any further.

The three, faceless, hallowed, figures appeared to Mozes as he started to gain control of himself. They seemed to prop him up, to give him support.

"Thank you. Thank each of you."

"What was that? What did you say?"

A voice focused Mozes, and the hallowed figures gave way to one man dressed in tattered, dirty, clothing. He sported a full beard and shoulder-length hair, both in the disarray of a person who lived on the street. As the man came into a sharper focus, Mozes recognized him as the local Penn Avenue vagrant. He knew him only as Murry.

"Murry, what're you doing?

"I'm helping you."

"You're helping me? Why are you helping me? You don't know me."

"That doesn't matter. I can still help you."

"Thank you."

"Everyone else moved out of your way. They only stared at you. You staggered and almost fell."

"I can manage."

"You can? You can control yourself! Like the other night?"

"What? What do you mean the other night?"

"Never mind. It's not important. It doesn't matter now. If you're okay, I'll go."

Mozes reached out to Murry and clutched some of the layers of his tattered clothing.

"What do you mean like the other night? Please tell me."

Murry removed Mozes' hand.

"I go now. Everything will be all right for you. My Father loves you. Bless you, son."

Murry walked off on Penn Avenue and resumed his panhandling. Not forced, just a mild-mannered panhandling.

Mozes stood on Penn Avenue and adjusted his clothing as he watched Murry walk off. He brushed off some lint and dust transferred to his finely, tailored, garments from Murry's old, worn-out, glove-covered, helping hands.

Mozes continued to his vehicle, unlocked it by pushing the keyless button on the door handle, opened the door, and entered. He sat there in deep thought. He rocked back and forth to comfort himself.

7   Breaking News

Tommy Slatski traveled back to his hometown to visit family and friends. He stopped for a coffee break, at the White Star Coffee Shop, in Bedford, a small town, the county seat of a predominately rural Pennsylvania farming area. He sipped his hot, black, coffee and checked his social sites on his smartphone. A posting on one of the news pages Tommy followed took his attention. The article referenced a grand jury report about the conspiracy to conceal sex abuse of hundreds of children by select members of the Roman Catholic Cloth.

Tommy used a search engine to search for the grand jury report and found a report that contained findings regarding the failure of a local diocese to report child abuse or related issues within parishes under its governance.

Tommy stopped and re-read a passage in the report from Section I, Introduction. He continued to read the report and stopped to re-read another passage.

Tommy just sat there as the phone involuntarily lowered to the table. He knew well the process of the grand jury and the intricacies of the grand jury process, from his days as a Federal law enforcement officer.

Tommy's thoughts echoed, "Priest alleged to be child predators went back to churches; they were assigned to other churches. A massive conspiracy to cover up wrongdoing by the Roman Catholic Cloth.

His hands trembled, a cold chill came over him, and he shook his head. He stared at the smartphone screen and the startling passage of the report which was displayed.

Tommy mumbled to himself, "The diocese, the priests, the Bishops, the hierarchy, they all conspired to avoid public scandal. To do so, they, the Cloth, cast away the well-being of children to protect themselves."

The diocese referenced in the Grand Jury report included Tommy's hometown, Windber, Pennsylvania and the governance of the local churches at which many of his childhood friends were members and attended mass. The churches were particular to European countries – Hungry, Poland, Slovakia, Ireland, and Italy. Two of the five churches, the Irish and Hungarian, were now closed.

Tommy thought to himself, "To have used a Grand Jury, an Investigative Grand Jury, that returned such a scathing report, people from the community, the people who made up the grand jury, very likely some were Roman Catholic by faith, must have believed the allegations. They must have found the state's evidence disclosed priest sexually abuse children. They believed there was a cover-up, a conspiracy to cover-up, the criminal acts by the hierarchy of the Roman Catholic Cloth."

Tommy raised his phone up and quickly scrolled through the report to the next-to-last page, Section VII, Conclusions and Recommendations and read more.

Tommy shook his head in disbelief. He briefly paused in thought, then continued to read the rest of the paragraph.

Shocked, he mumbled to himself, "The Grand Jury found the priest's acts criminal as was the cover-up by the Bishops. And the statute of limitations had expired, there could be no prosecutions. No prosecutions. The Cloth got away with evil, immoral, acts. Criminal acts codified by law."

This was shockingly brutal to Tommy. He sat there, held his smartphone, and within he wondered the question, "What do the people in Windber, some family, many friends, think about the conclusions of the Investigative Grand Jury?"

8   Command brief

Murry Stewart sat at his desk and stared at the file folders. The murders had him baffled. He had no leads, and the multiple homicides were quickly becoming cold cases. A situation no Detective wanted to report to superiors.

What made matters worse and created stress for him was the anticipation of the afternoon command brief. Today was Thursday. At one o'clock, every Thursday afternoon, Detective Stewart informed his superiors, his Lieutenant and the Assistant Chief of Investigations, on the progress of the investigations.

In turn, every Thursday at four o'clock the Assistant Chief of Investigations briefed the Acting Chief of Police.

In turn, every Monday at seven o'clock in the morning, in a one-on-one meeting in the Mayor's chambers, the Acting Chief of Police informed the Mayor on the murder investigations.

The investigation of the multiple murders had the attention of the Acting Chief due to the Mayor's intense interest. No one knew why the Mayor had such an intense interest in the multiple homicide victims, all with the same modus operandi. Chunks of flesh removed from the upper left shoulder and center of the lower back. Found in one of the three rivers. Naked bodies face up with their hands folded left atop right. All were unidentified. All with no leads

Detective First Class Murry Stewart, a fifteen-year veteran of the City of Pittsburgh, Bureau of Police (PBP) knew his Lieutenant was not going to like the brief this afternoon. There was nothing to report except the discovery of another homicide victim found the Friday morning past.

In the morning, at six o'clock, River Rescue found a female body. During a routine patrol of the three rivers to safeguard recreational boaters and commercial vessels, River Rescue discovered the naked female body floating face up near the Point State Park. They retrieved the naked female victim from the river water and transported her to the Point State Park boat tie up. From there the Office of Alleghany County Medical Examiner took possession of the body and transported it to the Medical Examiner facilities for a complete postmortem examination. There were no test results, the necessary testing not completed.

Detective Stewart checked his cellular telephone for the time. It was 12:55 p.m. He rose from his desk chair, slid it under his desk, and walked to the squad conference room. There he waited for the arrival of his Lieutenant and the Assistant Chief of Investigations.

At one o'clock sharp, the Assistant Chief and the Lieutenant of the Homicide Squad, in an authoritative gait, quickly walked into the squad conference room.

Absent the niceties of interpersonal communications, the Lieutenant's aged voice boomed.

"Do we need to sit?"

"No sir."

"Your report."

"Nothing to report on the previous homicides."

Before Detective Stewart continued, the Assistant Chief interrupted.

"Don't tell me there is another victim, another homicide."

"Yes, sir, there is."

The aged voice boomed again.

"I thought you said we didn't have to sit down?"

Detective Stewart was accustomed to the gruffness of the Lieutenant and Assistant Chief. He ignored it and continued.

"Last Friday, a nude female body was found floating face up in the Ohio River near the Point State Park. River Rescue discovered it. They pulled the body out of the water and went directly to the *Point* boat tie up. There they waited until the Medical Examiner office arrived and took custody of the body. The Medical Examiner office examination and test results not completed."

The Assistant Chief rambled.

"Great. The Acting Chief is not going to like this update. The Mayor, well that's the Acting Chief's problem. Is there anything else to report? The other homicides, is there anything else to report?"

"No, sir. There's nothing else."

With concern, the Lieutenant asserted.

"Are these cases cold? Don't let them get cold. Do we need to talk about that again Detective?"

"I'm doing the best I can. I'm talking to my informant's daily. I'm working the leads when I get them."

The Assistant Chief rumbled.

"You have leads? Good. What are they?"

"Sir, I don't have any leads. I mean I work the leads I get. I have no new leads to report."

The Lieutenant interrupted.

"Okay. Okay. We understand. You just work the investigations. Get out and talk to someone. Thank you, Detective."

The Lieutenant looked away from Detective Stewart and turned to the Assistant Chief.

"Sir, are you ready?"

The Assistant Chief looked at the Lieutenant then to Detective Stewart and back to the Lieutenant.

"Give me something guys. Come on. Give me something already. Thank you, Detective."

The Assistant Chief turned and walked out of the squad conference room, and the Lieutenant followed.

Detective Stewart remained seated. He exhaled in frustration because he was at a loss with these investigations. These were the most frustrating murder investigations he was ever assigned.

He rolled thoughts to himself.

"I know what the Medical Examiner is going to report for the latest victim, nothing. She is going to say nothing. It will be the same with this victim as with all the other victims. The Medical Examiner's postmortem examination and testing will disclose no leads. None. If I can't get a lead from the Medical Examiner, from whom can I get a lead? I just don't know what to do."

Again, Detective Stewart exhaled in frustration. He rose out of the rickety, conference room chair. He stepped behind the chair and rolled it back under the well-worn conference table. He checked the area to make sure he had all his materials from the meeting.

He thought to himself.

"The last thing I want is to lose control of the files and for them to get into the wrong hands. I don't want someone to leak this information to the media. To leak information about such sensitive investigations that are over a year old. Murder victims in which the Mayor has an intense interest and a gag order in place."

9   A note of hope

Detective Stewart turned and walked out of the conference room to his desk. He sat down and organized all the files, then stood and stored them back into the metal file cabinet to the right side of his desk. He took the long steel rod and slid it down through the drawer handles. He took the padlock from his desktop and affixed it to the top of the metal rod and the holder for the rod welded to the top of the file cabinet. He snapped the lock closed and pulled on it to test the security.

He momentary stood by the now secure file cabinet. He supported himself with his right hand rested on the handle of the second drawer. The drawer that held all the murder files to which the Mayor directed his interest. He paused to reflect.

He abruptly turned and walked toward the door. Detective Stewart left for the day. His tour of duty was over. He walked out the main entrance of the Homicide Squad and down the wide hallway to the ornate, oak, staircase. This was the only access to the three-story old city building. He walked down the rickety staircase to the first floor. There he continued to walk to the main entrance door to the street. He exited the city government building and pushed the door closed to make sure it latched.

The only building security was the electronic lock that controlled the main door. City employees used their access key cards to open it. Based on the needs of the city, employee access was temporary, for a period of time or permanent. Once inside the building through the main door, city employees or visitor accessed all three floors and all the offices on the floors.

71

There was no access control for the individual offices. One office, on the second floor, had no door because it was ripped off the hinges by an irate victim when asked to give a statement to a Detective.

The person who expected a visitor had to go to the main entrance and let the visitor in when they arrived. This included witnesses. The deplorable office conditions and work environment continued to negatively affect the morale of the police rank and file. The police union continually negotiated the issue with the city. The union was concerned for the safety of the officers and was very concerned about a breach to the city building by an active shooter.

Detective Stewart arrived at his personal vehicle that he routinely parked on the street. The city did not provide secure parking facilities, nor official take home cars. The latter policy was archaic, extremely counterproductive to efficient, effective, modern day policing.

Detective Stewart always performed a security sweep of his vehicle, an officer safety tactic. He walked around to survey it and the immediate area for anything unusual. As he rounded the front driver's side, he observed a piece of folded, yellow-lined, tablet, paper under the driver's side windshield wiper.

Before he retrieved it, he fitted his hands with latex gloves he took out of his right, rear, pants pocket. Now guarded against contamination, he retrieved the piece of tablet paper and opened it. He read to himself

"I KNOW ABOUT THE MURDERS OCCURRING AROUND THE CITY FOR THE LAST YEAR OR SO. I HAVE INFORMATION ABOUT THE MURDERS TO ASSIST YOUR INVESTIGATIONS FROM BECOMING COLD. I WILL BE IN TOUCH SOON. I WILL BE IN TOUCH AT AN OPPORTUNE TIME AND PLACE."

Detective Stewart leaned up against his vehicle. He stared at the printing on the paper. The note had a distinct aroma familiar to him. He thought about it as he raised the paper to his nose and slightly inhale. He mumbled to himself, "Coffee. It smells like coffee. That's odd."

He gathered himself, entered his vehicle, and sat in the driver's seat. Still holding the note in his left hand, he leaned over to the glove box and opened it with his right hand. He reached in and retrieved a clear plastic evidence envelope. He sat back up and gingerly worked the piece of yellow-lined, tablet, paper into the slightly larger plastic, evidence, envelope. He retrieved red evidence tape from the glove box and sealed the evidence envelope. With a fine tipped, black, marker pen, he marked it per police bureau policy. He returned the marker and evidence tape to the glove box and closed it. He laid the evidence envelope on the passenger bucket seat and started the car.

Murry removed the latex gloves as he checked traffic. He smelled the gloves and was sure of it. The pleasing odor was coffee. He drove off into the city traffic.

Of course, the secretive manner of the contact had Murry mesmerized. However, this was not the first time, as a detective or uniformed patrol officer, a witness contacted him in this manner. He knew he had to wait until the would-be witness wanted to talk to him, came out of the shadows. Besides, he had no information on which to make contact. Was this an important lead? No. It was just a note of hope.

10   Hometown grooming

As usual, when Tommy visited his hometown he made an appointment to get his haircut with Robi, his longtime barber. Tommy went to Robi for his hair grooming needs for over forty years. Tommy even maintained his loyalty to Robi when he lived in New Market, Maryland. Routinely, Tommy traveled the one hundred and thirty miles, one way, for a haircut. The loyalty was worth it. Robi always provided an exceptional cut.

This was not just Tommy's opinion. Many people commented and continued to comment on his excellent groom. There was a global consensus of this as well. Tommy received compliments from individuals during his work-related travels around the world. People from various continents and countries commented favorably on the excellent groom. There was even photographic proof of Robi's skilled grooming. A picture when Tommy greeted then Pope John Paul II, now a Saint Pope John Paul II.

Robi and Karolina were always friendly; they were warm and welcoming. They made their clientele feel at ease in their old, main street, business establishment. They made their clientele feel special.

When Tommy entered the shop, he received Robi's usual robust greeting.

"Hello."

"Hello," replied Tommy.

"I'll be right with you. I just have to finish here."

"Good. Take your time."

Robi turned his focus back to the customer's cut and the conversation they were having. Tommy sat to wait.

After Robi finished the cut and the customer paid, in a show of gratitude, he ushered the customer to the door. Then he turned to Tommy.

"Come on Tommy. Get in the chair."

Tommy rose and moved to the barber chair. Seated, Robi flung the barber's cape in the air, and as it fell into place, he adjusted it and began his craft.

As Robi cut Tommy's hair, they talked about the community. Tommy was confident the breaking news about the local diocese, and the priest pedophilia made public with the investigative grand jury report would be the topic. It was not. The conversation was the possibility the new owners of the town hospital were looking to purchase the entire block which included one of the three remaining ethnic-specific churches. Rumor had it the new owner needed the land to build a hotel for family members who came to support cancer patients when they received a new cancer treatment procedure.

Apparently, parishioners were not taking this rumor well. Past diocese commands included: The diocese merged the Poland and the Hungry churches due to a shortage of priests. Most recently, the Poland parish had to share a priest with the Slovakia parish.

These abrupt diocese changes appeared to strain the Polish community who were apparently a fickle group of people.

75

Something Tommy did not notice in his youth as his Polish mother paraded him around the Polish people.

Tommy wondered to himself as he drove off from another great haircut.

"Robi mentioned nothing about the alleged local diocese priest pedophilia. That was strange. Robi was a former parishioner of the Hungry ethnic parish. After all, it seemed a former priest to the Hungry church was at the center of the gut-wrenching breaking news. A revelation announced by the news media in the mid-1980s."

From his vast years of criminal investigative experience, Tommy's mind flooded with hunches. The thought of such horrid crime, in the midst of his hometown, which involved the Roman Catholic Cloth and possibly people he knew, maybe high school friends. This was disturbing to Tommy. Very disturbing.

The diocese sold the Hungry church property for the construction of a cancer research center. Again, Tommy's mind flooded with hunches.

"The Cloth knew the cancer center planned to demolish the church to build a new building engineered for their needs. Was this a ploy on the part of the Cloth? Was this a maneuver by the diocese to remove the scene of the crime? Was this to eliminate any possibility to gather lingering evidence of perverted acts or was this a sincere effort on the part of the diocese to heal the community by the removal of the large visual sign of the crime?"

Tommy shook his head.

"My hometown grooming didn't prepare me for such shocking, reality.

11   Once again on tour

Tommy merged onto Seventeenth Street from Railroad Street. At Seventeenth Street and Somerset Avenue, he turned right and coasted his bicycle along the *Wall* to a stop. While straddled over the bike, within, he rolled the past.

"Here was where I hung out with my brother and friends. The *Wall* was our meeting place. A meeting place at which we gathered and decided what we would do for the evening. Sometimes we just hung out and sat on the *Wall* and talked. We waved to the many friends who passed by as they toured the town. We made fun of others and each other. We laughed for hours. At times, gut-wrenching laughter that made our sides hurt. In the large field behind the *Wall,* we picked teams and played sandlot football against each other. Sometimes we played roughly which led to inter-friend fights. By the end of the game, we were all once again on the *Wall* laughing at the two who had fought. The inter-friend fights and roughhousing were nowhere near as intense as when we played Rummel. Those sandlot football games had action. Oh, yeah, particularly the *Turkey Bowls*. Now that was some action and all without protective gear."

The sound of a passing car's horn brought Tommy back. Tommy waved with a conditioned reflex; though to whom, he did not know. The car's brake lights engaged briefly as if the driver must have considered stopping. The car continued to the intersection of Somerset Avenue and 15th Street and continued straight on Somerset Avenue.

Tommy just finished a long bicycle ride. A loop from Windber, past the Windber Recreational Park, and back through the coal mine patch neighborhoods *42, 36* and *35*. He jumped up on the *Wall* to take a break. He reflected.

"I'm back on the *Wall* forty years later."

As he sat on the *Wall,* he noticed the car that passed and sounded its horn a few minutes ago, was coming by. This time the car slowed to the curb, brought to a stop, and parked at the curb across from the *Wall*. The driver's door opened. A short stature, strikingly beautiful, lady exited the vehicle. Her brown hair styled short. Her fashionable attire reserved. She walked with a somewhat soft but confident gait. She looked familiar.

Tommy thought to himself, "I should know her. Not again, like with Arnold when he stopped at my brother's house to say hello, and I didn't recognize him until he left."

The lady's approach was reserved. She crossed Somerset Avenue and stepped up from the roadway to the sidewalk. Tommy jumped down from the *Wall* to stand in her presences.

"Hello. How are you, Tommy?"

Tommy remembered.

"Hello MJ. I'm fine. How are you?"

"I'm well thank you. I haven't seen you..."

Tommy quickly interrupted, "Like thirty-five years. I tried to contact you for the class reunion. You didn't return my calls."

"I know. Sorry. How was the reunion?

"Good. More people attended than I thought. It was a combined reunion with the classes of 1974 and 1975. It was nice. It was good to see everyone."

"Good. I saw you here. I just wanted to come back to say hello."

"Yes."

"Thank you for the messages about the reunion. Please excuse me for not calling you back."

"Don't worry about it. I must say, you look wonderful."

"Thank you, Tommy. You were always so nice to me. Thank you. I have to go."

"We should get together sometime. Catch up after all these years."

"What? I don't know."

"How about tonight?"

"No, not this evening."

"How about Saturday night?"

Before MJ answered, a seventies era, red, Chevrolet Camaro came to a screeching stop in the roadway. The noise startled MJ. Even as the chromed out hot rod sat and idled, a thunderous noise came from what appeared to be three engines stacked on top of each other. The engine was so large; the hood had a hole cut into it. It appeared two of the three engines protruded through the hole. The thunderous noise vibrated inner organs.

Chivalrously, Tommy stepped between MJ and the Camaro as the passenger window descended. The driver leaned over toward the passenger seat and with great merriment shouted.

"Hey, Tommy. What are you doing? MJ, how are you?"

Tommy and MJ looked into the Camaro and saw a man with a big smile. The man laughed. Tommy and MJ recognized him and greeted him in unison.

"Hi, Gino."

MJ looked to Tommy and gazed for a moment before she said, "I have to go. Good to see you." She reached her hand out and gently touched Tommy's forearm and finished, "You take care."

Before Tommy replied, MJ quickly walked away, entered her car, and drove off.

Still smiling and laughing Gino shouted, "Get in."

"What?"

"You never rode in my Camaro since I redid it. Get in."

"I have my bike."

"Come on. Who's going to steal your bicycle in Windber? Besides, I know the Chief of Police. I'll tell him he has to find it for you. Or you can just take one from the Police Department lost and found."

"Okay."

Tommy got in the Camaro and said, "Great timing my friend. Great timing."

"Oh. Why?"

"I was talking to MJ."

"So."

"So. I was trying to get a date."

Gino roared with laughter. When he stopped laughing, he said, "Really."

Gino looked at Tommy and continued to smile.

Tommy reached over and punched Gino in the arm as he said, "What do you think, I'm too old."

"Ouch. No. I think MJ is too good for you," replied Gino.

"What."

Tommy reached over and punched Gino in the arm again.

"Ouch. Cut that out." Gino roared with laughter as he said, "I'm just kidding."

"Well, I wasn't. Since you interrupted my conversation and chased her off, you find her phone number for me. I think she was interested."

"After all these years, you think she was interested in you?"

"Yeah. Look at me." Tommy slowly moved his hand over his head. "And these are my cycling clothes."

"You keep dreaming my vain friend. Keep dreaming."

"You just get her number, Gino."

Tommy faked another punch, and Gino flinched.

"I'll see what I can do."

"No. You get the number. You say you know the Chief, right?"

"Yeah."

"Well, you get him busy on those law enforcement databases and get me the number. Where're we going?"

"For a tour. Like old times."

Gino accelerated the Camaro, which threw Tommy back into his seat. At illegal velocity, the rear wheels spun and smoked. The tachometer neared the red line, and the red and chrome Camaro trusted away from the *Wall*.

Tommy reached for his seatbelt and belted himself to the smooth, clean, shiny, black leather, bucket seat.

Motoring away from the *Wall*, Gino looked to Tommy and showed a half smile. He worked the clutch and shifted into third gear, and the rear tires chirped as the Camaro passed by the *Big Store*, the former main company store.

Gino blew the stop sign at Somerset and 15th Street. He had slammed fourth gear before they passed by the now vacant, former main office building for the coal company that founded Windber, on the right-hand side.

The two longtime, hometown, friends were once again on tour.

12   Springtime in the 'Burgh.

The dreary, cold, snowy, days gave way to mild temperatures.
The warm temperatures brought the Robins back into the city,
and it was in transition from winter to summer. Just as the
flowers and trees started to bloom from the warmer weather,
the Pittsburghers started to bloom as they peeled off their
winter layers. And as the Pittsburghers warmed up, they
became more pleasant.

The transition in the 'Burgh also brought the Pirates back. PNC
Park opened for business for another season of major league
baseball. This always brought excitement into the 'Burgh.
Pittsburghers were finicky fans. Finicky, loyal, fans.

With warmer temperatures, Mozes decided to walk over to
Gheorghi's Joe for his mid-morning coffee.

As he walked up the sidewalk on Penn Avenue, Mozes heard
his name. He stopped and turned around, but he did not see
anyone he knew. He turned back and continued to walk. When
he heard his name again, he stopped and moved to an open
space to a storefront. He leaned back on the brick wall and
scanned the sidewalk. He looked for someone who may have
called his name, but, again, saw no one he knew. A couple
minutes went by, and he bounced off the brick storefront and
continued his way.

When he arrived at Gheorghi's Joe, he entered and went
directly to the coffee counter.

"Good morning. May I have a large coffee? Just plain."

"Black?"

"Yes. Please."

The clerk handed Mozes a large coffee. When he turned to walk to the cash register, he bumped into a lady.

"Excuse me."

The lady was tall, with brown hair, in her mid-forties, and fashionably dressed. She wore expensive jewelry based on diamond size, gem size, and a Rolex watch.

"That was close. I almost spilled my cappuccino."

"I'm sorry," said Mozes.

"You're okay. There's nothing on my clothes."

"Here. Here are napkins. May I hold your cup while you wipe your hand?"

"Yes. Thank you. You're such a gentleman. I don't meet many gentlemen these days."

She handed her cup to Mozes, took the napkins, and wiped her hand. She extended her dry hand to Mozes.

"Hello. My name is Sofiya. You are?"

"Hello, Sofiya. My name is Mozes, pleased to meet you."

"Nice meeting you. Is this how you meet ladies? You try to knock their coffee out of their hand?"

"No. However, I met you. Maybe I should."

They both laughed.

Mozes felt comfortable with her. He was surprised because that was not his norm. Certainly, not this quickly.

"Would you like to join me at the table outside?" asked Mozes.

"Yes. Thank you."

"Let me pay for the coffees. Would you like to get the table?"

"Thank you. I will."

Mozes went to the rear of the checkout line as Sofiya went to the table on the street. Gheorghi came up to Mozes as he waited in line.

"Good morning Mozes."

"Good morning Gheorghi."

"I don't want to pry into your business, but do you know who she is?"

"Sofiya is all I know now. I hope to get to know her a little better over coffee. Isn't she beautiful?"

"Seriously, you don't know who she is? You're a police officer, and you don't know who she is?"

"Gheorghi, I'm not a police officer. I'm an Investigator."

"Yeah, okay. You should know who Sofiya is. You're in law enforcement."

"I don't know Gheorghi. Who is she?"

"Sofiya Zlatkov. She is the daughter of the reputed boss of the Bulgaria Crime Family in Pittsburgh. Come on, you don't know? They're in the news for their charitable work and donations. Sometimes they're in the news for their alleged involvement in political corruption. Come on, you don't know?"

"No. Next time we'll sit, and I'll tell you what I do."

The excitement was building in Mozes.

"Now I'll get to know Sofiya. I'll talk to you later."

"Mozes, be careful. Please. You're such a good man. I don't want people to take advantage of you. I don't want you to get hurt. And I don't mean by a broken heart."

Mozes took his change from the cashier and said, "Thank you."

Mozes looked back to Gheorghi. He smiled and said, "Springtime in the *'Burgh.'*"

13   A Pittsburgh socialite.

Mozes walked out of Gheorghi's Joe, directly to Sofiya, and sat down.

"Please excuse my carelessness. I'm sorry for bumping into you."

A thick Bulgarian accent sounded.

"Don't be silly. Please excuse my carelessness."

"This is nice, though. I get a chance to meet you."

"To meet me? Do you know me? I don't recognize you."

Mozes still felt comfortable with the lady. He used the contemporaneous intelligence Gheorghi shared with him.

"Who doesn't know you? Sofiya Zlatkov, Pittsburgh socialite, and daughter of Boris Zlatkov. The Zlatkov family is one of the wealthiest families in Pittsburgh. Yeah, I recognize you."

"So, you know me. Too bad."

"What do you mean too bad?"

"Too bad. You, like everyone else who knows of me, only know of my money. You all form your opinion of me based on my money. And those damn news reporters who display my father as a Bulgaria, crime lord."

Her Bulgarian accent grew thicker as she showed contempt for those news reporters.

"Sofiya, I'm not like everyone else. I only say what I know of you. I want to get to know you. Please give it a chance. Maybe I should go?"

"No, don't go."

She reached out and placed her hand on his.

"It's not often I get to meet a handsome man, a polite man. Tell me what you do."

"I'm an investigator for the City of Pittsburgh, with the Office of Inspector General. I investigate fraud, waste, and abuse by city employees, city program recipients or others involved with city programs or city money."

"Sounds important."

"I believe it is. And you, what do you do all day long?"

"I. Well I describe myself as a socialite."

"A socialite? What does a socialite do all day?"

"What?"

"What does a socialite do all day? You know. As an investigator, I investigate all day. What do you, a socialite, do all day?"

With a large seductive smile and proudness in her voice, she explained.

"Well, by day, I run my businesses. In the evening, I'm out and about society."

"Tell me more. I'm talking to a socialite, a Pittsburgh socialite. Give me the details. Don't let me walk away with the open content, online encyclopedia definition. Please, do tell."

"Are you interested in what I do?"

"Yes, I am. Why wouldn't I be?

"Well, you're the first gentlemen I had the pleasure to meet. The first with interest in what I do. Are you sure you don't want to brag on yourself? Make me listen to your grand adventures."

"Thank you for the compliment as a gentleman. Grand adventures? I don't know about that. Please tell me more about you."

Sofiya looked up from her cellphone.

"I'm sorry. I must go back to my office. I received a text from my personal assistant about an urgent matter."

"Perhaps another time. Here, please take my card."

Mozes extended his business card to Sofiya.

"Thank you. And here's mine. Please call me for lunch."

"Thank you. Yes, lunch. We must."

Sofiya rose from her chair, and Mozes rose with her. They shook hands with soft, gentle, touches. When Sofiya started to pull her hand back, Mozes tightened his grip and smiled playfully. Sofiya quickly responded with a seductive smile. Mozes released his grip, and they both said goodbye.

Sofiya turned and walked off on Penn Avenue. Mozes sat back down and continued to sip his coffee. He watched Sofiya disappear into the crowded Penn Avenue streetwalkers and fell into deep thought. The hum of the vehicular traffic did not interrupt him. Numerous pedestrians passed by, some brushed up against him as they navigated a congested sidewalk. He was not distracted from his titillating thoughts of the vivacious socialite.

Mozes came back to reality when his cellular telephone rang. He answered it and listened briefly. He ended the call and holstered the phone. He rose from his chair and walked off in the direction Sofiya walked. He thought.

"A Pittsburgh socialite and I felt comfortable."

As he continued to walk, his coffee cup in his left hand, he rubbed and massaged the nape of his neck with his right hand. He attempted to ease the tension brought on by the sharp pain that moved through his head.

Mozes thought to himself, "When will this end? It seems every time I meet a lady or think of the opposite sex I have this pain."

14 **A dream in a dream.**

Mo stood behind the tree. He placed a medium size, black bag at his feet. He stood motionless for three hours and just stared at the house. Occasionally, he rubbed his hands together to warm them. The spring chill in the air made his ungloved hands cold. Other than that, he did not move.

Mo contemplated what just happened as he stood motionless. He knew it was wrong and he was aware there were severe consequences for his actions. He knew he could never explain his actions to himself or others.

Once again, he found himself in torment. The extreme distress of his mind was the repeated affliction he experienced every time he listened to the hallowed figures.

At the first sound of his alarm, Mozes jumped out of bed. He walked to the bathroom to begin his morning routine. He stopped by the dresser and placed his right hand on it to support himself.

Within he wondered his thoughts.

"Another dream. It was vivid as always. Another dream."

He shook his head and continued to the bathroom.

As he made his way, he tripped and almost fell. Balanced he turned the lights on. When Mozes looked to the floor, he saw he tripped over a medium size, black bag.

Mozes thought, "This is strange; I never have anything out of place."

He bent over and picked up the bag. It was weighty. Though spooked, he put it on the bed and opened it. He peered inside and immediately jumped back. The decapitated head of Sofiya was in the bag.

The scene caused Mozes to stagger a bit. He mumbled faintly.

"No. Oh, Dear God, no."

Mozes fell to the wooden floor and cowered in a fetal position. He cried at the sight of the gruesome contents.

Mozes sat straight up in bed when his telephone alarm sounded at the usual time, five o'clock. He did not reach for the phone nor stop the blaring alarm. He slung the covers off and jumped to the floor. He quickly moved to the bedroom door and turned on the lights. He frantically searched every inch of the floor for a medium size, black bag. He looked on and under the bed. He moved to the oversize walk-in closet, turned on the lights, and continued to search. He found nothing.

He stepped outside of the closet and leaned up against the wall. He slowly slid down to the floor, drew his legs into his chest, and placed his folded arms on his knees. He lowered his head to his forearms. He rocked back and forth to comfort himself.

He rolled the past through his mind.

"I had a dream in a dream. The last time was in seventh grade. It happened when the gym teacher found me in a fetal position in the boy's locker room showers rocking back and forth. He took me to the school nurse's office, and they called my mother. When mother came to the school nurse's office, the nurse told mother she never handled such an event. The Principle recommended I visit a psychiatrist. In their presence, mother agreed.

As we drove through Windber, on Graham Avenue, on our way home, mother looked at me. She reached her right hand out, placed it on the nape of my neck, and spoke to comfort me.

'Mozes, you don't need to go to a psychiatrist. They just don't know. They just don't know.'

Her confident tone revealed the high school dropout knew more than the college educated, school district employees.

I should have asked her why. I didn't. On that day, bitterness showed in her eyes welled with tears. Tears she failed to hold in front of her son. Her sweet, comforting, smile turned to an expression of grief. Her eyes said she was somewhere else. A place far away. Perhaps a dark place. I should've asked before the state committed her. Once in the institution, she spoke to no one according to Aunt Llona. Was I to blame? I'm still haunted by that too."

Mozes sat on the floor and rocked back and forth. When the third alarm sounded from his telephone, he rose and walked to the bedside nightstand. He turned off the loud, sounding, alarm as well as the remaining two.

Mozes gingerly walked to the bathroom for his morning groom. He feared to bump into a medium size, black bag.

15 The first ride

There it was again. The low, sexy, Bulgarian-accented voice.
Today Viktorija blended it with enthusiasm.

"I caught you again Mozes."

"What?"

"I caught you checking yourself out in the mirrors again."

"Yes, you did."

"You know I do that too."

"Check yourself in the mirrors."

"No. Check you out."

Mozes blushed.

Playfully, Viktorija said, "I made you blush."

The elevator arrived at the third floor; the doors immediately
opened, and the passengers made room for two more. Mozes
motioned for Viktorija to enter first and he followed as the
doors closed behind them. The elevator jerked to a start, and
Viktorija reached out and gripped Mozes by the forearm to
steady herself. No one talked in the elevator as it descended.

At the first floor, Mozes motioned for Viktorija to exit first.
She continued to walk to the front door. As she did, Mozes

drew to her and stared at her curvaceous figure as it moved before him.

They exited the apartment building, and Viktorija turned to Mozes. She smiled as she caught Mozes looking at her patootie.

Mozes quickly redirected his eyes to her eyes. With trepidation, he asked, "May I give you a ride to your work?"

"Okay. That would be gracious of you. I'll have a break from the riffraff on the bus, not to mention the stinky people. I'm sorry but some of those people."

"You don't have to say anymore. I know what you mean. This way."

Mozes showed Viktorija to his car. He opened the passenger door, and Viktorija entered.

"Thank you, Mozes. You're such a gentleman."

"Thank you."

Mozes closed her door and walked around the vehicle to enter the driver's seat.

Viktorija thought to herself, "I knew he wasn't gay. He just checked me out. I knew it was just apartment building gossip."

After Mozes had entered the vehicle, Viktorija said, "Mozes, are you going to blush again?"

"Probably. Where may I take you?"

"To the *Strip* please."

"My office is near the *Strip* too."

"Why haven't you asked me to lunch then?"

Mozes blushed.

Before he could say anything, Viktorija continued, "There it is. I made you blush again."

"Yes, you did. Stop that."

"No, I don't think so."

Viktorija turned in her seat toward Mozes and looked at him. He looked at her but quickly looked away.

Viktorija, in a serious tone, continued, "Let me see if I can do it again. Mozes, would you like to have dinner with me tonight?"

Mozes blushed again.

"You're taking too long to ask me out. So, I'm asking. Will you have dinner with me tonight? What do you say?" prodded Viktorija.

"Yes. I say yes. You must let me plan it. I'll pick you up at six thirty at your apartment."

"Oh. You're going to plan it. Have you been thinking about asking me out?"

Mozes' tone lowered, and he became bashful as he replied, "Yes."

"How sweet. I don't know if I'll be able to work today. I'm so excited. I may just sit around and daydream about you, about tonight."

"Now the pressure is on. Thanks."

With a little force in her voice, Viktorija said, "The pressure is on. My expectations are high for such a flamboyant man. I just hope I have something to wear, so I don't embarrass you."

"You embarrass me. No. I don't think so. Let's do this. Let's just go somewhere casual tonight. Let's just relax."

"Good. That reduces the pressure a little. Turn right, at the next light, please. Then up on the left. You can let me out there."

Mozes steered the Porsche to the curb.

"How's that?"

"Good. Thank you."

Viktorija opened her door. As she moved out of the vehicle, she said, "See you tonight Mozes. Thank you for the ride. What a great start to my day."

"You're welcome. See you tonight. Enjoy your day."

Viktorija closed the car door, paused, and looked up and through the window. She locked eyes with Mozes; he could not pull away. She released Mozes when she playfully waved goodbye. She turned and with a smile, walked off toward the entrance to her office building.

Mozes remained and stared at Viktorija's curvaceous figure as it moved away from him.

When Mozes pulled away from the curb, in his peripheral vision, he saw Sofiya Zlatkov walking toward the same building. In his rearview mirror, Mozes observed Viktorija waiting by the entrance. She held the door open for Sofiya. By their facial expressions, it appeared they knew each other.

16   Detailed to the Homicide Squad

Mozes enjoyed the lingering scent of Viktorija's perfume as he continued to his office. Once at his desk, he turned on his computer. The password screen came up after it had cycled through the opening sequence. He entered his password and his home screen immediately appeared. He clicked on the email icon and began to review his inbox when he noticed an email from the IG marked urgent. He opened it first. It instructed Mozes to report to the IG as soon as he arrived for the day.

Mozes rose from his desk, walked to the IG's office, and knocked on the door.

"Come in," a voice sounded.

Mozes entered to the IG seated at his desk and the DIG seated at a small round table. He looked from one to the other as he greeted them.

"Good morning."

In unison, the IG and DIG replied, "Good morning, Mozes."

"You said to report to you as soon as I arrived."

"Yes. Thank you. Please sit down," replied the IG.

As Mozes sat in a low back, plush, black leather, conference table chair, the IG continued.

"I need you to handle a sensitive case for this office."

"Okay."

"I received a letter yesterday."

The DIG slid two clear, plastic, evidence envelopes, sealed with red evidence tape, across the small, oak, conference table. The IG continued.

"The postmark was from the Lawrenceville Post Office. The short informal letter, on simple plain white stationery, with a matching envelope, appeared to have computer generated printing. There was no date on it."

Mozes picked up the envelope first. He studied it, observed what the IG described and, noted the postal stamp dated three days earlier. He placed it back on the table.

Mozes picked up the letter, observed as the IG described, and nothing further. He read the letter to himself.

"SIR. I AM REPORTING THE MAYOR OF THE CITY OF PITTSBURGH IS PARTICIPATING IN A CONSPIRACY TO COVER UP MURDERS COMMITTED IN THE CITY THROUGHOUT THE LAST FOURTEEN MONTHS. MY FATHER LOVES YOU. BLESS YOU, MY SON. SAINT MICHAEL."

"Mozes, are you done?"

"Yes. This letter, this one sentence letter, requires an investigation. It requires an investigation of the Mayor."

"Yes."

"You declined to open investigations which I brought to you with way more evidence."

"Mozes, I received more evidence. Well, not evidence. A couple days ago, I received a request from the PBP Homicide

101

Squad to assign an investigator to a task force formed to investigate a yearlong murder spree in the city. I told the Lieutenant I needed some connection of city personnel or city money to assign resources. The letter was the evidence. So, I assigned you to the task force."

"Sir, you said a yearlong murder spree. I haven't heard anything about a murder spree from the news media."

"The Mayor placed a gag order on anything related to the killings."

"A gag order. When? How soon after the first or second murder?"

"I have your attention now."

"Yes."

"Good. I don't have the answers to the questions you're about to ask. You're better off asking the lead investigator of the task force. His name is Murry Stewart. He is expecting you at the first task force meeting tomorrow for a briefing."

"Tomorrow. Tomorrow is Friday, my compressed day off."

"Sorry Mozes. You must be at the in briefing tomorrow. It starts at 9 a.m. I'll send you an email with Stewart's contact information and the address for the meeting. This case is now your priority. I'll reassign all your other cases, and I'll be looking for your weekly case write-ups."

"Okay."

"Thank you, Mozes. Thank you for all your great work."

The meeting was ended with the compliment the IG always used to end a meeting. Mozes rose from his chair, gathered the evidence envelopes, and looked from the DIG to the IG, and said, "Thank you."

Mozes walked out of the office and back to his desk. He sat and contemplated his new assignment. He read the one sentence letter to himself again, then studied the letter. He sat and thought to himself.

"This is not much to go on, not much at all. I hope the task force members have a lot more."

Mozes secured the evidence in his safe and left his office for his morning coffee at Gheorghi's Joe.

17   Connection on Penn

Mozes ordered and paid for his coffee, then walked out to the street and stood near the building. He sipped his coffee and watched the people milling about. The *All-Seeing* quickly joined Mozes and hovered beside him. The slight breeze waved his vestments. He said.

"So, *Mo*, you have a date tonight?"

Mozes did not reply. He just looked at the *All-Seeing*.

The *All-Seeing* continued.

"Are you sure you want to go on a date *Mo*? You know what happens every time you go on a date."

Mozes said nothing. A voice sounded in the distance and made the hallowed figure fade away.

"Mozes, how are you?"

Mozes focused on the voice and brought himself back. He replied, "Murry. I'm fine. How are you?"

"Very well."

"Can I get you a cup of coffee?"

"No, not today. I have to go help someone."

"Okay. Next time."

"Yes, next time. My Father loves you. Bless you, my son."

Murry left at a fast pace zig-zagging through the people milling about Penn Avenue.

Mozes watched as Murry walked away. He took the last sip of his coffee, moved away from the wall, and walked toward the garbage can to discard the empty cup. He stopped in his steps and jerked his head in the direction he last saw Murry.

Mozes thought to himself, "Was it just uncanny or was Murry a lead."

He wanted to chase after him. He wanted to ask him some questions.

To himself, Mozes repeated what Murry said. "My Father loves you. Bless you, my son."

Mozes looked hard to find Murry. He thought, "That was the same salutation used in the one sentence letter. Was there a connection on Penn?"

18   Command brief

Detective Stewart circled the block for the third time. He looked for a parking space designated for the official vehicle he signed out when he began his shift this morning. Today, citywide construction and a heavy traffic flow for the Pirates afternoon game delayed him. He was concerned he would be late for his Thursday afternoon, one o'clock brief to his Lieutenant and the Assistant Chief of Investigations.

As he waited for an animal rescue truck to vacate a parking space, Detective Stewart checked his cellphone for the time. It was twelve fifty-five. He thought to himself, "There was no time to change out of my undercover street disguise. I just had to go over to the *Strip* this morning."

Detective Stewart quickly parked the undercover police vehicle. He slid out and scurried up the street to the main entrance of the old city building. He raced through the unsecured door and through the lobby to the large, oak staircase. He scaled the stairs two steps at a time to the third floor and continued to rush through the office space to the squad conference room. Detective Stewart entered the room and observed his Lieutenant, and the Assistant Chief seated, looking out the window.

The Lieutenant noticed Detective Stewart first.

"You're late."

"Yes, traffic was heavy. I just returned from the *Strip*. I spent a few hours there this morning."

"Your report."

"Nothing new to report."

"Nothing!"

"Nothing sir, except tomorrow is the first meeting for the task force."

The Assistant Chief rotated his chair from the window to the Lieutenant.

"A task force. What's this about a task force?"

"I told you we decided to stand up a task force."

"You did?"

"Yes."

"I don't know. What will the Mayor say?"

"I thought you cleared this with the Acting Chief and the Mayor?"

"Well not yet. Apparently, I forgot. These investigations aren't my highest priority."

Detective Stewart set his eyes on his Lieutenant then shifted them to the Assistant Chief and back to the Lieutenant. He moved his eyes and glared out the windows. He had no play in this conversation.

The Lieutenant defended their investigative strategy.

"I think we should proceed with the task force."

"No. No task force. You shut it down, now."

The Assistant Chief looked at the Lieutenant, raised his right hand, and pointed his index finger at him.

"No. Task. Force."

The Assistant Chief's adamant order surprised the Lieutenant.

"Yes, sir," said the Lieutenant.

The Lieutenant looked to Murry.

"No task force. Shut it down today."

"Yes, sir."

"Anything else Murry?"

"No, sir."

"Anything else Chief?"

The Assistant Chief looked toward Detective Stewart.

"Thank you, Detective."

Detective Stewart did not know how to interpret the Assistant Chiefs comment.

The Assistant Chief turned to the Lieutenant.

"This thing is slowing down. We don't want this to get cold. I have another meeting. I must go. No task force people. Understand?"

Abruptly, the Assistant Chief rose from his chair and walked out of the squad conference room.

The Lieutenant looked to Detective Stewart and shrugged his shoulders upward as he raised his hands with open palms.

"I don't understand either. Nevertheless, no task force. He seems off today. Not himself."

"Sir."

The Lieutenant cut Detective Stewart off.

"No task force. That's all."

The Lieutenant quickly turned and rushed out of the conference room. He needed to catch up to the Assistant Chief.

Detective Stewart stood dumbstruck. He walked over to the windows and stared out at the aged city. His view took in the two major league sports stadiums with city high-rises as the backdrop. PNC Park was active with the afternoon game.

The Detective thought to himself.

"No task force. Why not? And they want results."

Detective Stewart shook his head, turned, and walked out of the conference room, directly to his desk.

Murray pulled his metal desk chair out and sat down. He pulled himself to the desk, opened his top left-hand drawer, and took out a yellow, ruled, standard size, notepad. He annotated the top of the first page with the day of the week and date and continued to write notes for his morning surveillance activities from the *Strip*. His records needed to be contemporaneous to his investigative work; he needed to finish them before he ended his tour of duty. Finished, he filed the hand-written notes into the appropriate investigative file.

He swiveled in his chair a little to his right. He unlocked the top right-hand drawer, opened it, and retrieved a black, cloth bound, ruled, notebook. He opened it to the blank page marked by the attached silk, ribbon, page marker. On the blank page, in the upper right-hand corner, he annotated the weekday and date. He scrolled contemporaneous notes for the 1:00 p. m. briefing. Notably, the Assistant Chief's ordered not to convene a task force for the yearlong murder spree. He skipped a few lines and wrote OBSERVATION. On the line under it, he wrote, "I observed the Assistant Chief had a confused mental state today." He skipped a line and wrote, The Lieutenant's observation of the Assistant Chief today was, "He seems off today. Not himself."

Detective Stewart closed the notebook and returned it to the security of the drawer. He slowly closed the drawer with his *Cover Your Ass* material. Disheartening as it was, he had to create a record for his defense if needed. Just another sign the PBP continued to deteriorate as discussed by many inside and outside the once respected and coveted police organization.

Detective Stewart retrieved another file from his lower right desk file drawer. He opened it and started to scan the documents inside. He quickly closed the folder and replaced it in the file drawer.

"I'll review it tomorrow morning. I'm finished. This was a long day."

Detective Stewart closed and locked all his desk drawers. He returned the lanyard, with his office keys attached, around his neck. He rose from his desk chair, pushed it under his desk, and walked toward the main entrance to the squad room.

19   A sweet, strange man.

Mozes was ready for his first date with Viktorija. At the front door inside his apartment, he stood in front of the decorative full-length, mirror to take a final look at himself. He was content with his casual appearance.

Mozes stared at himself and went into deep thought. His thoughts concluded, "I'm visually ready, but I wonder if I'm mentally ready."

Mozes second-guessed himself. He encountered the *All-Seeing* today whose words were not hopeful. He continued his thoughts.

"Maybe the *All-Seeing* was right? Dates didn't go well for me after all these years. The few I had didn't work out well for her or me."

The *Guiding* appeared and hovered beside Mozes.

"*Mo*, you have to go on this date. You must keep trying. You must put the past behind you."

The Guiding disappeared, and Mozes encouraged himself.

"I can do this. I must do this. The *Guiding* is right. I must put the past behind me. I can do this."

Mozes closed the door behind him and locked it. He walked down the hallway, passed the elevator alcove, and stopped at the door for apartment 3C. He hesitated and then knocked lightly.

Viktorija immediately answered.

"Hello Mozes. Come in."

Mozes thought to himself, "I don't want this to happen. I don't want to go in. This is too much like the past."

He started to rub and massage the nape of his neck in an attempt to ease the tension brought on by the sharp pain that moved through his head. Mozes hesitated.

"Mozes, you're so shy. Come in."

With glee, Viktorija reached out and gently took hold of Mozes' hand. She ushered him into her apartment.

Slowly, Mozes moved through the doorway and closed it behind him. He felt uneasy and almost froze in the foyer.

He said to himself, "Help me *Guiding*. Help me."

Instantly, he felt a cool breeze and became calm. He continued to walk to the living room.

"Please have a seat. I just have to get my purse."

"Okay. Take your time."

Viktorija moved back the hallway and Mozes scanned the finely decorated living room. There was no clutter. In fact, and to his surprise, the furnishings were sparse. There was a couch, two small armchairs, a large circular coffee table, and two floor lamps. A larger painting hung behind the sofa. Another piece of art hung between the two large windows fashionably covered with fabric curtains. Three symmetrical paintings hung on the third wall. The painted walls had a hint of gray just enough so you knew it was not white. The ceiling was painted white. The entire room accented with ornate, woodwork, trim painted white. Everything was color coordinated as if straight out of a home design magazine. The room was light and airy. This was not consistent with the darker colors typically used in Pittsburgh home decor. Curiously absent were family pictures. Not a one positioned in the living room. The room made Mozes comfortable, something not often experienced by Mozes.

Viktorija returned to the living room.

"I'm ready now."

Mozes looked up from the comfortable chair.

"I don't know if I want to go. I'm comfortable right here. You have a lovely home; it puts me at ease."

"Thank you."

With a hint of disappointment in her voice, Viktorija continued.

"I suppose we can stay here and order in if you wish."

Mozes rose quickly from the comfortable chair and moved toward Viktorija.

"Oh, no. I'm taking you out tonight. Look at you. You look beautiful. You look so cute. I'm taking you out to make everyone envious of me, the guy with the gorgeous lady."

Viktorija moved closer to Mozes. She looked up to his eyes, reached out, and placed her hand on his broad chest.

"Mozes you're so kind."

They briefly locked eyes before Mozes became uncomfortable and pulled back a bit. This struck Viktorija as an odd reaction. Certainly, not the response she tried to induce. Disappointed, she turned and walked toward the door.

As Mozes followed, he thought to himself, "Did I just repeat the same ruinous actions? Did it happen again? Why can't I have a regular date? A normal relationship? Though how would I know what that is. My affliction continually intercepts normal."

Mozes fixed his eyes on Viktorija as she led him out of the apartment. She was dressed casual but elegant. She wore a black, button down, silk shirt. The top two buttons were undone and exposed cleavage from her bosomy figure. Slightly faded blue jeans profiled her derriere as it moved side to side with her confident gate in black, leather, flats. She accented herself with a single strand, black pearl, necklace, a matching bracelet, and single black pearl earrings. And of course, there was the sweet aroma of Viktorija's spellbinding perfume. The sweet scent was sure to linger in Mozes' olfactory organ.

They walked to the elevator alcove, and curiosity got the best of Viktorija.

"Where're we going?"

"Carson Street food trucks."

Mozes pressed the down button to summon the elevator.

"Carson Street food trucks."

"Have you been there before?"

"No. Wasn't there a shooting there? Weren't two people murdered there a couple of days ago?"

"So, you don't want to go to the Carson Street food trucks."

The elevator arrived on the third floor. When the doors opened, Mozes motioned for Viktorija to enter first. He followed her in and pressed the first-floor button.

"If you planned to go there. You said you wanted to plan our date."

"I would like to go there. I'll protect you if anything happens."

"I'm sure you will."

"I'm just kidding."

Viktorija cocked her head, looked up to Mozes, and said, "You won't protect me?"

Mozes chuckled. He like her wit.

"You'll see when we get there. This is my plan."

Viktorija smirked.

"No. I think we should go to the Carson Street food trucks. I don't want you to think I'm uppity."

"I don't think you're uppity. I was thinking about this place all day."

"You weren't thinking about me all day."

Mozes said nothing. He never lied. If he replied, he had to say he thought about her all day. In his mind, that sounded a little creepy to say on a first date. He also risked a disturbing thought in her mind, so he remained silent.

He thought to himself, "Thankfully she is kind and polite. She just let the question go. However, I have a hard time deciphering when she is serious or joking. Does she have sarcastic humor? Could I be so lucky? On the other hand, is it just the stress of the first date? The stress, for her or me. I think it's me. She seems so relaxed and confident."

The elevator stopped at the first floor, and the doors slowly opened. Viktorija moved out, and Mozes followed as they walked to the apartment door. Other tenants just arrived at the building and held the door open. They all exchanged cordial greetings as they passed. Mozes continued to lead Viktorija to his Porsche where he opened and held the door for Viktorija to enter. He closed it and walked around to the driver's side and entered.

Mozes drove the Porsche out of the parking lot, turned right onto Miltenberger Street, and then left onto the Boulevard of the Allies. He stayed on Route 885 and turned right to descend into the Southside. As he descended under the parkway, he glanced in the rearview mirror. In the back seat, seated three abreast, were the *All-Seeing*, the *Teacher*, and the *Guiding*. His face affixed a blank look.

Viktorija noticed the look on Mozes' face and said, "Mozes, are you okay?"

There was no reply from Mozes. When the green turn arrow showed, the sound of car horns focused his attention on the traffic. He turned left onto 2nd Avenue.

"Mozes, are you okay?"

"What?"

"Are you okay?"

"Yes, I'm okay. Why?"

"You looked distant like you were deep in thought about something."

Mozes cautiously looked back into the rearview mirror. The hallowed figures were gone.

"No. I'm okay."

"This is Hot Metal Bridge. Here's the turn to the Carson Street food trucks."

"We're not going there."

"Where're we going?"

"You'll see."

Mozes continued to operate the Porsche on 2nd Avenue, along one of the three rivers, the north-flowing Monongahela.

Viktorija remained a good sport. She had no idea where Mozes was taking her but did not press him. The mystery made him more interesting still.

Mozes turned the Porsche left onto Greenfield Avenue and immediately left onto Saline Street.

Curiosity got the better of Viktorija. She could not help herself.

"Where're we going?" she asked again.

"Patience. Patience. We're almost there. Here we are."

"We're here? Where? Are we eating at one of your relative's houses?"

Mozes laughed.

"No. On the corner. Grande Giacomo's Ristorante. This place was featured on one of those TV food shows."

"This was a featured dive?"

"Come on give it a chance."

"I will. I'm just joking with you."

Mozes slid out of the Porsche and walked around to open Viktorija's door. He again thought to himself.

"I'm having a hard time here. Is she serious or joking? I just can't tell."

It was self-seating, and Mozes walked through the restaurant to a table off in a corner. Mozes was disappointed, it was not busy for a Thursday night. He hoped more people would have seen him with the beautiful Viktorija.

Seated and with a menu in hand, Viktorija looked around the restaurant. She studied the restaurant's motif which was not updated since the 1970s. She fixed her eyes on Mozes, but her gaze went unnoticed. She studied the menu.

After the meal, wine, and conversation there was silence in the Porsche as Mozes retraced the route back to their apartment building. Mozes parked the Porsche in his assigned parking spot, and they made their way into the building and to the elevator.

Mozes pushed the up button to summon the elevator. He felt Viktorija's gaze and returned it with a smiled. She swayed his way, but Mozes just smiled and pulled away. She stopped herself and smiled.

The elevator doors opened, and Mozes motioned for Viktorija to enter first. As she entered, he looked in and saw the *All-Seeing* standing in the corner. He froze and the elevator doors closed.

The doors reopened. Viktorija stepped forward and said, "What are you doing?"

"Joking with you. I'm just joking with you. Let me get in."

There was silence in the elevator on the way to the third floor. When the elevator doors opened, Viktorija took the lead.

"After you. I don't want to lose you again."

Mozes laughed as he stepped out first. He paused for Viktorija, and they walked down the hallway. At her apartment door, Viktorija gazed up into Mozes' eyes and said, "Would you like to come in?"

"Yes."

Viktorija opened her door and walked in. Mozes followed and closed the door behind him. When he turned around the *All-Seeing* stood in front of him and shook his head to indicate no. Mozes froze again.

Viktorija was in the living room when she looked back and saw Mozes still in the foyer.

"Mozes you can come into the living room."

There was no reply.

"Mozes you can come in here."

"I have to go. I'm sorry. Thank you for a lovely evening and warm company. Thank you."

Mozes quickly turned to the door, opened it, and rushed out.

Viktorija just stood in her living room. She was baffled. She swiftly walked toward the door. She thought she would chase after him. She placed her hand on the doorknob but stopped. She simply locked the door, turned back toward the living room, and leaned up against the door. She thought to herself.

"Strange. Very strange. He's sweet. Just my luck, a sweet, strange man."

Alone, she slowly walked off to her bedroom.

On the other side of the door, Mozes released the door knob and made it two steps before he fell to one knee from the pain.

He said to himself, "Every time I meet a beautiful lady this happens to me. God help me."

The pain subsided enough for Mozes to stand up and walk to his apartment. Once inside, he closed the door and leaned up against it. He slid to the floor exhausted from the pain.

20   The Task Force

Mozes woke up to the vibration of his cellphone alarm. He patted and crushed his pockets until he found his phone and fumbled with it to turn off the alarm. He looked about. He was confused because he did not recognize anything. A chill came over him. He looked about again, and things started to come into focus. The chill was caused by the opened front driver and passenger windows. He leaned up to observe he was in the fully reclined driver seat of his Porsche. It appeared he slept in the Porsche. He looked back at his cellphone for the time which displayed eight o'clock.

There was no time for his morning groom. He had to wear the same clothes he wore on his date last night. The fact he woke up in his car. The fact he was out in public without his morning groom. All this had him in more than a tizzy; he repulsed himself, but there was no other option.

Mozes adjusted the driver's seat, started the engine and slid the gear selector into drive. Today, he did not have time to let the Porsche warm up; he had a nine o'clock appointment at the task force and had to cross the morning rush hour traffic to get to the north side PBP offices.

Mozes looked over to the vehicle's watch as he navigated onto the parkway. It was eight-twenty. He opened the center console and retrieved an emergency red light. He affixed it to the center of the dash and plugged it into the power port. It began to rotate, and traffic started to yield the right of way to the makeshift emergency vehicle. He quickly reached the Ohio Boulevard exit and turned right to continue toward the PBP

123

building. He became flustered when he remembered this city building had no employee parking.

He thought, "Where will I park?"

At that instant, his cellphone rang. He pushed the answer button on the leather steering wheel.

"Hello."

"Mozes."

"Yes. This is Mozes."

"Mozes, this is Murry. Murry Stewart. We are to meet today at nine o'clock for a task force briefing."

"Yes."

"I'm unable to meet with you today. I have an emergency call to go on."

Just then, an unmarked police vehicle with flashing emergency lights passed Mozes at a high rate of speed. It traveled in the opposite direction on Ohio Boulevard.

"Okay. Let me know when you can reschedule. I hear your siren; let me hang up."

"Thank you, Mozes. I'll call you."

The call disconnected and Mozes pulled the plug to stop his emergency light. He slowed, pulled to the curb, and parked. He reached up and took the emergency light off the dash and gently placed it back in the console. Since the meeting was canceled, Mozes had his day off back. He had to decide what to do, but he knew he had to go back to his apartment for his morning groom. He drove off from the curb.

Mozes' mind struggled to disclose why he woke up in his car. As he drove along the Allegheny River, he looked over to the passenger seat and noticed a red color stain on the leather. He reached out and rubbed it. It was dry.

"Now what? What is this red stain from?"

As he focused back on the roadway and the morning traffic, he noticed the faceless, hallowed, figures appeared in his car. They were seated, one in the front passenger seat and two in the rear seat. He listened to the *All-Seeing*.

"*Mo*, you did well last night. Thank you for your help again."

The *Guiding* and the *Teacher* agreed, and they both congratulated *Mo* for his dutiful work last night.

Mozes listened to the *Teacher*.

"You tried again last night with Viktorija. It didn't work out, just like the other times when it didn't work for you. We groomed you from an early age to be like us."

The *Guiding* added.

"Yes, *Mo*. You did well last night. You fought this long enough."

Mozes pleaded.

"No. This is wrong. You should help me do the right thing. You only want me to do the wrong thing."

Mozes sat straight up and looked around. He was in his bedroom, in his bed, alone when he awoke from a dream. He reached to his bedside stand, picked up his cellphone, and pushed the button to display the time. It was seven o'clock. He touched the alarm app to turn off the alarms, but no alarms were set. He placed the phone on the bed, got out, and walked to the bathroom to start his morning groom. He had to be at the task force for a nine o'clock meeting.

Finished with his morning groom, he took a final look at himself in the decorative, full-length, mirror by the front door. He was content with his appearance. His morning routine made him visually suitable to engage the day, and he left the apartment for the meeting.

To avoid a chance encounter with Viktorija, Mozes used the stairs at the opposite end of the hallway from the elevator and apartment 3C. At the first-floor fire door to the lobby, he peered through the small square window to make certain there was no Viktorija. He quickly opened the door and with purpose walked through the lobby, out the door, and to his car. He pulled away from the apartment building.

Mozes navigated the parkway traffic as he crossed town to the north side, made his way through the north side traffic, and arrived at the PBP office. He circled the block several times before he found a parking space. Parked, he took a few minutes to compose himself for the meeting.

Mozes swiped his employee badge at the main entrance to the city office building. The electronic lock sounded, the door opened, and he entered, moved across the lobby to the oak staircase and walked up to the third floor. He walked into the Homicide Squad Office suite and directly to the conference room. Mozes was familiar with the building layout, particularly the location of the Homicide Squad conference room. It was in

126

the conference room Mozes interviewed three homicide detectives, subjects of a Personnel Investigation. It was alleged they stole narcotics from the apartment of a suspected murderer during the service of a search warrant.

Mozes entered the conference room.

"Detective Stewart?"

"Yes. Mr. Olah?"

"Yes. Please call me Mozes."

"Murry. Please call me Murry."

Murry extended his hand as did Mozes and they greeted each other with a firm handshake.

"Come in. Please sit. Thank you for coming."

"Thank you."

"Shall we get started?"

"Don't you want to wait for everyone else?"

"Everyone else is here. This is it. Just me and you."

"Oh. I thought there would be more agencies."

"No. Just us. Just me and you."

"Okay."

"Over the last thirteen months, nine mutilated bodies were discovered in the city. Three adult males, three adult females, and three minor females. The commonalities of the victims included: The position of their bodies, they were all found in one of the three rivers. The bodies were all positioned on their back with their hands folded left over right. All the victims were found nude. The last victim was discovered this morning at seven o'clock. None of the victims were identified. Forensics did not determine the specific cause of death for the victims. There was nothing at the crime scene to identify them. Their Fingerprints and DNA were not in our databases.

A couple weeks ago, I received a note on my personal vehicle when it was parked outside this building. It stated:

I KNOW ABOUT THE MURDERS THAT HAVE BEEN OCCURRING AROUND THE CITY FOR THE LAST YEAR OR SO. I HAVE INFORMATION ABOUT THE MURDERS THAT SHOULD ASSIST YOUR INVESTIGATIONS FROM BECOMING COLD. I WILL BE IN TOUCH SOON. I WILL BE IN TOUCH AT AN OPPORTUNE TIME AND PLACE.

The Mayor took a personal interest in this matter and demanded weekly briefings. To accommodate the Mayor, a briefing chain was established. Every Thursday afternoon, at one o'clock, the Assistant Chief of Investigations and my Lieutenant were briefed by me. The Acting Chief of Police was briefed every Thursday afternoon, at four o'clock, by the Assistant Chief. Every Monday morning at seven o'clock, the Mayor was informed by the Acting Chief of Police, in a private meeting in the Mayor's chambers. Between you and me, the cases have gone cold. Even today's discovery."

"Oh. Another victim? Today?" Mozes inquired.

"Yes," answered Detective Stewart and continued.

"Today is my day off. A mandatory day off so I don't run up the overtime. If it's okay with you, I would like to stop here for today. On Monday, I will have all the file folders out for you to review. It should only take you three or four hours to read them all; there's not much in them. You can jot down your questions, and we can discuss further then."

"Okay. Sounds good."

"One last point. This is not a task force."

"What do you mean?"

"Yesterday, at the command brief, the Assist Chief ordered my Lieutenant not to convene a task force. Understand?"

"Okay. How are we going to work together? Under what authority are we working together?"

"The complaint your office received in the mail. You should have a case opened. I'm more than willing to cooperate and work with the IG's office. Right. Isn't that what city policy states?"

Murry paused a moment. He expected to receive resistance from Mozes, but Mozes gave none.

Murry continued, "Give me a minute. I'll walk out with you."

"Okay."

Murry and Mozes walked out of the third-floor office. They walked down the stairs, across the lobby, and out the front door.

"Do you have access to this building?"

"Yes."

"Oh, yeah. The Mayor gave you guys complete access citywide. I forgot."

Employed by the IG, Mozes had access to all city property. Since the inception of the OIG, there was contention between all the departments, bureaus, and organizations under the Mayor's leadership. The PBP voiced the most and loudest. BPB leadership professed the OIG was a duplication of services. The PBP internal affairs investigated fraud, waste, and abuse within their organization and their investigative squads investigated all matters involving other city departments, bureaus, and agencies before the OIG was created. This included all criminal violations by city employees, residents or others. PBP command failed to see the need for the OIG and the related financial expenditures to run the office. Of all the city's leadership, the Chief of Police which continued with the Acting Chief gave the most push back to the OIG and their investigation of alleged wrongdoing by the PBP.

Mozes extended his hand as Murry did the same. They shook hands and concluded their meeting.

"I've parked up the block. Until Monday."

"Yes. Until Monday."

They walked off in different directions.

In his car, Mozes sat and reflected on the meeting.

"How does he know the OIG has an open case and a complaint? No task force. What will the IG say? This is starting out in a strange way. Another victim today and he goes home. How do they set their priorities?"

130

Mozes made his way from the north side to the Parkway. He moved slowly on the Parkway, construction of the Squirrel Hill Tunnels backed up the usual heavy Friday traffic on the eastbound lanes. He started to rub and massage the nape of his neck in an attempt to ease the tension brought on by the sharp pain moving through his head. He looked into his right-hand, side, mirror to check traffic before he changed lanes. He pulled back with surprise. The *Guiding* was seated in the right front passenger seat.

"Now what?" said Mozes.

The *Guiding* continued to look straight ahead.

"*Mo*, you can't work on these murder investigations. We can't afford for you to get caught. You need to remain reclusive as much as possible. You work for the OIG to gather information, so we don't get caught. You don't have to work. You have no financial needs with the amount of money you receive from the monthly payments. You don't want for anything."

From the left, a car horn sounded and brought Mozes back to focus. When Mozes looked to the left, he saw a motorist gesture at him with his middle finger. Mozes realized he did not let the person merge into the exit lane. Mozes quickly looked back to the right; the hallowed figure was gone.

21   Chance occurrences

Mozes sat straight up in bed. He looked at his Rolex and saw the time was one thirty. Friday afternoon he came home from the meeting with Detective Stewart and decided to lay down for a few minutes. He fell asleep at two o'clock and slept until one thirty Saturday afternoon.

He rubbed his face with both hands. He slung his legs over the edge of the bed to the wood floor. He sat there and cradled his head in his hands.

Shortly, he rose from the edge of the bed and walked out of the bedroom to the kitchen. He stopped at the sink, supported himself, and thought.

"A windowless kitchen. How fitting. Just like me. I have no windows. I can't see out. I can't see out to my past. I know a few things, only a few."

A knock on the door brought Mozes out of his deep thought. He pushed off the sink and walked to the door. He was still a bit groggy from his twenty-four-hour sleep and his deep thought of his past – his brief childhood in Windber and the coal mine patch neighborhood, the reticence of his mother about his childhood, his father's coal mining accident at *Mine 40*, and his doctor visits at the company hospital. What always took Mozes into his deepest thoughts was his mother's commitment to the Somerset State Hospital. Nothing was more troubling to Mozes. Mozes' mother was confined there from a Commitment Order signed by a doctor at the company hospital. That was all Mozes knew. All Aunt Llona told him.

When his mother was committed, Mozes was uprooted from Windber and brought to Pittsburgh by his mother's sister, Aunt Llona, his Godmother. She was a pleasant lady and treated Mozes with the utmost affection and love.

Mozes did not want for anything. It was an understatement to say he was spoiled. He always dressed in the latest styles and designer labels or private labels. He always drove new, fancy sports cars or SUVs. He attended an affluent independent preparatory school in Shadyside.

From there, he continued his studies at a major university local to the 'Burgh. Though he was late to apply, he was accepted to the regional, residential campus near his birth town. Aunt Llona, with no explanation, was adamant he would not go there. Mozes thought it cool to attend college so close to his birth town. Aunt Llona did not agree. Unannounced to Mozes, through friends of friends, Aunt Llona pleaded her request to the university and Mozes was granted an exception. Mozes received a second letter which stated he was accepted to attend the main campus in Oakland. Mozes never knew about Aunt Llona's intercession.

Mozes knew Aunt Llona routinely visited his mother at the state hospital, but she never took Mozes. Sometimes Mozes asked to go, but Aunt Llona did not take him. It was the only time she was agitated and short with him. On those days, Mozes sulked about the large, ornate, Victorian home in the affluent Shadyside neighborhood of Pittsburgh. He so much desired to visit his mother.

Sometime around his graduation from high school, Mozes observed Aunt Llona stopped her monthly trips to visit his mother. He never asked her why because he did not want to agitate her. At the age of eighteen years, he understood how kind and giving his Aunt was to him.

133

Deep in thought about his past and still groggy from a long sleep, Mozes walked directly from the kitchen to the door and flung it open. He did not check through the one-way peephole.

Viktorija stood there.

"Well. Do you always answer your door like this? It's kind of cute for me. I wonder what the cable guy might think."

Mozes looked down at himself. Embarrassed he stuttered.

"Ah." That was all he said. He repeated, "Ah."

Viktorija covered her mouth with her hand and laughed. It was an effort for her not to stare and size Mozes up while he stood there in his tight-fitting, black, athletic boxers. What also showed was his unclothed muscular torso, bulging biceps, and pecs. All accented with a ruddy hue. She slowly looked up and trained her eyes on his.

Already embarrassed Mozes acted cool.

"Would you like to come in?"

"That may be dangerous."

"What do you mean dangerous?"

"Me coming in and you only in your boxers. I don't know."

Mozes reached out and took Viktorija by her hand and pulled her into the apartment.

"Come in."

"Okay. If you insist. I'm not responsible for what happens."

He shut the door behind her.

"I'll go put clothes on. I was just about to make coffee. Make yourself at home. Sit and relax."

Mozes disappeared down a short hallway to his bedroom as Viktorija stretched to watch his tight, muscular, buttock move with every step. He quickly dressed into casual faded blue jeans and a novelty t-shirt. He returned to the edge of the living room.

"Would you like a cup of coffee?"

"Yes. Please."

Mozes walked to the kitchen to make the coffee.

Viktorija teased Mozes.

"Who is that in the kitchen?"

"What?"

"Who is that in the kitchen?"

"What do you mean?"

"Faded blue jeans. A novelty t-shirt. If I saw you out somewhere in those clothes, I wouldn't recognize you."

"What? This. These are my inside clothes.

"I don't know. You look sexy. I think you should wear jeans and a t-shirt more often."

"No. You wouldn't catch me out with these clothes. This isn't even my t-shirt."

"What do you mean it's not your t-shirt?"

Mozes ignored her question and asked, "Cream or sugar?"

He did not want to explain he never wore t-shirts because of his youthful commitment he made to himself. He only had them in his closet for the fare Pittsburgh ladies in case they stayed over. So was his longtime, lusty, desire to spend the night together. Then, in the morning, the lady would lounge around in the t-shirt, braless.

"Just black please."

"You like the natural taste of coffee. Good for you."

With a coffee cup in each hand, Mozes walked from the kitchen to the living room. He gave Viktorija a cup as she moved to her right to give him room to sit next to her. Mozes went to and sat in the armchair opposite the couch.

Mozes looked over his cup and sipped his coffee. He watched Viktorija as she looked about the apartment.

"What do you think?"

"What do I think?"

"Yes. What do you think of my apartment? You're looking around."

"I am?"

"Yes, you are."

"I am. It's impressive. It's a pleasant surprise. Who is your decorator??"

"My Aunt decorated it for me."

Laughing, Viktorija steadied her cup with both hands.

"Mozes. It's okay. You can tell me one of your girlfriends decorated it. You're Aunt. Come on."

"No. I'm serious. It was my Aunt Llona."

"Okay, for now, we'll just call her Aunt Llona."

"Why don't you believe me?"

"Because. A man like you. You probably have many girlfriends. Maybe many at one time."

"You have me all wrong. Why do you think of me in that way?"

"Look around. Look at your apartment and its décor. Other men's apartments don't look like this. They struggle to have furniture in the living room. Look at the paintings? The prints hanging on the wall? Look at your lamps. They match. That's a first for me. Feel this leather. Again, a first for me. Falling through lawn furniture is my experience. One place had camping gear in the living room. A camping stove in the kitchen."

Mozes smiled and held back laughter.

"You have me all wrong."

"We'll see. We'll see."

Silence took the conversation. Viktorija sipped her coffee. Mozes stared at the painting on the wall behind her.

Viktorija broke the silence and said, "If I have you wrong, then let's go to a movie right now. Let's just go. You're dressed. I'm ready. Let's go."

"I'm not ready. I can't go like this."

"See."

"See what? See I like to be visually presentable when I go out in public."

Again, silence took the conversation. Viktorija held her coffee cup with her right hand and rested it on her right thigh. Viktorija looked at Mozes and tried to lock eyes, but Mozes shifted his.

Uncomfortable, Mozes rose from the chair and walked toward the kitchen. He passed a print on his way. From a reflection in the glass, Mozes saw Viktorija gently shook her head. He did not know what the head shake meant.

"Would you like some more coffee?"

"No. I think I should go."

"Go. Why?"

"I don't know. You confuse me."

"Confuse you. I'm not trying to confuse you."

Viktorija rose from the couch. Mozes watched her, with keen attention, as she walked to the kitchen and placed her cup in the sink. Mozes continued to look at her as she walked up to him in the hallway to his bedroom. She encroached the customary distance for a conversation and stopped six inches from Mozes. Mozes heard her heart beat. It pounded with such intensity, her voluptuous breast rose and fell in rhythm with the beat. She looked up and into his eyes, but Mozes looked away and moved back the hall to create distance from her. She stopped and lowered her head as she walked off to the front door. Viktorija paused with her hand on the doorknob, then opened it. Halfway through, she stopped, turned, and looked at Mozes.

"See. You confuse me."

She turned back, walked out the door, and gently closed it behind her.

Mozes just stood in the hallway and thought to himself.

"Another chance occurrence with Viktorija. She looked so sad."

Mozes walked to the armchair and sat. In one hand, he held his coffee cup. In the other, propped on the arm of the chair, Mozes supported his head held low. He mumbled out loud with anger.

"Why me? Why me God! There is deadness in my soul. Why do I deserve deadness?"

He raised his head and fixed his eyes on the painting. The painting seemed to soothe his soul. He sipped his coffee and continued to stare at the painting on the wall.

His stare was quickly interrupted by three, faceless, hallowed, figures who appeared on the couch. They sat three abreast, and the *All-Seeing* spoke.

"Forget her *Mo*. Forget her just like the others. Your soul is ours. We create the deadness in your soul. We control you."

He set his coffee cup on the round coffee table. He drew back into the chair, lowered his head, and cradled it in his hands. He sat there and wept not for his pain, but for the pain of the others. The pain he caused to the others. The pain he caused Viktorija. His desire was not to hurt her; his desire was her.

22   On my way to renouncing them

Aunt Llona never talked in detail to Mozes about his mother or
father, nor the events that brought him to Pittsburgh to live
with her. She did not know why Mozes never asked her any
questions. This relieved her but kept her on edge. She too
desired to shield Mozes from the atrocity.

Aunt Llona uprooted Mozes from '*40*' to protect him from the
vile diocese. Mentally difficult, she kept to his mother's
religious practice. She made sure Mozes attended church every
Sunday and holy days of obligation. She dutifully took Mozes
to the Hungarian ethnic church in the Baldwin area of
Pittsburgh. This was a distance away from their Shadyside
home, but Aunt Llona wanted Mozes to attend an ethnic church
to maintain his ethnic Hungarian traditions. She wanted to ease
Mozes' transition to Pittsburgh and thought it helpful for
Mozes to attend an ethnic Hungarian church like the one he
attended in Windber.

Sunday church was always followed by a family meal prepared
by Aunt Llona. This too was a family practice of her sister and
Aunt Llona wanted to continue it for Mozes and for respect to
her sister.

Mozes was up early today and quickly groomed himself to
make the nine o'clock morning Mass. He took a final look at
himself in the decorative, full-length, mirror. Content with his
appearance, he left the apartment.

Mozes drove toward downtown to the Liberty Bridge, across
the bridge, and through the Liberty Tunnels. He made his way

to Route 51 South, Saw Mill Run Boulevard, which turned into Clairton Boulevard.

As he drove south, he rolled the past through his mind.

"All those years Aunt Llona and I went to church, she abruptly stopped going in with me when I graduated high school. Then she waited outside in her car parked in the parking lot. This was at the same time she stopped going to visit mother. That was peculiar. When I graduated college, Aunt Llona stopped taking me to church. That was also peculiar. There were many peculiar things about my life. I needed to sit Aunt Llona down and talk to her. I needed answers to many questions, the many unusual things. She was seventy now. I needed to have a conversation with her. Once she was gone, God forbid, I had no one else. As far as I knew, there was no one else."

Mozes arrived and parked his Porsche in the rear parking lot. He walked to the front entrance of the church, entered, and walked through the ornate vestibule. Inside the church, he dipped his three fingers into the holy water and genuflected. He took his usual seat on the right-hand side a third of the way to the front. He knelt and prayed. Finished, he sat in self-reflection. He rubbed and massaged the nape of his neck in an attempt to ease the tension brought on by the sharp pain moving through his head.

Throughout the mass, Mozes felt someone watching him, looking at him. Occasionally he glanced about but observed no one he knew. After the congregation said the *Our Father* and extended each other the sign of peace, Mozes saw. On the left-hand side, near the rear of the church, Viktorija stood next to a man. He risked detection but took a long look anyway. The two seemed chummy. He looked away to bring his attention back to the mass.

The priest gave the final blessing, and the choir began the final hymn, as the priest, deacon, and altar servers processioned to the rear of the church.

Mozes stood in final self-reflection while the attendees filed out of the church. Deep in self-reflection, he was startled by a gentle touch to his shoulder. He jerked, looked, and saw Viktorija.

"Good morning Mozes."

"Good morning Viktorija. So, nice to see you."

"Thank you. I didn't know this was your church."

"Yes. I have been a member here since I moved to Pittsburgh. And you, you're a member here too?"

"No. I'm a member of the church on Washington Place. It's closer to the apartment."

"Yes. This is a little way from the apartment. You look beautiful as always."

"Thank you. Mozes, are you trying to make me blush? You know I'm to do that to you."

"And you do. You do."

"I see your gentleman is waiting for you. You should go. It was nice to see you as always."

"Who Tommy? He is a friend of mine. Would you like to join us for brunch?"

"A friend?"

"Yeah. He's in Pittsburgh to do research for a book he's writing. He's an aspiring author, and he's here to get a perspective of a Hungarian Roman Catholic. Whatever that is to a writer. I didn't ask him."

"Hm."

Come on, join us. I want you to."

"You do. After yesterday is that possible."

"Yes, Mozes it's possible. I enjoy your company. Wait, do you think there's something between us? Tommy and me. There isn't; he's just a friend."

"Okay. Thanks. Where you all going?"

"Tommy likes the Royal Brewery when he's in Pittsburgh. Will that be okay with you?"

"Yes. I'll meet you there."

Viktorija replied with an excited tone, "See you there."

In the nave, Viktorija moved closed to Mozes, extended her right hand and gently rested it on Mozes' left shoulder. She smiled and winked at Mozes, then turned and walked back to Tommy. Together, Viktorija and Tommy walked through the vestibule to exit the church.

Mozes had a butterfly feeling in his stomach. He stepped out of the pew, genuflected, and turned to leave the church. He walked to his car. Seated with the car running he was brought to a pause by a vision. The *All-Seeing*, the *Teacher*, and the *Guiding* appeared. They said nothing. Mozes rocked back and forth and fought hard to make the vision go away.

Mozes mumbled, "Not today. It's Sunday. I went to church. When I'm leaving the church, you all appear in my car. No. No. Not today."

The *Guiding* spoke.

"Don't you want to stay after church? Don't you want to play in the nave? You know. Like in the nave when you were young."

Mozes rocked faster and harder. He wanted the vision to go away. He slowly opened his eyes to see if they were still there and they were not. He placed the shifter into drive and drove off.

As Mozes walked up to the main entrance to the Royal Brewery, he heard his name called. He hesitated to turn, in fear it would be another vision. When his name was called a second time, he cautiously turned and looked. He saw Viktorija and Tommy were walking behind him.

When they reached him, Viktorija said, "Mozes this is Tommy Slatski. Tommy this is Mozes Olah."

Mozes and Tommy extended and shook hands as they talked over each other.

"Pleased to meet you."

Mozes opened the door and motioned for Viktorija and Tommy to enter. He followed them to the hostess stand.

Tommy asked, "May we have a table for three on the porch?"

"Sure. Follow me please."

They followed the hostess and were seated.

"There should be less noise out here. It can get noisy inside," said Tommy.

After they all had been seated, Mozes inquired.

"Tommy, you're an author?"

"Yes. A debut author."

"What have you written?"

"A novel. *Operation Red X.*"

"What's that about?"

"A contemporary fiction political thriller. An assassination team conspired to kill all the members of the United States Presidential Cabinet, through a false flag operation that implicated the Republic of Poland as the perpetrator."

"Sounds interesting."

"The ending is a plot twister. So, readers say. I won't tell you."

Viktorija added, "Sounds interesting. How is your research for your second book going?"

"It's going well. The setting will be Pittsburgh of course. I'm getting out to visit some of the sights and landmarks to refresh my perspective of the locations."

"Good."

Tommy inquired of Mozes.

"How do you pass your time?"

"I work for the City of Pittsburgh's Office of Inspector General. I investigate fraud, waste, and abuse with city programs and money."

"That has to be interesting."

"I think so."

"I think you have some good material for a book or two."

"I suppose. I've thought about it. Just the political machine alone."

Viktorija reached to Tommy and jokingly poked his ribs.

"What is your second book about? Can you tell us? Or do we have to wait."

Laughing, Tommy slowly and gently pushed her hand away. He moved about in his seat as he answered.

"You have to wait. I'm still in the research phase. I don't even have an outline yet."

Viktorija, Tommy, and Mozes continued to converse, eat, and drink. They finished their brunch and visit and finally made their way to the front door. Tommy looked to Mozes.

"Mozes, it was a pleasure to meet you. Maybe I can shadow you for the first-hand perspective of white collar crime in the *'Burgh*. Maybe I could get some ideas for my second book. Perhaps a third."

They shook hands.

"I may be able to work it out. Let me see what I can do."

Tommy looked to Viktorija.

"I always enjoy our visits."

Tommy reached out and hugged Viktorija. They cheek kissed.

Tommy looked back to Mozes.

"Would you mind giving Viktorija a ride back to her apartment. I understand you two live in the same apartment building. Sure would help me. You don't mind Viktorija?"

"Okay," replied Mozes.

"Thank you. You two just go and enjoy each other today."

Viktorija looked to Mozes.

"That sounds like fun to me. Mozes did you have other plans?"

"No. Just back to the apartment."

"Okay. See you all later."

Tommy smiled and walked off.

"Mozes, you know I have my car."

"That's what I thought."

"I don't know what Tommy was thinking. I drove him here."

She paused for a moment.

"Wait. Okay. I get it."

Hesitantly, Mozes asked, "Would you like to go for a walk along the river?"

Viktorija was still thinking of Tommy's slyness.

"Wait till I see him again. Sure, Mozes. What a pleasant surprise. And would you like to go with me?"

Mozes cocked his head as he looked at Viktorija. He began to speak when Viktorija started to laugh.

"I get it," said Mozes.

Mozes laughed with Viktorija.

Mozes and Viktorija walked down to the paved riverside walkway. Viktorija interlaced her right hand over Mozes' left forearm. They slowly strolled along the river in the warm, Sunday, afternoon, sun.

Mozes thought to himself, "What a nice day. Sunday church, lunch, and Viktorija along the river. This will definitely ease the Sunday night depression sitting alone."

Mozes looked at Viktorija and smiled. Viktorija felt his gaze, looked up at him and smiled. They didn't say anything to each other; they didn't have too. They knew each was content, at the moment.

Again, Mozes thought to himself, "Am I on my way to renouncing them?"

23   File Review

When Mozes arrived at the PBP, he went directly to the third floor. Murry was already in the homicide squad conference room and had laid out all the investigative reports.

"Good morning Mozes. I trust you had a good weekend."

"Yes, I did. And you?"

"I did too. Relaxing. Now back at it. Please read through all the files here. I have a couple of things to do this morning. You should be finished by lunch. Please note your questions for when I return."

"Okay. Sounds good."

Murry left the conference room.

Mozes set his black, leather, Tumi letter pad on the conference table. He took his suit jacket off, inspected it for lint, then held it with his left hand and reached to the inside customized pen pocket and slid his black, Monte Blanc pen out and placed it atop the letter pad. He put his suit jacket on the chair back and adjusted it, so it did not wrinkle.

He pulled out another chair and sat at the conference table to begin his review. He picked up the Monte Blanc pen and twisted the top. He opened the Tumi letter pad and dated the top sheet of paper in the upper right-hand corner in European format. Below the date, he annotated PBP File Review.

He set the pen down and picked up the government green file folders. He counted them. There were eleven. They were not thick which reminded Mozes of what Murry said on Friday, the cases have gone cold.

He thumbed through the files and saw they were in numerical order by case number. He sat the stack off to the left. He pulled the top file folder off the pile and placed it on the table in front of him. He opened it with his left hand. With his right hand, he slid his leather pad to his right. He picked up the Mont Blanc and across the top of the page wrote the headings: Date Found, Name to be preceded by an A for the adults or C for the children, Sex, Race, and Distinguishing Marks. He used the far left-hand column to label each victim with a V and the consecutive number one through eleven. He first reviewed all the case files and completed the headings.

V1	12/26/2015	A-Jane Doe	Female White None
V2	1/12/2016	C-Jane Doe	Female White None
V3	2/15/2016	C-Jane Doe	Female White None
V4	2/20/2016	A-John Doe	Male White None
V5	3/3/2016	A-Jane Doe	Female White None
V6	4/7/2016	A-Jane Doe	Female White None
V7	4/18/2016	A-John Doe	Male White None
V8	4/29/2016	C-Jane Doe	Female White None
V9	5/12/2016	A-John Doe	Male White None
V10	5/23/2016	A-Jane Doe	Female White None
V11	6/1/2016	C-Jane Doe	Female White None

Mozes stacked all the case files together. He tapped them on the table, so they were all in line. He set them to his left ready for a second review. This time, he looked for anything the victims had in common. He started with the ME's reports and made another heading, ME Reports Disclosed. He used it for all males and females, youth or adult victims, collectively. He wrote:

1. Found naked.
2. Found floating in one of the three rivers.
3. Face up with their hands folded left over right and placed atop their body.
4. In an unskilled manner, all the victims had parts of their flesh removed, all in the same locations – upper left on the back and in the center of the lower back. The upper left was a four by four area and the center lower back was an eight by four area.

Mozes shuffled the files together and tapped them on the table, so again they were all in line. He set them to his left. He sat back in his chair and wondered to himself.

"Flesh removed in an unskilled manner from all the victims in the same locations on their bodies. Adults and children. What was removed, perhaps a tattoo? Or was it some type of ritual marking?"

For a third review, Mozes moved to the Investigative Write-ups (IW). He opened the first file and paged through it. There was no IW. He set the file to the right. He opened the second file, paged through it, again no IW. Such was the case with all the remaining nine files. This struck him as odd. He pondered the absence of the IWs as he shuffled the case file folders for a symmetric alignment.

He wondered, "No IWs? Surely Murry knows PBP's policy requires an IW even if it is one sentence. Murry must know the IG, Office of Audits, performs unannounced city department audits to assure adherence to departmental policies. The lack of timely IWs is an actionable offense. All actionable offenses impact the department head's bonus which of course trickles down to the subordinates' performance evaluations."

There was nothing else in the case files for Mozes to review. He twice checked himself for entries of the press coverage. There was nothing. He slid the black, leather, letter pad in front of him. Pen in hand, he began to write questions to discuss with Murry. He started with the obvious:

IWs?
Media coverage entries?
Efforts to ID the victims?
Local, State and Federal Indices checks – Fingerprints?
   DNA, Photographs?
International Indices - Interpol, Europol?
Perpetrator psychological theories (PPTs)
   by PBP Investigative Psychologist?

Murry entered the conference room and broke Mozes' concentration with the thorough case review.

"How're you doing?"

Because of the lack of details in the file folders, Mozes skipped the nicey-nicey.

"Okay. I have questions."

Murry sat down in a chair next to Mozes.

"Okay."

"Where are the IWs?"

"There are none. I had nothing to write up."

"You know you have to enter something, even if it's one sentence. Even if the one sentence says, 'Nothing to report.' That's PBP's policy."

"Okay. I'll write them up this afternoon. I have eleven IWs to write. They'll all say the same thing, nothing to report.

"Where are the media coverage entries?"

"There was no media coverage. My Lieutenant, at the direction of the Mayor, declared these cases under a press blackout. He noted some goofy Executive Order by the Mayor."

"What effort did you take to ID the victims?"

"Well, nothing. I was waiting for the ME reports."

"How about fingerprints? DNA? Photographs?"

"Those were all negative."

"Negative. That's not in the case files."

"Okay, but the PBP database checks were negative."

"International indices. Did you check with Interpol? Europol?"

"No. Neither."

"And did the PBP's psychologist provided a Perpetrator Psychological Profile?"

"No. I didn't make the request yet."

"From what I reviewed this was not a race thing."

"Why do you say that?"

"The victims are all white. Even if the perpetrator is black, it's not a race thing. Whites are a non-entity."

"Oh."

"No politician cares when it's a white victim. All the victims are white with these cases. Politicians can't make a political statement with that fact. That fact will not garner votes or support for their personal agendas."

"Okay."

"So why the Mayor's keen interest to the point of weekly briefings from the Acting Chief?"

"I don't know."

"What are your thoughts on the body mutilation? The ME's report describes all eleven victims, adults and children, have parts of their flesh removed, in an unskilled manner. All in the same locations, upper left on the back and in the center of the lower back. Even the males."

"Perhaps something was removed. Maybe tattoos."

Mozes reflected out loud.

"That's what I thought too. But even the children? I don't follow. Is it possible for the children to have tattoos? Did their parents tattoo them? Is it even legal to tattoo a minor? Is there an age limit before someone can get a tattoo?"

Mozes paused momentarily, then continued.

"Also, consistent, with males and females, adults and children. They were all naked. They were all found floating in one of the three rivers. Face up. Hands folded left over right."

"Perhaps there's some type of ritual aspect with the murders."

"That's what I thought. That's all we have? Maybe tattoos were removed and a possible ritual aspect. That's not much at all."

Mozes oral case review brought silence to the conference room, which he finally broke.

"I'm going for today. You have more work to do before I continue with you."

"Okay. I will bring everything up to date today. I'll stay until I finish."

"Good. I don't know how else to say this, so I'll just say it. Everything we do must be at one hundred percent per the rules and regulations. I will not be a part of a sloppy investigation. I also think there are things you are not telling me. I'll wait to read the IWs before I discuss that with you. I'm not going to keep things from you; I ask for the same respect. Please."

When Mozes mentioned there were things Murry was not telling him, Murry kept his head down and stared at the table.

Mozes closed his materials, slid the case files over to Murry, and rose from his chair. He pushed it under the table and paused with his hands on the back of it. The case review raced through his mind. He released the seat back, turned to his suit jacket, and removed it from the chair. He inspected it, put it on, and adjusted the custom fit. He picked up the Monte Blanc, turned the top to retract the point and returned it to the customized pen pocket on the inside of his suit jacket. He picked up his materials and walked out of the room.

24   The next day

"Good morning Murry."

"Good morning Mozes. I completed all the IWs yesterday. They're ready for your review."

"Good. Thank you. I'll read them now."

Mozes sat in a chair opposite Murry at the conference table. He took out his pen and positioned it with his leather letter pad on the conference table.

A voice boomed and broke the silence of the room.

"So, this is the guy from the IG's office."

Murry jumped up from his chair.

"Yes, sir. It is. Let me introduce Mozes Olah. Mozes, this is my Lieutenant."

The Lieutenant walked around the table to Mozes as Mozes rose from his chair. They both extended their hands for a hearty handshake and at the same time said, "Hello. Pleased to meet you."

The Lieutenant continued.

"Welcome to the homicide squad. We can use the help. Now you're not here to secretly gig us on bullshit regulations, are you?"

"No, I'm not here for that. Although, as I told Murry yesterday, everything we do must be at one hundred percent per the rules and regulations. I will not be a part of a sloppy investigation. I also think there are things Murry isn't telling me. I'm not going to keep things from you all. I ask for the same respect, sir. Please."

"Murry, shut the door please," commanded the Lieutenant.

"Yes, sir.

Murry walked to the door and closed it.

Mozes thought to himself.

"Here it comes. The Lieutenant is going to tell me how great this unit is. How uncomfortable it is for his unit to have me here working on a murder case. How some of the detectives remember me from a personnel investigation of three suspects, three detectives, suspects in the theft of illegal narcotics from an alleged murderer's apartment during the service of a search warrant. An investigation I worked right out of this conference room and proved the allegation of three, then accused, now terminated and incarcerated detectives."

The Lieutenant looked at Murry and then to Mozes.

"Please sit."

He focused back to Mozes and continued.

"Mozes, we don't know each other. I ask for your loyalty and commitment to finding the perpetrator or perpetrators of these murders. Frankly, the Mayor hinders Murry's investigative efforts. I could not get any of my superiors to commit the necessary resources, human or financial, for the murder investigations. They all say the Mayor is not approving my requests. I know the Mayor selects murder victims and monitors those investigations. Those same investigations are under a gag order, by the direction of the Mayor."

The Lieutenant paused and maintained eye contact with Mozes. He continued.

"Now, if you're here to gig this unit, then please go back to the IG, back to your office. If you're here to work as a team member with Murry, then please stay. We need help. We want your help."

The Lieutenant paused again. Mozes said nothing.

The Lieutenant continued.

"Of course, I checked you out. You were highly recommended. Your reputation was impeccable for getting the job done in a fair and efficient manner."

Mozes used a lull to speak.

"Sir, thank you for clearing the air. I'm staying. I'm here to work as a team member. The IG knows I have a stubbornly persisting drive to prove or disprove allegations. In this case, to find the murderer or murderers. As well as my penchant for ensuring the rules are followed, both by me and those, I work with."

"That the IG emphasized to me. The IG and I have known each other since our parochial school days in Brooklyn. I wanted you to know I was glad you were assigned to this investigation for just that reason."

"Great."

The Lieutenant continued.

"I have a gut feeling this investigation is going to be complicated and involve prominent employees and/or residents of the city. And that may just be the beginning."

"Thank you, sir."

"Murry, you have anything to add?"

"No Lieutenant. Only that I too appreciate your help, Mozes. I sure can use it."

"Okay. We're all in agreement then. Let's get these murderers. Murry, finish your brief to Mozes."

"Okay. This is the remaining information we have.

I didn't complete the IWs because we didn't want the case information in the files in the event a mole breached the files.

I received a note on the windshield of my personal vehicle when it was parked on the street here at work. The hand-written note stated,

I KNOW ABOUT THE MURDERS OCCURRING AROUND THE CITY FOR THE LAST YEAR OR SO. I HAVE INFORMATION ABOUT THE MURDERS TO ASSIST YOUR INVESTIGATIONS FROM BECOMING COLD. I WILL BE IN TOUCH SOON. I WILL BE IN TOUCH AT AN OPPORTUNE TIME AND PLACE.

No one has come forward yet.

I personally conduct an undercover surveillance operation in the Strip District as Murry, the vagrant. There's a connection to the *Strip* and the murders. A business or businesses. A person or persons. Everything that happens in Pittsburgh touches the *Strip*, somehow, some way.

160

We identified one victim. V11. Rhonda Popa. I recognized her from Gheorghi's Joe when in my undercover role. This was our first big lead. The ME listed her as Jane Doe.

And now you Mozes, Murry finished."

"Me."

"Yes. Mozes, what is your relationship with Sofiya Zlatkov?"

"I met her once. It was on the *Strip* at Gheorghi's Joe's. I bumped into her. Literally bumped into her as I turned with my coffee to pay at the cashier. She seemed to be flirtatious, so I pursued. We sat outside Gheorghi's Joe's, talked and drank our coffee. It was brief. She received a text and had to go back to her office. We exchanged business cards and mutually agreed we should go to lunch. My only encounter with her."

"Do you know who she is? Do you know who her father is?

"She is a Pittsburgh socialite and daughter of Boris Zlatkov, one of the wealthiest families in Pittsburgh. They're always in the news and in the papers. She is constantly about town."

"And you know her father, Boris Zlatkov, is the reputed boss of the Bulgaria Crime Family in Pittsburgh. It's alleged he controls his global criminal enterprise from right here in the hills of western Pennsylvania."

"I didn't know all that."

"You have to stay away from her. Will you be able to stay away?"

"Of course."

"Okay. Why did you faint on the *Strip* the other week? Do you remember when I caught you, helped you?"

"I do. It was nothing."

"Nothing? It looked like you were bent over in pain?"

"No. It was nothing."

"Okay. If you say so."

The Lieutenant interrupted, "Well then, we're done for today?"

Mozes looked to the Lieutenant.

"I had one more thing to add. An unknown person sent a letter to the IG. It was postmarked from the Lawrenceville Post Office. The short printed informal letter was on simple plain white stationery. The envelope was the same. It was undated. It read,

SIR. I AM REPORTING THE MAYOR OF THE CITY OF PITTSBURGH IS PARTICIPATING IN A CONSPIRACY TO COVER UP MURDERS COMMITTED IN THE CITY THROUGHOUT THE LAST FOURTEEN MONTHS. MY FATHER LOVES YOU. BLESS YOU, MY SON. SAINT MICHAEL.

The letter, the allegation, gave the IG the authority to assign me here."

The Lieutenant quickly looked to Murry.

"I got this."

The Lieutenant looked back to Mozes.

"I sent the letter. I needed help from your office, the clout of the IG's office. I saw nothing wrong with such an approach.

The facts were true. The Mayor's Directive encouraged city employees to report wrongdoing by city employees. Even to report it anonymously."

Mozes cut the Lieutenant off before he finished.

"You did nothing wrong. Thanks for your candor."

The Lieutenant requested, "Murry anything else?

"Nothing further from me sir."

The Lieutenant looked to Mozes and requested, "Mozes, anything else?"

"Nothing further here."

The Lieutenant finished, "Okay if I don't see you sooner, I'll see you both at the Thursday command brief."

The Lieutenant rose from his chair and walked out of the conference room.

25 Father's Day

Mozes drove his usual route to church. His mind wondered to last Sunday and the pleasure he had when he met Viktorija at church and her afternoon company.

Mozes entered the church through the vestibule. He moved to the nave and surveyed the church with a desire to see Viktorija. No Viktorija. Mozes chose a pew, bowed, crossed himself and moved in. He knelt and prayed. When he finished, he sat back in the pew and raised the kneeler with his foot. It was Father's Day which moved Mozes to reflect.

"A few memories of my father were all I had. Mother talked about father only a few times. When she did, it was short. I knew he died in a coal mining accident at the mine in '40'. What were the circumstances? Was it an explosion? Was it a cave in? I never met any of his family, if he had a family. Aunt Llona never talked about him. She never mentioned him."

Mozes carefully looked about the church at the end of mass. He hoped to see Viktorija but was disappointed as he retraced his path out of the church.

On the way to his car, he heard his name called. He turned and saw Tommy, Viktorija's friend.

Tommy rushed toward Mozes.

"Mozes. Good morning. It's Tommy."

Mozes cut him off.

"I remember. Viktorija's friend. Good morning. How are you? Happy Father's Day."

"Thank you. Happy Father's Day to you."

"I'm not a father," replied Mozes

"Surely you're a father figure to someone?"

Out of politeness, Mozes smiled. He quickly thought to himself.

"No, I'm not a father nor a father figure to anyone. Not sure how that would work out for me."

It appeared out of politeness Tommy changed the subject too.

"What are you doing today? Would you like to have lunch? My treat. I'd like to pick your brain for my book."

Reluctant, as though he had something better to do, Mozes replied, "Okay. Where would you like to go?"

"I don't care. You pick. It's your city. I prefer a local place as to the national chain restaurants."

"Good. I'll meet you there? How well do you know the city?"

"I don't have a car. That's why you saw me with Viktorija last week."

"Okay. Get in. I'll decide."

Both Mozes and Tommy entered Mozes' car. Mozes adjusted the air conditioning and drove away.

Mozes asked, "Where's Viktorija today?"

"Visiting her father in her hometown."

"Where's her hometown?"

"About eighty miles east of here. Did you ever hear of a coal mining town called Windber?"

"Yes," replied Mozes.

"Yes. You know Windber? Viktorija's hometown. I'm from there too. That's how I know Viktorija," said Tommy.

Mozes pushed back into his seat, and his hands gripped the steering wheel. He cocked his head toward Tommy.

"What a small world. I too am from Windber. Well, born there. I moved to Pittsburgh when I was fourteen."

"Yeah. Where did you live back there?"

"A coal mine patch neighborhood outside of Windber. We called it '*40*'."

"What? No way. That's where I lived. Where I grew up. On Wissinger Road. House 934."

"I lived at the top of Third Street on the left-hand side. I don't remember the number."

"Olah. I don't remember the name. Sorry. Hey, did you go to the sandlot baseball field behind Third Street?"

"No. My mother was protective of me after my father's mining accident."

166

"Oh. I understand."

Mozes changed the topic.

"I know a place on Carson."

"Sure. Good."

After seated on the patio, for less noise, they placed their orders.

Tommy continued their conversation.

"So, you were saying, your mother was protective of you. Your father was involved in a mining accident?"

"Oh, he wasn't involved. The coal mining accident killed him."

"Mozes, I'm so sorry. I didn't mean to dredge up the sad past on Father's Day."

"No. I was eight when my father was killed in the industrial accident. I guess they called it that. I knew little about him. I was told less about the accident."

"Is your mother still in '40'?"

"No. When I was about fourteen, my mother was committed to the Somerset State Hospital. That's when I came to Pittsburgh. My Aunt Llona, my Godmother, brought me here."

"Talk about a rough childhood. You lost your father. Your mother was committed. I'm so sorry

"What are you sorry for? You didn't do anything."

167

Tommy sensed the conversation about Mozes' childhood, his parents, and his life difficulties troubled him. Mozes showed signs of stress such events inflicted on people.

Mindful of the stress Tommy continued.

"I have to ask, but you don't have to answer. Did you ever visit your mother? How tough that must have been."

"No. I never did. My Aunt Llona visited her then stopped. She never offered to take me. I didn't think it was my place to ask. The few times I asked to go, I was rebuffed."

"Why?"

"Aunt Llona was so nice to me. Everything I had was from my Aunt Llona. And when she got ready to go visit my mother, she got upset. I didn't know why, but I didn't want to add to the confusion. I certainly didn't want to upset her more. I didn't ask."

Their food was served to them.

"Anything else for now?" asked the waiter.

Both Mozes and Tommy looked at the waiter and replied, "No thank you."

The waiter walked away, and they began to eat.

Tommy abruptly stopped and placed his utensils down on the salad plate. Mozes looked up from his food.

"What's the matter? Is there something wrong with your food?"

"No. It's actually pretty good."

"What's wrong then?"

"I have to tell you. I hope I don't upset you."

Mozes sat back still holding his fork in his right hand.

"If you have something to say, just say it."

Tommy continued, "The Somerset State Hospital was closed in 1995. It was converted to a minimum-security correctional facility to house older males with geriatric mentally challenging issues."

Mozes sat up taller. His facial expression of interest changed to shock.

"What? What are you saying?"

"In the capacity of a mental ailment hospital, it was closed in 1995."

"How do you know?"

"I read it in the newspaper back in 1995, when I visited family in Windber. The local newspaper articles about the minimum-security correctional facility caught my attention, and I read them."

"It was in 1995," inquired Mozes.

"Yes. 1995."

"That's when Aunt Llona stopped going to visit my mother."

"It was. Are you sure?"

"Yes. Somethings are vivid to me. Somethings I can just recall about my mother and father. One is when my Aunt stopped going to Somerset to visit my mother."

"Did you ever think about investigating your parents? To get everything straight in your mind. You're an investigator."

"No. I never did."

Before Mozes finished, Tommy talked over him.

"Boy, I would. The investigative psyche would be in overdrive for me."

"I suppose I could start with my Aunt Llona. She is seventy years old. Her mind is still sharp."

"Was your mother older or younger than her sister Llona?"

"Younger. My mother would be sixty-eight, two years younger than Aunt Llona."

"If I may suggest, maybe you should take Viktorija with you when you talk to your Aunt Llona. Having a supportive female with you may make your Aunt Llona more conducive to open up and talk about this."

Mozes went silent.

Tommy continued, "Again, I know I may be way out of line here. Viktorija likes you. She's taken by you."

"What? No way."

"Oh, yes. You don't see it?"

Mozes did not respond. Tommy directed the conversion back to Mozes' parents.

"Anyway. If I follow this correctly, Viktorija is near the age of your mother at commitment. Aunt Llona is seventy you said."

"Yes, seventy."

"Viktorija's presence may be helpful. A powerful subliminal motivation for your Aunt Llona to tell you all she knows. Maybe."

"Wow. This's a lot for me to process. After all these years."

Mozes started to rub and massage the nape of his neck.

Tommy saw the strain in Mozes' face. The stress that the conversation about his parents seemed to bring to him.

"Are you all right Mozes?"

Mozes did not answer.

"Mozes, are you all right?" Tommy asked again.

A blank stare came over Mozes' face. He stared passed Tommy at the three, faceless, hallowed, figures.

Tommy continued, "Mozes. Mozes are you all right?"

Tommy reached across the table and shook Mozes by the arm.

"Are you all right. Mozes?"

Finally, Mozes looked at Tommy,

"What? What did you say?"

"I said, are you okay?"

"Sure, why not."

"It looked like you were about to pass out. Your face turned white."

"I'm okay. Where's the check? I want to go."

"I got the check. I said this was my treat. I enjoyed our conversation and your company for lunch."

"Thank you."

"You should talk to your Aunt. You really should."

Now on the sidewalk in front of the restaurant, Mozes turned to Tommy.

"Where can I drop you?"

"I'm okay. I'm just going down a few blocks to a coffee shop. I'm going to write. I want to walk to clear my mind."

"Are you sure?"

"Yes. Thank you."

"Okay. Thanks for lunch. We'll see you later."

"You're welcome, Mozes. And, if I can be of any help with your family history just ask. Even if you just want to talk. I have some close friends in Windber, they might be able to help."

"Thanks. I'll keep that in mind."

They walked off in opposite directions.

26   Command Brief

Murry and Mozes took seats on the same side of the conference table. It was twelve forty-five. They huddled early to discuss any last-minute issues with the murder investigations before the usual Thursday afternoon one o'clock brief to the Homicide Squad Command.

Precisely at one o'clock, the Assistant Chief and the Lieutenant appeared in the squad conference room. The Lieutenant spoke his predictive opening.

"Do we need to sit Murry?"

"No."

"Your update?"

"No change to the investigations."

The Assistant Chief exclaimed.

"Come on already! No change. That's getting old."

An uncomfortable silence came over the room. Mozes began an impatience shift in his chair.

Murry looked directly into the eyes of the Assistant Chief.

"No change sir."

The Assistant Chief looked to Mozes.

"Is that how you see it, Mr. Olah?"

"Yes, sir."

"Well, I would have thought *Hotshot MO*, the hotshot investigator from the IG's office, would have solved all eleven murders by now."

Mozes looked up at the Assistant Chief and held his gaze for a minute. He then looked at the Lieutenant and held his gaze on him for a minute. Murry watched Mozes and kicked Mozes' foot under the table. Mozes ignored the kick of caution.

"Sir, I don't follow you. I understand the *'Hotshot MO.'* The hotshot investigator part, I am. Thank you."

Murry kicked Mozes again. Mozes ignored the second kick of caution and continued.

"But as I say to everyone, good guy or bad guy, I follow the rules. And I'm very productive closing cases with that as my professional foundation. I don't understand what you mean when you say, '...solved all eleven murders by now.' Please explain, help me understand your comment."

The Assistant Chief just stood there. He was stunned by Mozes' dialog. It was evident he was not accustomed to such candor.

Mozes continued, "I want to be a team member, a team player. Please explain to me. I want to solve these murders, and I will help Murry solve them."

The Assistant Chief looked at Murry still bedazed.

Mozes continued, "Do you have something you would like to get off your chest? Something you find necessary to tell us regarding the murders?"

Now the Assistant Chief glared at Mozes. His right hand, by his side near his duty weapon, started to shake. He moved it into his front pants pocket.

"Thank you, Mr. Olah. Your cockiness is most interesting," sounded the Assistant Chief.

"Sir, please don't confuse cockiness with confidence because they both begin with a C. I will help Murry solve these murders. I shouldn't make you nervous."

The Assistant Chief turned and glared at the Lieutenant.

With a slight nervousness to his voice, the Lieutenant interrupted Mozes.

"Anything else Murry?"

"No, sir."

"Then we shall go."

The Lieutenant put his hand on the shoulder of the Assistant Chief.

"We're done here. I'll take care of this later. This is my responsibility."

He ushered the Assistant Chief out of the squad conference room as he looked back at Murry and Mozes.

Murry, with the command out of hearing distance, looked to Mozes.

"What the hell are you doing?"

"I'm tired of such posturing. Talk down to me. I have a hunch about the Assistant Chief."

"Talk down. A hunch. Are you crazy? He's the Assistant Chief. An Assistant Chief!"

Murry stopped talking and looked away. He immediately looked back to Mozes.

"What are you doing to me?"

"Helping you solve the murders."

"Like that!"

"He puts his pants on one leg at a time just like me. Just like you. Talk down to me. Murry, that's a pet peeve of mine."

A little calmer and with a quizzical tone Murry inquired, "A hunch. What do you mean?"

"The guy knows something. I get the sense he knows the answer to the questions he asks."

"What?"

"His posture displays boredom. Like, I know what you're going to say, hurry up and say it so I can go. He doesn't know what I know. He's unsure of himself with me. His interest isn't to solve the murders, I can tell you that. But I have to get the proof."

177

"I'm not following you."

"Murry, today I want to leave it as a hunch. I want to leave it at, he knows more than we do. Give me some time."

"Okay. I don't have any other choice."

"Well you do, but you're too professional. You have a lot of questions to answer, and you won't stop. You won't give up. You're tenacious."

"Thank you. I guess."

"You're welcome."

27   Information brief

"Thank you for meeting me today Cipő."

"You're welcome. How are you?"

"Good. And you?"

"Very well."

"How's business? Are you still publishing the magazine?"

"Business is going well. I am."

"Thanks for meeting me here at the Potomac Avenue Grill. I know this is out of your way. I didn't want anyone on the *Strip* to see us together."

"This is unusual."

"Cipő, I have…"

Mozes was interrupted by the husky toned waitress, with a voice that evidenced at least two packs of cigarettes a day, possibly three.

"Good morning. Two coffees?" The waitress coughed.

"Yes. Please," Cipő and Mozes both replied.

As the bullish waitress poured their coffees, she continued, "Do you know what you want or you need more time?"

"I think we're ready. Go ahead Cipő."

"I'll have two eggs, over easy. Bacon. White bread not toasted. Dry." Cipő looked up to the bullish waitress with a smile. "Thank you."

In a tone of dislike for a customer who cannot decide on a menu item, the waitress turned and looked to Mozes.

"And you. What will you have?"

"I'll have the egg sandwich. No bacon, please. May I substitute a slice of tomato and a generous slice of white onion?"

"I suppose if you want me to break the rules."

She snatched the menus from them and scurried off.

Cipő commented, "I wonder what kind of sandwich you're going to get."

"I don't know. Whatever it is, I'll just eat it. If not, I'll put it in my pocket and say it is good."

They both laughed. Then stopped abruptly when the waitress returned unexpectedly. She looked to Mozes.

"You said no bacon, right?"

"Yes. No bacon. Please."

The waitress turned to Cipő.

"Do you want his bacon?"

"Yes. Please. That was sweet of you to ask."

"Yeah. I'm such a sweet old gal."

She scurried off again.

Mozes and Cipő laughed at the sarcastic humor from the husky, bullish, waitress whose disarrayed white dress uniform appeared to be two sizes too small.

Mozes continued to smile while Cipő continued, "I think she has an eye for you. I already gave her your number. That was her way of thanking me."

"Yeah, you would."

"So, what do you need Mozes? How can I help you?"

"I need information."

"Information. You law enforcement types; you all need information, all the time. Information about what?"

"First I need your word you won't talk about this to anyone. No one."

"You know you have my word. If I can help, I will. I don't need to broadcast I support law enforcement, that might not be good for my business. You have my word."

"Thank you. Over the course of about a year, the Mayor selected eleven murders. Four adult females. Three adult males. Four children females. He directed a gag order on the killings; there was no media coverage. He required a weekly case update brief from the Acting Chief of Police. The ME was slow in processing her examination of the victims. She finally released the fact all eleven victims, in an unskilled manner, had parts of their flesh removed. All in the same locations, upper left shoulder and in the center of the lower back. Only one of the victims was identified.

"Excuse me."

The waitress was oblivious to interrupting Mozes.

"Now you had two eggs over easy. There you go. And you had the egg sandwich."

She placed the food on the table and towered over.

"Will there be anything else?"

"I don't think so. Thank you," replied Mozes and Cipő.

"Well if you need anything just give a yell."

She looked at Mozes and rubbed his shoulder.

"Anything. Anything at all."

She walked off with a huge smile on her face.

Suppressing laughter Cipő looked at Mozes and smiled. He maintained a smug silence and began to eat his breakfast.

Ignoring the bullish advance, Mozes continued.

"We have the identity of one victim, Vic 11. Her name is Rhonda Popa. She worked at Gheorghi's Joe. This was our first substantial lead."

"Did she work the coffee counter?"

"Yes. Rhonda was friendly. Had a lot of energy."

"What a shame. Rhonda was helpful. You're right, always perky."

Cipő set his fork done. He lowered his head.

"Rhonda, may she rest in peace."

Cipő crossed himself. He picked his fork up and continued to eat.

"And that's what we have."

Mozes picked up his coffee, took a sip, and gently set the cup back down on the saucer.

"I know I'm not a detective, but you don't have a lot."

"That's why we are here. I have a hunch."

"A hunch."

"Yes. I think the political machine is involved with the murders."

"The political machine. The good old Pittsburgh political machine. You sure you want to go there."

"Someone must. We don't even know the identity of the other ten victims. Yes, I want to go there."

Cipő pondered for a moment. "Do I want to go there?"

"You can say no, but I need an answer this morning by the time we finish here."

"No pressure. Thanks."

"Cipő, if anyone can help me, you can. How well I know."

"Why? Is Murry, the vagrant, coming up empty?"

"Excuse me. What did you say?"

"I don't know what he's going to do now."

Surprised, Mozes set his utensils down on his plate. He sat back in his chair and exhaled. He looked at Cipő.

"What?"

"You heard me. Murry was made about a week after he started his undercover escapade on the *Strip*."

"Oh."

"Yes. The business owners love it. They feel the bad guys know too and the bad guys stay away from conducting their criminal activity on the *Strip*. The business people aren't going to blow his cover; that's why Gheorghi gives him free coffee. Gheorghi likes when he hangs around his store."

"Oh, boy."

"We all wonder why he's undercover on the *Strip*. Now I know."

"You can't tell anyone."

"I won't. I won't do that to you. I won't do that to Murry. My word is me."

"Thanks, Cipő."

Cipő took a bite of his bacon and held it in his hand.

"You said all the victims had parts of their flesh removed."

"Yes. The ME said it was cut out in an unskilled manner. It was the same two places for all the victims."

"Even Rhonda?"

"Yes."

The conversation was interrupted by the waitress. She topped off their coffee, and said, "Gentlemen. Can I get you anything else?"

"No, I don't think so. Just the check. Please," said Mozes.

The waitress looked carefully at Mozes.

"Too bad. Here's your check. You pay at the cash register. Thank you."

She smiled and walked off.

"I bet she put her telephone number on there for you."

Mozes chuckled at the humor, then continued with a serious tone.

"All eleven victims, in an unskilled manner. All in the same locations – upper left shoulder and in the center of the lower back."

"Someone removed tattoos. I'm sure you thought the same."

"Yes. We thought the same."

Mozes picked up his coffee, took a sip and cradled the ceramic, white, logo, coffee cup as he continued.

"Do you know the Zlatkovs?"

Cipő with a tone of disgust responded, "Who doesn't know them? The reputed Bulgaria crime family. Boris Zlatkov, the father, rumored to operate his global criminal conspiracy from Pittsburgh. Right on the *Strip*. Out of the businesses owned by his daughter. A front for the father's criminal activity."

"His daughter Sofiya?"

"Yes. Boris' daughter. Sofiya. The Pittsburgh socialite."

"I met her."

"You met her?"

"Yes. I literally bumped into Sofiya at Gheorghi's Joe."

"You didn't meet her."

"Yes, I did. We sat and had coffee at the table on the street in front of Gheorghi's Joe."

Cipő used the authority of a well-informed informant.

"No, you didn't meet her," said Cipő. "Listen to me. You don't meet her. That isn't how it happens."

"Oh yeah."

"Don't flatter yourself. No one meets Sofiya unless she wants to meet them or her father wants her to meet them. Did you see the security she travels with?"

"Security?"

"Yeah. There's a team of seven bodyguards. My god, they're so obnoxious."

"Bodyguards?"

"One time on the *Strip,* her guards pushed me off the sidewalk to get me out of her way. Not physically pushed me. I stepped off the curb to get out of their way. They weren't moving. What an obnoxious bunch."

"She was by herself when I met her."

"No way. You sure you met Sofiya Zlatkov?"

"She introduced herself as Sofiya Zlatkov. Her business card read the same. And Gheorghi said she was Sofiya. He also cautioned me about her."

"No way. She was out and about, naked? No bodyguards? Yes, she wanted to meet you. You met her, but it wasn't by happenchance."

"So, like a romantic interlude?"

"What? Romantic interlude? Are you Bulgarian?"

"No."

"Then no. No romantic interlude? Are you an arrogant fool? People of Bulgarian descent are the only ones for her to see. They're not going to mix their blood. They're old country."

"You seem to know a lot about them."

"Yes, I do."

"They seem to upset you."

"Yes, they do."

"Why?"

"I have my reasons."

"Care to share?"

"No."

Cipő seemed to go into deep thought. There was a history there; it was evident, but he was not going to share the history today.

Cipő brought himself back. His eyes now showed a keen interest in the murders and in helping.

"So, your hunch is the Zlatkov family participates in the killings? The Pittsburgh political machine engages in a conspiracy perhaps?"

"Yes, that's my hunch. I think this reaches the Mayor's office. The Mayor, possibly others. I believe the Mayor is directing other city department heads to do little if anything to investigate the murders. I believe he's obstructing their offices, their duties. Obstructing justice."

"Okay. That's why you're involved. The IG is required to investigate this."

"Yes. We don't get involved unless city employees or city assets are involved. Or, as in this case, the IG receives an anonymous allegation."

"Okay. I see. I understand."

"I'd like a lot more information on the Zlatkov family and their possible involvement in the murders. Anything you can get on any city employees and their involvement with the murders would help. Information on a cover up or intentional delay of their official duties to hinder the murder investigations."

"Well, that's not too much I suppose. I'll need some time. I'll do what I can. I'll help you."

"Thank you Cipő."

"I'll be in touch when I have something for you."

"Great."

The two rose from the table. Mozes picked up the check and took it to the register. Cipő continued out the front door.

Mozes paid and went back to the table. He left a generous tip for the time he spent at the table.

Cipő stood on Potomac Avenue and waited for Mozes. As Mozes emerged from the restaurant, Cipő extended his hand and two shook hands.

"I'll talk to you soon. Thanks for breakfast."

"Thank you Cipő. I look forward to your call."

189

"Oh, no. The call will be to arrange the time and place for lunch, maybe dinner. It's going to cost you a little more to entertain me. In fact, you may want to start to save for those Pirates tickets. I think a ball game would be good cover for our rendezvous. It will be the usual fee schedule too. I'm giving you a discount on this one. Old Boris."

Cipő smiled and walked to his Mercedes Benz. He entered and drove off toward Liberty Avenue.

Mozes stood on Potomac Avenue and reflected on the meeting. He continued to see Cipő's eyes deep in thought after he asked him about the Zlatkov family.

Mozes thought to himself, "Cipő's keen interest to help me after he learns of my hunch, he must explain that to me. I need to know his history with the Zlatkovs. And, should I tell Murry his cover is blown?"

28   He fled the interest of his innocence

Mozes picked up his cellphone from the bedside stand. He held it in his left hand as he laid in bed thinking if he should call Viktorija. He closed his eyes, and her beauty appeared. Vivid was her bosomy, curvy, silhouette in his memory, her scent lingered in his olfactory organ, and he felt the warmth of the sun as he did during their river walk on Sunday. His nerves on his forearm still felt her soft, gentle, touch from that day.

He thought to himself, "I was so comfortable. I was so at ease with Viktorija. I even had butterflies in my stomach, just like a teenager, I suppose."

A supposition was all Mozes had; he only speculated about dating. He did not date in his youth, while in high school, college or after. His innocence was only pinged three times for his fifty years, and all three times, it was awkward for him and for the ladies.

The first date was senior prom. A date arranged by Aunt Llona. She arranged for Mozes to take the daughter of her best friend. It went so horribly wrong Mozes blocked the date and the girl's name from his mind.

The second date was the summer between his sophomore and junior year in college. It went much better. They went to a movie where they shared popcorn and soda. They snuggled a bit. Afterward, they went to his place of summer employment, the local hot dog shop and hang out in Oakland where they had a late-night bite to eat. They even got a little frisky in the back-corner booth on the second floor.

191

Unfortunately, there was no second date. Three days after the date, while Mozes worked an evening shift at the hot dog shop, his Shift Supervisor directed him to wipe the tables on the second-floor dining area. He obediently went to the second floor to comply. After Mozes had cleaned three tables, he saw her. On the second floor, in the back corner booth, he saw her with another girl. He got excited at the opportunity to talk to her again. He took two gleeful steps and was immediately stopped from what he witnessed. She was embraced with a girl in the same booth he and she shared on their date. Mozes watched their hands moved about the body of the other with intense exploration. They were locked in passionate kissing, and their steamy sexual emotions were undeniable.

The girl unknown to Mozes noticed he was staring at them. She quickly became uncomfortable and pushed her partner off her. She said something to her companion in a quiet tone. The girl of Mozes' second date turned and looked his way.

She rolled her eyes and said, "Hey Mozes. What's up?"

She turned back to her partner and the two giggled. She pulled her partner into her, and they resumed their passion.

Mozes said nothing. He fled the scene as he ran downstairs, out the front door, and all the way to the Cathedral of Learning. There he curled up in a bed of flowers. The campus police found him curled in a fetal position and he was still wearing his work apron. Ultimately, his Aunt Llona came to the campus police station and retrieved him from the psychological event. This event caused his interest in females to wane further.

For his third attempt with the ladies, Mozes was older, in his mid-thirties. He met a woman at a church function, the parish annual summer bazaar. They were volunteers and worked together in the kitchen as dishwashers. Mozes sensed a connection.

They joked back and forth, playfully sprayed each other with the dish sprayer, and bumped into each other, for Mozes, on purpose. The dish washing area was a confined work space which created an arousing environment. Because of the hot dishwashing water, rinse water, and spraying, the lady, periodically stopped working. With one hand, she balanced herself on the sink edge. With the other, she dramatically wiped the sweat from her neck and exposed chest area before it ran down her cleavage. From the humidity and moisture, her clingy white t-shirt revealed her voluptuous, curvy torso. Little was left for Mozes' imagination.

Mozes asked her out right in the church basement as they dined together on their break from their volunteer work. She said yes and gave him her telephone number. When Mozes called the number to arrange the date, he received a recording that stated the number was disconnected. He took the hint and avoided her at future church functions.

All three events had one thing in common, visions of three, faceless, hallowed, figures. The dominance of the images, after each event and they appeared to Mozes for months after the events. They laughed at Mozes. It was as if they mocked Mozes.

Mozes often reflected, "Why do I have the visions? Oh, God, why me?"

The repetition of the visions dissuaded Mozes from dating. After his third attempt, he fled the interest of his innocence.

29   A complicated guy

It was not awkward now. There was not nearly as much pain, and the visions subsided. It was if Viktorija kept the images at bay; as if she pushed the pain away. Had Mozes found his guardian angel?

Mozes was brought out of his dreamy sleep by the vibration of his cellphone in his left hand. He looked at the text message on the screen. It was from Viktorija.

"I'M HUNGRY."

Mozes felt comfortable enough to joke with her.

"WHO IS THIS?"

"YOU KNOW WHO THIS IS."

"ARE YOU SURE YOU SENT THIS TO THE RIGHT PERSON?"

"I'M SURE MOZES. I'M SURE. WELL?"

"WELL, I SEE YOU'RE HUNGRY."

"MOZES. ARE YOU HUNGRY?"

"YES. WHAT ARE YOU HUNGRY FOR?"

"I DON'T KNOW."

"DO YOU WANT FORMAL OR CASUAL?"

"MORE ON THE CASUAL SIDE AND NOT THE CARSON STREET FOOD TRUCKS."

"CARON STREET FOOD TRUCKS? WHO WOULD EVER TAKE YOU THERE?"

"OH, I DON'T KNOW."

Mozes continued.

"DO YOU WANT SOMETHING BIG?"

"WHAT?"

"DO YOU WANT SOMETHING BIG OR SMALL? HOW HUNGRY ARE YOU?"

"JUST HUNGRY."

"HOW ABOUT THE PRETZEL PLACE?"

"UMM. YEAH. OKAY. GOOD IDEA."

"OKAY. CAN WE SIT OUTSIDE?"

"SURE."

"GREAT. I NEED 30 MINUTES TO GET READY."

"YOU'RE WORSE THAN A WOMAN. I'M READY NOW."

"I'LL KNOCK IN 30."

"OKAY."

Forty-five minutes later Viktorija mumbled to herself, "Where is he? I'm hungry. I'm starving now."

She left her apartment and locked the door behind her. She walked down the hall to Mozes' apartment. She passed the elevator alcove when she saw Mozes on the floor half way out

195

of his doorway. She rushed to him and knelt beside him. She shook him and called out.

"Mozes. Mozes."

There was no answer. Vicktorija shook Mozes and called his name again. Nothing. She checked for a pulse. He had one, but it was faint. She took out her cellphone and dialed 911.

An operator announced.

"911 what is your emergency?"

"I need an ambulance."

"What's the address?"

"Third Floor. The Fifth Place Lofts, 1865 Fifth Avenue. Third floor. Apartment 1C. Hurry please."

"Okay. Hold on with me. I'm going to dispatch an ambulance. Stay with me. Don't hang up."

"Okay."

The 911 operator came back online with Viktorija.

"The ambulance is on its way. Hello. Hello."

"Yes. I'm still here."

"Tell me what happened."

"I don't know what happened."

"Is there any blood?"

"No. I don't see any blood."

"Who's the victim?"

"Mozes."

"Mozes who?"

"Mozes Olah. White Male. Fifty years old."

"Do you know of any illness?"

"No."

"Are you his wife?"

"No. I'm a friend."

"Your name."

"Viktorija."

"Hold on with me Viktorija. I'm going to relay this information to the emergency team on the way. Hold on don't hang up."

The 911 operator came back.

"You still with me?"

"They're here."

"Okay. Good. I'm going to hang up now."

"Okay. Thank you."

As the Emergency Service personnel rushed down the hallway, one commanded, "We'll take it from here. Please move away."

The EMTs began their work. They had checked Mozes before they readied him for transfer from the floor to a backboard. Once on the backboard, they braced his neck and fixed the straps tight to hold him in place.

An EMT directed.

"On three. One. Two. Three."

The two EMTs lifted Mozes and the board to the gurney.

One of the EMTs called out.

"Who knows this guy?"

"I do," responded Viktorija.

"What is your relation?"

"Friend."

"We're taking him to Mercy Emergency."

Viktorija pleaded, "What's wrong with him?"

"We stabilize and transport."

The EMTs said nothing more. Prohibited by Federal law, they ignored Viktorija's pressing question. The EMTs wheeled the gurney down the hall to the elevator alcove. They moved directly into the waiting elevator they locked out with their emergency key. The doors closed and the elevator descended.

Viktorija locked and closed the door to Mozes' apartment. She went to the stairs and rushed down to the first floor. She continued directly to the front door and to the street. She looked for a cab, flagged one down, and instructed the driver to take her to Mercy Hospital, the Emergency Entrance. When she arrived, she paid the taxi and swiftly walked inside.

She continued directly to the admittance desk and in a demanding tone inquired about Mozes.

"Mozes Olah. What room is Mozes Olah in?"

In a harsh tone, the attending admittance clerk was short with Viktorija.

"And you are?"

"I'm Viktorija."

"Are you his wife?"

"No."

"Are you a family member?"

"No. I'm a friend."

"I can't tell you anything. I'm sorry."

"Okay. I can see Mozes though?"

The admittance clerk paused for thought.

"Yes. Let me check."

Viktorija thought to herself.

"I don't even know who to call. I don't know any of Mozes' family. We never talked about friends or family."

She became emotional from her inability to help, not knowing what was going on or who to contact.

Viktorija thought again.

"Aunt Llona? Was he serious then? Does he have an Aunt Llona?"

The clerk interrupted, "Viktorija, you can see him when the doctors are done."

"Doctors."

"Everything is all right. The Doctors just need to finish their examination. Please sit down over there. I'll come get you when you can go back. You can help us by waiting over there. Please."

"Thank you," replied Viktorija.

Viktorija moved to the emergency waiting room. She sat near the back. Seated only long enough to catch her breath and collect some thoughts, a doctor sat down with her.

"Hello. Are you Viktorija?"

"Yes."

"I'm the emergency room attending physician for Mozes. I understand you're his friend?"

"Yes, I am."

"You're not family?"

"No. I'm just a friend. We date."

"Oh. I can't tell you anything other than Mozes is okay. He's stabilized for now. We found nothing wrong with him. We're going to keep him overnight for observations. If all remains well, we'll release him tomorrow morning."

"That's good to hear."

"How well do you know him?" queried the Doctor.

"The same apartment building. We passed each other in the hallway. It started with small talk. Things progressed. I asked him out. We went out a few times. In fact, I was on my way to his apartment to see if he was ready to go out tonight. I found him on the floor."

"Do you know anyone who knows him? Family?"

"No. I'm embarrassed. Our talks never go to those topics. Why? Is there something wrong?"

"You know I can't tell you without the patient's permission. There are laws. I sense your concern, so I will say, there are no physical injuries."

"No physical injuries."

"No. None."

"No physical injuries. But there's something?"

"Well yes. Yes, there is. I can't tell you."

"If it's not physical then it's mental. Some type of psychological problem?"

The Doctor rose from his chair and looked down to Viktorija.

"I can't tell you. If you find any relatives, please let us know. If you find any information, please tell the attending nurse. So, the attending nurse can annotate the file. If you're going to help him home tomorrow. Thank you."

"Thank you, Doctor."

The Doctor walked off. Viktorija positioned herself deeper into the chair. She sat there deep in thought about what the doctor said. Shortly, the admittance clerk interrupted.

"Viktorija."

"Yes. I'm sorry."

Viktorija looked up to the clerk.

"You may go back now. Mozes is sleeping. The doctor has him under a sedative to help him sleep. You can go back and see him."

"Thank you."

Viktorija collected her things and followed the clerk through the doors to Mozes' room. The clerk showed her in and said "How about five minutes. The doctor wants him to rest."

"Yes. Okay, five minutes."

There was nothing Viktorija could do. She just stood there and looked at Mozes. He had an intravenous injection in his right arm. His left-hand index finger was affixed with a heart monitoring device. The life monitoring machines sounded their urgent beeps. The environment and event beckoned a tear from Viktorija's dazzling blue eyes.

After five minutes, Viktorija left the room and retraced her route in. She passed the admittance desk and spoke to the clerk.

"Thanks."

The clerk waved to acknowledge her courteous manner.

Viktorija slowly walked to the entrance/exit doors and to the street. A cabby asked if she wanted a ride. She declined and opted for the solitude of a walk.

As she began her walk home, she thought to herself, "What a complicated guy."

30 The tale of Mozes

Viktorija was up early Sunday morning after a restless night. She laid awake more than she slept. Alone, in the solitude of her bedroom; alone, in her bed, her thoughts were still on Mozes.

"What am I going to do? I have an intense interest in Mozes. I don't know if Mozes is interested in me. With two dates is he ever going to make a move on me? A good night kiss is all the sign I need. He shows interest, just not a sexual interest. Of course, I measure him by the others. I know I shouldn't. Can he be old fashion? Is it just an old fashion respect? Does he have values? A rare quality these days?"

Viktorija looked at the large wall clock that showed seven o'clock. She threw the white satin sheet off and moved to the edge of the king-size bed, rose, and walked to the bathroom. Groggy from the sleepless night she supported herself on the granite sink top. She took a deep breath, undid her skimpy, silk, black, nightie and left it to drop to the floor. She removed her panties and dropped them to the floor. She moved into the doorless shower, turned the water on and leaned against the wall while the water warmed.

Finished preparing herself, Viktorija left her apartment to retrieve Mozes from the hospital. She walked out to Fifth Avenue and hailed a cab. As the cabby proceeded to Mercy Hospital, she stared out to the Monongahela River. A plethora of boat activity near the south side shore caught her attention. She fixed her gaze on it.

The cabby, from a glance in the rearview mirror, observed Viktorija stared at the activity in the river.

"You see all the action over there?"

"Yes. What is it?"

"I don't know. There's nothing on the radio news about it."

"Maybe it's a boating accident."

"Could be. Here you are. Eight fifty please."

"There you go. Keep the change. Thank you."

"Have a nice day."

Viktorija slid out of the cab and walked into the emergency waiting area. She went directly to Mozes' room. When she opened the door, she was taken aback. Mozes was not in there. In fact, the room was cleaned and readied for the next emergency. She quickly walked to the nurse's station and abruptly interrupted the attending nurse.

"Where's Mozes?"

The attending nurse was irritated by the abrupt interruption.

"Who?"

"Mozes. Olah."

"Who are you to him?"

"A friend. Just a friend."

"Well friend, he's gone."

"What time did he check out?"

"He didn't. He just left on his own."

"What do you mean?"

"He was not in the room at the 3 a.m. patient bed checks."

"So, what does that mean?"

"He didn't check himself out; he just left. That was how we wrote it in the discharge summary."

"And you all let him?"

The attending nurse's patience was slipping.

"Honey, we can't force people to stay. To have treatment. There's no law giving us the authority to force treat an individual."

"Did he say where he was going?"

"Again, he just left. He didn't check out, process out, per hospital policy. He just left. No one had talked to him before he left."

"Okay. Thank you."

"You're welcome."

Viktorija slowly walked away from the nurse's station. She walked through the double doors, across the emergency waiting area, and out the main doors. Her gate continued slowly down the walkway to Forbes Avenue.

She thought, "With what the doctor said last night. He walked away early this morning. What was going on with Mozes?"

Viktorija, in the cold summer air, started to walk back to her apartment. She continued along Forbes Avenue. The air was refreshing. She knew she would be able to clear her mind as she walked. Quite often she walked to think, to aid in difficult decisions.

At Miltenberger Street, she turned right. She continued to walk toward the Boulevard of the Allies. A bench on the corner gave way to a vista of the South Hills and the river. Often, she found herself there and sat by herself. From the bench, she gazed out at the view and rolled her thoughts through her mind. Today she had a few thoughts to roll.

As she passed Edna Street to her right, the bench came into view. To her disappointment, it was occupied by a lone person. She continued with hopes the individual would soon be on their way.

As she came closer to the bench, she was stunned, the person was Mozes. She stopped and looked again. It was Mozes Olah.

She thought, "Now what. Do I go and sit down by Mozes or do I turn around and go home?"

She stood for a moment and collected her thoughts. She decided.

"I'm going to sit down by him. And this is either going to continue or end. Right here. Today."

Viktorija continued to walk toward Mozes and the bench. The road noise covered her approach and Mozes did not notice her until she sat down.

Mozes slid to his left. Viktorija did not know if Mozes moved not knowing who she was or if he moved to create distance between them as he always did.

He glanced her way and exclaimed with surprise, "Viktorija! What are you doing here?"

He made a gesture as if he was going to hug her. She wanted him to hug her. She wanted to hug him back. She moved into him sensing he wanted to hug her, but he pulled away and caused yet another awkward moment.

"I was just coming back from the hospital."

There was excitement in Mozes' voice.

"Did you go to check on me? Did you?"

"Yes, I did."

"I wanted to call you, but I didn't have my phone," Mozes said.

"Oh."

"Yeah."

"Look. I know you just got out of the hospital, but we need to talk or at least I need to speak. I need to figure some things out."

Mozes stuttered, "Oh."

"Yeah. I don't understand you. You confuse me."

"What do you mean?"

"We know each other for about a year now. You're always so pleasant to me. Polite. Well, I don't know how else to say it. To ask."

"Just say what you want to say Viktorija."

"The thing is this; do you have any feelings for me? Do you think you could have feelings for me?"

"I think the world of you."

"Stop. Please answer the question for me. I know what I want the answer to be. I can also accept the answer you give me."

"It's complicated."

"Come on. I deserve better."

"No, it's complicated. It's not a line. It's complicated."

"Well then, let me get comfortable." Viktorija mimicked adjusting to a comfortable position. "I'm ready now. Take your time."

"There you go with your sarcasm. Which I like. I think it's cute."

"Come on, say what you have to say."

"All right. I don't know if you're going to like what I say."

"I'm a big girl. Give it to me Mozes."

Mozes moved a little closer to Viktorija. He looked into her eyes, held his gaze, and then looked away to the river. Conditioned by his law enforcement years, he began.

"What did the emergency room doctor tell you?"

"Nothing. The Doctor couldn't say anything. Medical privacy laws."

"All right. I never did this before."

Viktorija's patience was thinning. Her tone turned sharp.

"Well, today is the day then."

"I have a problem. I have a problem with women."

"So, you're gay. That's okay. If you don't like women. I understand. Disappointed. But I get it."

Mozes jerked his head toward Viktorija.

"No. I'm not gay. You go there first. Come on."

"What? What did you expect me to think?"

"I don't know. Not that. I'm not gay. It's difficult for me to be intimate with women."

Viktorija cut him off.

"Dear God did you have an accident. Did something happen? An incident from your police work?"

Mozes had a rare moment of authority with a female.

"Please, let me talk. Just let me talk."

Viktorija's facial expression turned to concern.

"Okay. Sorry. I'm sorry."

"From what I know, what I can piece together, I suffer from Posttraumatic Stress Disorder. The Traumatic incident was..."

Mozes paused. He lowered his head. Viktorija placed her left hand on his right shoulder. Mozes pulled away, demonstrating his PTSD turmoil.

"Mozes, I'm just trying to help," said Viktorija.

"I know Viktorija. You do. Our walk along the river, so pleasant. When I sit in your living room, I'm so comfortable. You relax me."

Mozes paused and fixed his eyes on the south hills to continue.

"And I have visions. Images of three, faceless, hallowed, figures, dressed in the vestments of Roman Catholic priests, appear to me. Psychotic episodes I believe they call them."

He paused again. He raised his head and gazed to the south hills. It was as if he was embarrassed to look at Viktorija.

Viktorija sat there and said nothing. She knew no comforting words. She started to reach her hand out to comfort him with a gentle touch but quickly drew it back as she remembered her attempt to comfort him a few minutes earlier.

Mozes continued his gaze to the south hills.

"I'm so comfortable when I'm with you. I don't know."

"What don't you know?"

"It's not fair to you. You deserve someone who has no problems. Let alone..."

Viktorija cut him off.

"And who would that be Mozes? Who would have no problems? If you feel good when you're around me, then you should be around me. I want you to be around me. I want to be around you."

Mozes' voice sounded with excitement, "You do?"

"Yes. You must decide. I'm willing to try. I want it to work."

Mozes sat straight up. He slowly turned his head to look to Viktorija.

"You do! Viktorija I want that too. Oh, how I want you."

"Well then."

"No. No. There is more I must tell you. A lot more."

"I'm not going anywhere. Take your time."

"Not today. I just want to."

Mozes stopped talking and acted. He reached over with his right hand, cupped Victoria's head, and pulled her to him. He kissed her. A long passionate kiss. They were brought out of the embrace by the sound of car horns from the cars on the Boulevard of the Allies.

Mozes drew back and continued to cup Vicktorija's head. He savored Viktorija's smile. His hand sank into her soft, supple, shoulder-length, brown hair. Their eyes locked. He was hypnotized, and a smile emerged on his face.

They held their pose until it was interrupted by the young voice from a passing car.

"Get a room old man."

They both laughed. Then Mozes spoke.

"So now maybe you understand my behavior a little better. There's more to tell you. A lot more, but not today."

Mozes rose from the bench. He took Viktorija's hand.

"Come on."

Viktorija bounced up from the bench. A smile appeared below her confused eyes. She wondered to herself, "Where is he taking me? What's on his mind? The same thing that's on my mind, perhaps? Hopefully."

They walked hand in hand up the old, uneven sidewalk on Miltenberger Street toward their apartment building. There was an urgency to their walk led by Mozes.

As the brisk walk continued, Viktorija ran her sexual thoughts through her mind. Curiosity got the best of her. With her sexy Bulgarian accent, she inquired, "Where are we going, Mozes?"

With excitement, Mozes replied, "To watch the game. The Steelers play the Ravens today."

31   Command Brief

"Hello, this is Mozes."

"Good morning Mozes. This is Murry.

"Good morning Murry. How are you?"

"Fine thank you. Where're you at?"

"What's that?" replied Mozes.

Mozes stalled for time to think of an answer and continued.

"Where are you? Are you at the office? I'm on my way to you now," said Mozes.

"On your way to me. I'm on vacation."

Mozes' tone was one of a savvy, cool, nonchalant, law enforcement officer.

"Where're you at?"

A little more comfortable with his new partner, Murry ignored the question.

"Can you stop by the ME office now and pick up all the reports they have on all the murder victims. And make sure they give you at least the preliminary report for the last one."

"Vic 11?"

"No. Vic 12.

"Vic 12."

"Yeah. Saturday night or early Sunday morning. Out of the river. The Monongahela. Near the south side."

"Okay."

"Can you get all that, so it will be at the office this afternoon for today's one o'clock brief?"

"Yes, sir."

"Okay. Look I'm a little short with you today because I have to interrupt my vacation for the briefing."

"I'll see you later."

"No. There's another thing I need. Can you have your computer set up in the conference room so I can call into the brief?"

"Wow. High tech Murry."

"Come on. I didn't even think of the brief. I'm on vacation, and the Lieutenant knows. You think he would skip the weekly brief. No. I receive a telephone call from the Lieutenant about an hour ago. The Assistant Chief must have the brief."

"Okay. I'll take care of everything. You call me at twelve fifty. We'll make sure everything works."

"Thanks. Talk to you later."

Mozes ended the call and holstered his telephone. He signaled to turn left on Ohio Avenue and rerouted himself back across the city to the ME office on Penn Avenue.

When he arrived at the ME office, he circled the block several times before he found a parking space. He walked to the main entrance and with his law enforcement credentials, identified himself to the security checkpoint attendant. The security guard studied the credentials then handed them back to Mozes. He instructed Mozes to step around the checkpoint and go on.

Mozes walked directly to the Law Enforcement Liaison Office of the Medical Examiner Office. This was protocol. This was the only office to process requests from the law enforcement community. He found the window unattended, so he tapped the bell taped to the small counter.

From within the office, a perky voice sounded.

"I'll be right there. Hold on."

Mozes recognized the voice, so he repeatedly tapped the bell. The voice sounded back annoyed.

"Okay. Okay. I know you're there. I'll be right with you."

Immediately after she finished, Mozes rapidly tapped the bell again. The voice sounded louder and with a tone of anger.

"I hear you. You can stop ringing the bell. Please."

Mozes heard the clerk move through the room toward the window. He wanted to ring the bell again but refrained from pushing the patience of Lakeisha.

Lakeisha arrived at the window and saw it was Mozes.

"I should've known. You know how I hate when people keep ringing the bell."

She reached over and pressed the electric lock release.

"Get your white ass in here, boy."

Mozes shuffled to the door and pushed it opened. Inside, he turned and pushed the door closed. When he turned back, he was greeted by a huge hug. Lakeisha held the hug to the point of becoming uncomfortable.

"I haven't seen you for a while. You haven't visited me."

"I'm busy. You know how busy these government jobs keep us."

"Bullshit. That's just an excuse."

With a Pittsburgh accent, Lakeisha mimicked Mozes.

"I'm busy. I'm busy."

Mozes laughed.

"You need to visit me more often. Don't make me come down to your office and embarrass you in front of all your co-workers."

"Oh."

Mozes and Lakeisha met during a personnel investigation in which Lakeisha was the subject of a sexual harassment complaint. It was alleged, by an anonymous complainant who called the IG Hotline, she made repetitive unwanted sexual

217

advances to her first line supervisor, and she wanted to use the unwanted sexual advances to get promotions and pay raises.

As the investigation progressed, it disclosed just the opposite. Lakeisha's boss made unwanted sexual advances to her. She never reported her boss in fear of his reprisal in the form of losing her job, demotion or reduction in pay. She deflected her boss's unwanted advances and put up with his sickening touching and sexual innuendos. She had four children and all the monthly payments typical of a hard-working, lower-middle, income household. Even with her husband employed as a PBP patrol officer her income was essential for the solvency of the family finances.

Lakeisha's husband worked in the same PBP district stationed. He even witnessed some of their mutual boss' advances and touching. On one occasion, her husband confronted their mutual boss, a PBP Lieutenant. The Lieutenant ordered her husband to his office. Behind a closed door, the Lieutenant told the patrol officer to encourage his wife to give in to his desires so they both could get promoted. Finally, her husband reported the matter to the IG's office.

The second case was also assigned to Mozes. Mozes encouraged, her husband pleaded, and finally, Lakeisha agreed to wear a recording device to record the Lieutenant's unwanted sexual advances. She wore the recording device over the course of a month every day she went to work.

The IG demanded thirty consecutive work days of recordings and the installation of a hidden camera to record the touching. Over a thirty-day period, Mozes met Lakeisha in the capacity of a cooperating witness, prepped her with the recording device, and debriefed her at the end of her work day. This interplay developed a close co-worker type relationship.

Because of Mozes' cunning interrogation techniques, he extracted a confession from the offending Lieutenant. The Lieutenant admitted, among other facts, he logged the anonymous Hotline complaint with the IG office. He hoped to use it as leverage to get Lakeisha to acquiesce to his desires. The Lieutenant was ultimately fired.

Typical to personnel investigations, the victim was also punished. Lakeisha was transferred to her current position, and her husband was moved to a different district which increased his commute. As they both told Mozes a few months after the investigation when they all saw each other at a Pirates baseball game, their stress was reduced, and they were much happier. They were both grateful for Mozes relentless pursuit which disproved the allegation levied against Lakeisha.

"How are you getting along? You and the children?"

"You mean since my husband was murdered?"

"Yes. Such a tragedy."

Mozes reached out and gave Lakeisha another hug.

"Two years now," said Lakeisha.

"I know," replied Mozes.

"Yeah. Everything's as good as can be. We adjust as time goes. Now, it's only every once in a while, I think of my husband when something comes up that he would typically handle around the house. I guess it will take more time."

"Yes. Some things just need time to go away. How I know. How well I know."

"Thank you for your concern. You're so sweet."

Lakeisha paused from a swell of emotion.

"Yeah, murdered while he was parked in his patrol car. He sat in his cruiser on Ohio Avenue on the north side, on patrol, as he protected the city. Just another unsolved murder of the many as the media reports daily. And called what?"

Lakeisha sighed.

"Cold cases," said Mozes.

Lakeisha sounded with heavy sarcasm.

"Yeah, cold cases. The Homicide Squad worked hard on his murder."

Mozes said nothing. They both discussed it in the past, and they both believed her husband was killed in retaliation for the Lieutenant's firing. That aspect of the investigation was never pursued.

Lakeisha drew them back to Mozes' visit.

"So, what brings you to the ME's office? Is there a murder of a city employee at his desk I didn't hear about?"

"No. Not a city employee. I am investigating some murders. Eleven of them. No twelve. There was another one this past weekend."

"Oh, yeah."

"Yeah. Detective Stewart sent me over to gather all the ME's reports and the preliminary on Vic 12."

"Let me check the box. Sit down. I'll be right back."

"Okay. Thank you."

Lakeisha walked off and out of sight. Mozes sat in the chair by her desk to wait.

Lakeisha returned and said, "Mozes, I don't know what Detective Stewart is talking about. There's nothing in the homicide outbox. I didn't hear about these murders? Twelve you say?"

"You didn't hear about them?"

"No."

"Did you check your confidential files?"

"How do you know about those? Oh. You work with the IG's office. Sorry. I was just about to look."

She sat down at her desk, adjusted herself, and pulled the computer keyboard to her. She tapped on the keys and then studied the screen.

"Okay."

She stretched her hand out and with her index finger scanned down the screen.

"I see. You want all the final reports."

"What do you mean final reports? These cases aren't closed."

"In our office, these cases were settled. In fact, there is a notation since there were no family members to identify the victims, the victims were cremated."

"What? Cremated? These are active investigations.
Lakeisha, are you reading the files correctly? I mean. Even Vic 12?"

"Yes, I'm reading this correctly. I'm printing the reports for you."

"Even Vic 12?"

"Yes, Vic 12 too. Closed. Cremated."

"Who ordered that? Does it say who ordered that?"

"Let me get the printouts."

Lakeisha left her desk and quickly returned. She sat down, shuffled through the printouts, organized the reports, and handed them to Mozes.

"There you are. The final reports for all twelve victims."

"Does it say who closed the ME's case?"

"Look."

Mozes shuffled through the reports and looked at all twelve. In the box, *Case Closed By,* the name was the same for all twelve."

Lakeisha interrupted Mozes.

"Do you have any questions for me?

Mozes said nothing. He was still staring at the reports.

Not sure Mozes heard her, she repeated.

"Do you have any questions for me?"

Mozes looked up from the reports.

"How could she close the files?"

"I cannot answer that question. Per the reports, the bodies were cremated. The cases were closed. The ME was the official at this office who closed the cases."

Mozes talked over Lakeisha.

"I can see who closed them in this office. I can't believe this."

"Well, I didn't make your day, did I?"

"No. But thank you. Thank you for your help. It was nice to see you again, Lakeisha."

"Good to see you."

Mozes rose from the chair as Lakeisha rose from hers and came from around her desk. The two hugged again.

"I guess I'll be seeing you soon."

Mozes had a puzzled look on his face.

"What do you mean?"

"You're not going to let this slide. I know you. You'll be back to investigate this. Even I can see the glaring mismanagement and violation of city policies with those reports. With the cremation of the bodies."

"Yeah."

"For the record, there were no formal requests to close the cases. There were no homicide forms. No one from the Homicide Squad submitted *Request to Close Case* forms."

"Well, they shouldn't have. I must go. Thanks again."

"Your welcome."

Mozes turned and walked to the door he entered earlier. Frustrated, he slapped the green square button on the wall to release the magnetic lock. He pushed the door open and walked off.

In the car, Mozes pulled his phone from its holster. He unlocked it, mashed the *Contacts* icon, and scrolled down to Murry's name. He flicked the name. The contact listing appeared. He flicked the number. It rang once and went to voice mail.

"Great!"

He listened to the voice mail greeting and prompts, then left a message.

"Murry call me as soon as you get this. We have a problem."

Mozes ended the call and holstered his phone. He continued to drive to the north side PBP Homicide Squad.

When Mozes arrived at the Homicide Squad, he immediately parked on the street in front of the building. He checked the time. Twelve-fifteen. He exited his car and walked directly to the building, entered, and continued to the third floor. There he moved directly to the Homicide Squad conference room. He took out his official laptop computer and powered it up. He worked through the sign in screens and then clicked on the telephone icon. It filled the screen. He processed through the commands; all was in working order. He waited for Murry to call in.

As he sat in the conference room, Mozes turned to the windows and stared out. His thoughts drifted to Viktorija and the weekend. As typical three, faceless, hallowed, figures appeared aloft outside the windows. Then they seated themselves in the conference room chairs across from Mozes.

The vision was interrupted by the chime of the telephone icon. Mozes turned to the computer and saw it was Viktorija. He was surprised.

"Hello."

"Hello to you. I didn't know if you would answer."

"I can't talk. I'm waiting for a call to go into a teleconference."

"Oh, big man."

"You look beautiful."

"Are you flirting with me, Mozes?"

A voice sounded and interrupted the call.

"Is that official business Mozes? We can wait outside."

Viktorija sounded from the computer, "Who's that?"

Mozes quickly replied, "I have to go. I'll talk to you tonight."

"Okay."

Mozes ended the call and stood up out of respect for someone entering a room.

"Sorry. Good afternoon Lieutenant. Chief."

"Good afternoon to you."

The Assistant Chief, in a smug manner, said nothing. He just walked over to the windows and stared out.

"Sir, we are waiting for Murry to call in."

"A computer call? Hm. Okay."

The Lieutenant pulled a chair out and sat across from Mozes. Mozes sat there and stared at the computer screen. He thought to himself.

"Now what do I do? Should I bring up the MEs reports without first telling Murry? Should I bring it up without briefing the IG?"

The telephone app sounded. Mozes responded.

"Hello, Murry. Everyone is here."

"Very well."

Mozes turned the computer, so the Lieutenant and Murry saw each other.

"Hello, Murry."

"Is the Assistant Chief there?"

"I'm here. Go ahead."

There was a troubled, concerned, tone to the voice of the Assistant Chief. He continued to stare out the window.

"There's nothing new to report."

The Lieutenant repeated, "Nothing new to report."

"Nothing. I've been on vacation all week."

"Okay. Thanks."

"Your welcome."

Murry abruptly ended the call, and the computer screen immediately went blue, back to the app start screen. Mozes slid the computer back to face him.

The Lieutenant rose from his chair and pushed it under the table. He looked to the Assistant Chief.

"Sir, are you ready?"

The Assistant Chief slowly turned and faced the Lieutenant.

"You can go. I want to talk with Mozes. Alone."

Caught off guard, the Lieutenant was slow to answer.

"Okay."

The Lieutenant turned and walked out of the conference room and closed the door behind him.

The Assistant Chief walked over to Mozes.

"Sir, with all due respect, I don't think we should talk without someone else in the room," said Mozes.

"Why didn't you bring up the reports?" sounded the Assistant Chief.

"What?"

"Why didn't you bring up the ME reports?"

"Sir. If you persist, I have to read you your rights."

"To hell with my rights. My rights. I gave my rights away when I took the money."

"Sir, please. I must have you acknowledge you understand your rights and waive them. Please sit down so we can talk about this. We can work this out. Take some time to talk with me. Let me help you."

"Talk with you. Why? You think you can help me. You can't help me. No one can. You better help yourself."

The Assistant Chief corrected his posture and stood taller almost at attention.

This Mozes thought unusual. An uneasy feeling came over Mozes. He slid his right hand to his right side and moved his coat away from his duty sidearm. He gripped the Beretta and pressed the holster's release button with his right index finger. He slid his duty weapon from the holster and rested it on his right thigh. He was about to stand when he observed the Assistant Chief reached to his right side. The Assistant Chief's hand shook as he gripped his exposed duty weapon.
Mozes immediately pushed himself back from the conference table and tilted himself out of the chair onto the floor. In

conditioned defensive tactics form, Mozes quickly crawled away to create distance between him and the potential assailant, the Assistant Chief. As he did, he heard a lone gunshot. It echoed through the conference room, then he heard a thud. From the floor and through the legs of the conference table chairs Mozes saw the Assistant Chief laid on the floor. Still, in a defensive posture, Mozes rose to his feet, stayed in a low, defensive, crouched position, and tactically moved around the table to a point where he saw the Chief's body. The Chief did not move. Mozes continued around the table now his Beretta fully extended in front of him with a two-handed grip. He kept it aimed in on the motionless Chief while he studied the Chief closer and saw no rise and fall to his chest.

Mozes was almost to the Chief when the conference room door flung open. No one was visible, but a voice shouted.

"Gun down. Gun down."

To prevent a blue on blue shooting, Mozes placed his gun on the floor and raised his open hands. He stood upright and announced.

"It's down. It's down."

The Lieutenant, with his gun in a low ready, eased into the room and continued to scan the scene. He commanded.

"Mozes keep your hands up. I must do my job. Keep your hands up."

Mozes quickly composed from years of training for such events and his experience with other self-defense shootings.

"Yes sir," Mozes replied.

229

The Lieutenant advanced farther into the room. He was followed by two other plain clothes detectives. Their guns fully extended in front of them and trained on Mozes. Mozes did not move. He held his hands high in the air, palms faced forward.

The Lieutenant moved directly to the Chief. He pulled the Chief's gun from his right hand and slid it back to the detectives who followed him to potential harm. One detective picked it up and sounded.

"Weapon secured."

The Lieutenant moved to Mozes' gun. He picked it up and slid it to the detectives. The same detective sounded.

"Weapon secure."

The Lieutenant yelled.

"Clear. Clear. Everything is clear."

He holstered his weapon and commanded.

"Mozes put down your hands. Relax. Relax. It's over. Here sit."

Mozes slowly lowered his arms to his side and sat down in the chair the Lieutenant pulled out and turned away from the Chief. The Lieutenant rested his left hand on Mozes' left shoulder. He turned to the other detectives and commanded.

"Shut this place down. This is a crime scene."

"A crime scene!" Mozes exclaimed.

"Per regulations and policy Mozes. Per regulations and policy. You know we must do this. Relax. Relax."

At 9:30 p.m., Mozes was released from the scene. He took his dismissal as a sign the PBP Internal Affairs investigative team saw this for what it was, a workplace suicide. The team did not confirm this when Mozes asked; they only instructed he was free to go.

As Mozes walked out of the squad room, the Lieutenant called out.

"Mozes wait up."

Mozes stopped and turned, and the Lieutenant came up to him.

"Are you okay? Can you drive?"

"Yes, I'm fine. I can drive."

"Let me get a black and white to take you home."

"Thank you. No. That's not necessary."

"You sure?"

"Yes."

"I told them what I saw."

"What you saw?"

"Yes. I watched through the window in the door. I didn't like the Assistant Chief's tone with you. I watched through the window."

"Thanks. I had a witness. There was a witness. Thanks. And they said what?"

"Nothing. You know they're not going to say anything. No matter. There's no way they can spin this into anything other than a workplace suicide."

"Thanks, sir. I'm going to go. This turned into a long day."

"Okay. If you need anything, call me. Call me anytime."

Mozes paused, then turned and walked out of the squad room. He walked down the oak stairs and out of the building, directly to his car, and drove home.

Inside his apartment, he sat at the edge of his bed and took his shoes off. He was so exhausted, he laid back to rest before he changed. As he laid there, the *Guiding* appeared and sat on the edge of the bed. Mozes sat up.

The hallowed figure spoke, "*Mo,* maybe you should do the same. Instead of telling people about your youth, perhaps you should mimic the Assistant Chief."

32   The past questioned

Mozes woke up and looked at his Rolex. It was eight thirty-three. He looked down and saw he was still dressed in yesterday's clothes. He sat up, collected himself, and then rose out of bed. He walked to the kitchen to make coffee. He added a few extra scoops today; he wanted the coffee strong.

As he stood in the windowless kitchen waiting for the coffee, his mind played back yesterday's event as he shook his head.

"Suicide. The Assistant Chief committed suicide right in front of me. I can't imagine what he was involved in. How deep he was in. The fact was, the ME report showed in the notes section for all twelve murder victims, he was the person, the official who commanded the ME to close their investigations and cremate the bodies. The command came from the Assistant Chief of Investigations. Was he just following orders? If yes, did the order came from the Acting Chief of Police. Perhaps it came from the Mayor to the Acting Chief, then to the Assistant Chief. The circumstances were unfortunate, but this was the first thread to unravel."

Mozes poured himself a cup of coffee and took it with him to the dining room table. He sat and took a cautious sip of the hot coffee then set the cup on a saucer on the table. He reached for his black, leather, Tumi letter pad, opened it and mumbled out loud.

"All that is going to have to wait. I'm going to use my time off to investigate my past. Tommy is right."

233

Yesterday, while Mozes was detained by the detectives at the scene of the Assistant Chief's suicide, the IG stopped to see him. The IG was concerned for the wellbeing of his employee. He talked with Mozes for about a half hour and two things netted out of their conversation. One, Mozes was placed on the required administrative leave pending the outcome of the investigation. This was per OIG policy for traumatic events. Two, Mozes was commanded to see a Psychiatrist for a fit for duty evaluation. This was per the City of Pittsburgh, Civil Service Regulations for traumatic events.

Mozes took pen to paper. He created a timeline for his life.

1966   Born Windber, PA.
1973   Visions first appeared. First doctor's visit possibly?
1974   Father's coal mining accident.
1975   First memory of vivid dreams of murders.
1979   Incident at Windber Area High School gym shower.
       Possible doctor's visit??
1980   Mother committed to Somerset State Hospital.
       Moved to Pittsburgh by Aunt Llona.
1984   Graduated High School.
       Aunt Llona stopped going to church with me.
1988   Graduated College.
       Aunt Llona stopped taking me to church.
1995   Aunt Llona stopped going to visit mother.
       Somerset State Hospital closed.
       State Hospital converted to a correctional facility.

He paused and reviewed the list. He dropped down a few lines, annotated the heading UNKNOWN and continued.

Any of my father's family history.
Any more details of mother's family history.
The source of Aunt Llona's wealth.
Why are there things I don't pay for????

Mozes set his pen down, reached for his coffee cup, and took a sip. He held the cup, sat back in the chair and thought.

"This isn't adding up. What is going on? I know absolutely nothing about my family history. I live in the lap of luxury. Why?"

He rose from the chair, walked over to the large dining room windows, and looked out.

He continued to wonder thoughts within.

"I'm so conditioned to wealth and comfort. Sure, I work, but the money flow, my expenses, are beyond my earned income. I only see this now, after all these years. The clothes, the cars, the luxury apartment. My free college education. Ever since here in Pittsburgh; ever since Aunt Llona, money seems to be endless. Money is infinite to me."

Mozes rubbed and massaged the nape of his neck in an attempt to ease the tension brought on by the sharp pain that moved through his head. He went to the living room, sat in the armchair, and stared at the painting across the room.

33   The left shoulder tattoo

"Mr. Olah. Welcome."

The maître d' did not study his seating chart. Nor did he gather menus.

"Sir. Madam. This way please."

The maître d' led Mozes and Viktorija through the table area of the *La Belle Vue*. As they approached a table next to the wall of windows with the best view of the Pittsburgh skyline, the maître d' turned to them.

"Your usual table sir. I trust this is satisfactory."

Mozes responded in a shy tone, "Yes. Thank you, Walter."

The maître d' pulled a chair out.

"Viktorija, please."

Viktorija was surprised the maître d' knew her name. She sat and adjusted her pose, as the maître d' controlled and moved the chair to accommodate her.

Mozes waited until Viktorija was seated before he sat next to her. Their positions focused them to the city skyline soon to be a sparkle with lights.

"Thank you, Walter."

"You're welcome, Mr. Olah. Enjoy your evening,"

Walter walked away. Immediately, they were greeted by another staff member.

"Mr. Olah, good evening."

"Good evening George. How are you tonight?"

"Fine, thank you. Will you begin, as usual, sir?"

"Yes. Please."

"Shall I ask the Chef to begin or do you and your guest wish to enjoy the view?"

"Please ask Chef Dubois to begin."

"As you wish."

George walked away with a dutiful gait.

Viktorija slowly turned her head from the view and looked at Mozes who was also enjoying the view. Mozes felt Viktorija's look and looked her way. He blushed as he smiled.

"What?"

"What? Where do I start? I'm impressed."

She abruptly stopped talking.

"What's wrong? Why did you stop?"

She leaned into Mozes and whispered.

"She's just standing there."

Mozes looked to his right. The direction Viktorija motioned with her eyes.

"Jane, good evening. Sorry."

Good evening Mr. Olah. May I?"

"Yes."

Jane stepped forward and presented the bottle of wine to Mozes. Mozes gave it a quick glance.

"Yes. Good."

She stepped back and turned her back and worked at the bottle. She turned back around and stepped toward Mozes. She poured a small amount into Mozes' glass.

Mozes did not taste it. In a humble tone, he said, "Fine Jane. Thank you."

Jane dutifully moved to Viktorija and poured her wine. She then moved back to Mozes and poured his. She stepped back from the table, placed the wine bottle in a holder, and walked off.

Viktorija looked to Mozes.

"I'm a little nervous here. I'm not accustomed to such service. I hope I don't embarrass you."

"You're fine. You can't embarrass me. Relax and enjoy the view. And thank you."

"Thank you. Me. For what?"

"For your company, tonight."

"Mozes, I don't want to pressure you. Would you like to talk more about your past? If you want. I want you to know I'm here for you. To help."

"I know you are Viktorija. And I'm way more relaxed thanks to you. Not tonight. I just want you to enjoy the evening. We'll talk soon. I want to talk with you; I think it will help me."

Their attention was taken from each other from a stir of commotion at the maître d' station. Mozes 'conditioned law enforcement officer instincts forced him to look to the commotion to analyze it for possible threats to his or Viktorija's safety and security.

He observed two large men dressed in dark suits with two-way radio ear pieces in their left ears. It appeared they were in a heated conversation with Walter, some type of disagreement between them. They all took a quick glance in the direction of Mozes then back to each other and continued their conversation.

Walter walked away from his station in the direction of Mozes and stopped at Mozes' table.

"Mozes, excuse me. This is embarrassing. Would you mind if I move you and Viktorija to another table?"

"Why Walter?"

"I have someone who wants this whole area. I'm only at liberty to say it's a security matter."

"Who's the VIP?"

"I'm not at liberty to say."

"This is highly irregular for you."

"Yes, it is Mozes. Please accept my apology."

"Walter, I don't want to move."

Walter stuttered when he said, "Sir. Please. Is there any way you would help me?"

"Yes. If those protection guys want this area, let them come over and ask me."

"Sir. You don't want that. Let me deal with them."

"No."

A strained troubled look came over Walter's face. He swiftly walked away, back to his station. He briefly engaged the dark-suited gentlemen. Both gentlemen looked in the direction of Mozes and walked off from Walter.

As they approached the table, Mozes rose from his chair. Not out of respect, to position himself in a defensive posture. He did not know who or what was coming his way.

At the table, the person who seemed to be in charge spoke.

"Sir is it possible for you and your guest to take another table."

Mozes postured for authority.

"So, you're not law enforcement. Private bodyguards. For whom?"

"Sir, we're not at liberty to say. We ask for your cooperation please."

"Who are you and why do you ask?"

"Sir. It is imperative for the security of my client to have this entire area of the restaurant for her dining pleasure."

"No. It's imperative I know who I am accommodating."

"I can't tell you."

"I can't accede to your request. Thank you. Enjoy your evening."

The dark-suited bodyguard spoke into his left sleeve.

"Roger. Negative. Working on it."

He nodded to his dark-suited partner and they walked away.

Mozes sat down and looked to Viktorija.

"Please excuse the rude interruption. This has never happened to me here. I'm sorry."

Jane approached the table with the bottle of wine in her hand. This time, without waiting for approval, she topped off their wine glasses. Her left hand shook as she laid a small folded note card to the right of Mozes' silverware. She stepped away, placed the wine bottle in a holder, and nervously moved off.

241

Viktorija gasped at this point. She spoke in her true to form sarcasm.

"What is going on here? Wait, I know. This is entertainment. This is one of those murder mystery dinners."

"No, Viktorija. Sorry. This is just getting out of hand. This should not be happening at the *La Belle Vue*. I don't come here for this."

Mozes picked up the note card, opened it, and read it to himself.

"PLEASE EXCUSE THE CONFUSION. SOFIYA ZLATKOV WILL BE SEATED NEXT TO YOU. I OWE YOU AN EXPLANATION. WALTER."

"What does it say?"

Mozes handed the note card to Viktorija, and she read the card to herself. Finished, she looked to Mozes.

"Do you know who she is?"

"Yes."

"Do you know I work for her?"

"I didn't know that. Do you want to move?"

"Only if you do. It doesn't matter to me."

"Let's just stay. We shouldn't have to move."

Just then two labor staff from the restaurant came to the area. They carried portable screening and began to set it up to divide the area. They rushed to get the screen in place. They were polite and courteous and kept the disturbance to a minimum.

242

They said nothing to Mozes or Viktorija. When finished, the screen obstructed Mozes' and Viktorija's view of the skyline.

Mozes looked to Viktorija.

"I'm so sorry."

"Stop it. You have no reason to apologize. We're here together. Let's just enjoy each other's company."

"You're so understanding. You're so sweet."

Mozes reached out to Viktorija and gently caressed her left shoulder. His touch moved her clothing about and revealed a tattoo. He looked twice, the second longer than the first. He estimated the size to be approximately four inches by four inches. It was the same size and at the exact location of the removed flesh of all twelve murder victims. He tried to study the tattoo to decipher what it represented. The words. The symbols. He tried to get a better look. He was at the wrong angle.

He thought, "This cannot be."

"Sir, may we present," sounded a voice to the right of Mozes.

"Yes George, please."

George directed two other staff members to begin. As they set the course of food before Viktorija and Mozes, George explained the appetizer.

"Will there be anything else, sir?"

"No, George. Unless you can take the screen with you? Thank you."

243

George snickered. He knew it was unbecoming of his position with the *La Belle Vue*. He quickly composed himself and moved away from the table; then he abruptly stopped, turned, and went back to Mozes.

"Mr. Olah, please accept my apology for the screen. Walter is beside himself; he is upset by this. It's out of his control. Excuse my boldness."

"George, everything is fine. Please tell Walter not to worry. I know it's out of his control."

Mozes and Viktorija were left to enjoy their appetizer.

"Sir, may we clear?" sounded a voice from Mozes' right.

"Yes. Thank you."

The wait staff cleared the ware used for the appetizer course and continued to serve the second course.

As Mozes and Viktorija enjoyed the second course to their dinner, two dark suits moved their way. One spoke into his left sleeve.

"Clear. Come on in."

They positioned themselves one on each end of the screen.

Momentarily, Sofiya Zlatkov appeared near the maître d' station. Walter moved to greet her. He was intercepted by the first dark suit who stopped him with an open palm thrust to his chest and controlled Walter away from Ms. Zlatkov.
Two other dark suits followed directly behind Ms. Zlatkov. As choreographed, one of the dark suits from behind Ms. Zlatkov

took the lead substituting for the one that controlled Walter. He led Ms. Zlatkov to her table.

Mozes looked to Viktorija.

"I guess you're accustomed to this?"

"What do you mean?"

"You said you work with her. This must go on around you all day."

"Oh, no it doesn't. I'm shocked. I've never seen this. These dark suits. These guards."

"Come on. That's not what I hear."

"What do you hear?"

"Just what I see. A team of seven bodyguards. I count five in here, and I'm sure two drivers remain in the vehicles outside."

"This is a surprise. This is the first time I see this. It's entertaining."

Mozes was interrupted by a sexy voice with a thick Bulgarian accent.

"Mozes. I thought that was you. Viktorija. Hello. You two together? Hm."

Mozes rose from his chair, in respect for a lady.

"Sofiya. Good evening," responded Mozes.

"Good evening. How are you?" Sofiya said.

"Fine thank you."

Sofiya looked to Viktorija.

"Good evening Viktorija."

"Good evening Sofiya."

"Did you all have this screen put up?"

Mozes' tone was stern.

"No. Your obnoxious security detail did."

"What?" She turned and with a look summoned one of the dark suits.

"Did security put this ugly looking screen up?" inquired Sofiya.

"Yes," replied the bodyguard.

"Why?"

The bodyguard did not immediately reply. Mozes quickly injected.

"Sofiya, it was because I wouldn't move to another table."

Sofiya jerked her head to the direction of Mozes.

"What?"

"I wouldn't move to a different table so you could have this entire area to yourself."

Mozes turned and glared at the dark-suited bodyguard who made the request to him.

Sofiya followed his eyes to see who spoke to him. She turned her attention back to the lead dark suit and commanded.

"Get rid of this screen. Now!"

She turned to Mozes and Viktorija.

"I apologize for my security. Sometimes they get a little rambunctious. I'm sorry. I'll take care of everything for you tonight. Let me apologize."

Mozes talked over her.

"No. That's not necessary. I can't let you do that."

"Why?"

"It's just not necessary."

"Because you are a big city investigator. What's the agency? OIG, right? Some people refer to you as '*Hotshot MO.*' You have a reputation out there. Did you know?"

Sofiya's comments started to bother Mozes. He was done talking to the obnoxious Sofiya.

He thought, "She is much different tonight than at Gheorghi's Joe."

He looked directly into her eyes.

"Sofiya, it was good to see you again. I have a lady waiting. As you know, a gentleman never keeps a lady waiting."

He turned from her and sat down in his chair.

Viktorija took a sip of wine and set her glass down.

"*Hotshot MO.*" Viktorija giggled. "Are you going to start now?"

"What do you mean?"

"There's a story here, and I must hear it *Hotshot MO.*"

"Okay. Please don't call me *Hotshot MO.* It's *Hot Mozes* for you."

They both laughed.

"And yes, there's a short, short, story here. I'll tell you back at the apartment, not here."

Mozes reached for his smartphone.

"I have to do this. I'm not rude. I have to make sure Sofiya doesn't take care of this for me."

Mozes unlocked his smartphone and flicked the *Messages* app. He quickly composed a message and sent it. Immediately his phone sounded receipt of a message. He read the reply message and removed his phone from the table.

"Okay, took care of it."

Viktorija took another sip of her wine and emptied her glass. She twisted the long stem wine glass between her thumb and index finger. She longingly gazed at Mozes. Her dreamy thoughts were interrupted by a voice from her right.

"May I?"

Jane stood with the bottle of wine.

"Yes please."

Jane poured the wine and stepped back.

George appeared at the table.

"Sir, may I serve the main course?"

"Yes, George. Please."

With a nod from George, two other staff members began. They removed the ware from the second course and neaten the table. The main course was placed as George described it and finished with, "Will there be anything else?"

"No, George. Thank you."

George walked off.

After dessert, Viktorija and Mozes sat. They talked and finished the second bottle of wine as they enjoyed the view of the Pittsburgh skyline. The screen removed.

"Would you like anything else Viktorija?"

"What more could I possibly want here." Viktorija paused. "No nothing else for me here. Thank you."

There was flirtation in her voice. Mozes seemed to ignore it.

"Shall we go?" Mozes said.

"Yes."

Viktorija thought to herself.

"Once again no response to my flirtation. And where's the check? I can't ask; that's not proper etiquette. I guess he knows what he's doing. Does he have an account here? On a city investigator's salary? A city employee's salary? Is he a gigolo! He talks to Sofiya like they know each other. What did I get myself into? I may have had too much wine."

Mozes rose out of his chair first. He moved behind Viktorija, controlled her chair, and assisted her up. As Viktorija adjusted her clothing from being seated, Mozes caught another glimpse of the tattoo on her left shoulder. No details were discerned; it was covered too quickly. They walked away from the table, and neither Mozes nor Viktorija acknowledged Sofiya as they walked by the area she occupied.

Walter, at the maître d' station, lowered his head as Mozes and Viktorija walked by. Mozes gently touched Viktorija's arm to get her attention, and she looked his way.

"Give me a minute, please."

Mozes turned to Walter.

"Walter, everything was great as usual. Thank you."

Walter looked to Mozes.

"You're such a gentleman. You're kind. Thank you."

"I'll see you next time, Walter."

"Will there be a next time?"

"Yes, there will. I'll expect the same grand service."

"You're so kind."

"Good evening, Walter."

"Good evening, Mozes."

Walter looked to Viktorija.

"Good evening, Viktorija."

"Good evening, Walter," replied Viktorija

Mozes controlled the door for Viktorija as they walked onto Grandview Avenue.

34   Session One

"Good afternoon Mozes. My name is Joseph Polanski. I'm the Psychiatrist retained by the City of Pittsburgh to help city employees."

"Good afternoon, sir."

"Welcome. You are here today because of a City of Pittsburgh Civil Service rule. It requires all employees to have at least one session when they are involved in a traumatic event."

"Yes."

"How do you feel about the session? The compulsory attendance."

"It's a rule. I'm here. It's no big deal."

"Do you think you need to be here?"

"No."

"Why not?"

"I witness a suicide. I don't understand why someone takes their life. I don't feel I need to know why. It's part of the profession to witness traumatic events, to be part of traumatic incidents. An occupational hazard. I accept it."

"Your profession. Why were the two of you together that day?"

"A criminal investigation."

"Of what? What was the crime? The allegations?"

"I don't know how much I can tell you about the investigation. It's an ongoing criminal investigation."

"You can tell me anything; I'm here to help you. All our communications are confidential between you and me. They are covered by the confidentiality privilege of doctor-patient."

"Sounds good. But, frankly, I'm skeptical."

"Please, Mozes. You're going to have to trust me. I need for you to speak with me freely and openly. I'm not here to judge you. I'm not here to report back to your superiors. I only sign the Fit for Duty Certificate. To do so, you need to talk to me. I need to be certain you're ready to go back to work."

Mozes paused for thought.

"Okay. Ask away."

"What was the crime?"

"Murder. And conspiracy to commit murder."

"What was the allegation?"

"Unknown perpetrator or perpetrators committed twelve murders. Eleven of the twelve victims were unidentified; one of the victims was identified. I was assigned to the PBP Homicide Squad because the OIG received an allegation the Mayor was involved in the cover-up of the murders."

"Was the Assistant Chief a suspect?" asked Dr. Polanski.

Mozes continued, "The morning of his suicide, I discovered evidence that made him a person of interest. He violated BPB policy when he requested the ME to close their files and cremate all twelve victims. He either acted on his own, under duress or he followed an order from someone in his chain of command."

"Did you question him? Did you acknowledge to him you suspected him?"

"No."

"Why not?"

"I discovered the evidence in the late morning of the day of his suicide. I had a meeting with him at one o'clock. I told no one about the evidence. I needed more time to plan an investigative strategy. I wanted to gather more evidence or information before I confronted him. He was a high-ranking officer, and I needed to be certain."

"To be sure of yourself."

"I needed to be certain of the facts. To be sure of the facts."

"Did you draw your duty weapon?"

"Yes."

"Why?"

"I feared for my safety."

"Why?"

"The demeanor of the Assistant Chief. A gut feeling."

"Did you fire your weapon?"

"No."

"Did you point your weapon at the Assistant Chief?"

"I drew my duty weapon and rested it on my thigh. When the Assistant Chief pulled his pistol, I rolled out of my chair and created distance. I sought concealment and cover. As I moved to the body, to check for life, I had my weapon pointed at the Assistant Chief."

"Do you have dreams about it? Do you have dreams about murder?"

"I don't dream about his murder."

Dr. Polanski tone was inquisitive.

"Do you dream about a murder?"

"I don't know if I should answer."

"Should answer. Well, you have too."

Mozes inquired.

"And our conversations are confidential?"

"Yes. I told you that."

"I have dreams of murders."

"Murders."

"Why are you writing that down?"

Dr. Polanski ignored Mozes' question and continued.

"When did the dreams of murder start?"

"Since my childhood. Is this relevant to my work?"

Mozes' question was again ignored by Dr. Polanski.

"Do you hallucinate?"

"What? Hallucinate."

Mozes stopped talking and looked away from the Dr. Polanski.

Dr. Polanski broke the pause with a soothing tone.

"Take your time Mozes. We're not in a hurry."

Mozes continued to look away. Dr. Polanski sat there in a long awkward silence.

Still looking away, Mozes finally replied.

"No. I don't hallucinate."

Mozes paused as if to recompose himself though he did not show any emotion to recompose. He continued.

"I have visions."

"How long have you had visions?"

"Since my childhood."

"Please describe the visions."

"I see three, faceless, hallowed, figures. They are dressed in the vestments of a Roman Catholic priest," explained Mozes. "Sometimes just one. Other times two. Most often all three."

Dr. Polanski prodded.

"What happens in the visions?"

"There's a conversation, they chant, or they just stand or sit in silence. Sometimes the figures are aloft, hover."

"Where do these visions occur?"

"Wherever I'm at. In my bed, apartment, car. On the sidewalk. In the hallway of my apartment building. In my friend's apartment. Other places. Wherever I'm at."

Mozes briefly paused.

"Except in church."

Mozes appeared to have surprised himself.

"You know, in church, I've never had a vision. Outside the church, the church parking lot, but never in the church."

Dr. Polanski prompted.

"The dreams of murders. Please describe them. Tell me about them."

Mozes paused and looked away. He seemed to be in deep thought. Dr. Polanski sat in silence and gave Mozes time with his thoughts.

"Dr. Polanski, the murder dreams are vivid. The faceless, hallowed, figures are in the murder dreams. They command me to do things. Things that are very, very, very bad."

"Do the faceless, hallowed, figures try to control you?"

"Yes. Yes, they do. It's as if they mock me. Taunt me. They tell me I'm one of them. I shouldn't date women."

Dr. Polanski wrote that down too.

"Mozes, what is your sexual orientation?"

"What does that have to do with my employment? Fit for duty?"

"Nothing. It's relevant to me helping you."

"Why does everyone think I'm gay?"

"Who thinks you're gay?"

"I fancy women. Okay. I'm heterosexual."

"Who thinks you're gay?"

Mozes looked away. His face displayed anger, and his hands tighten on the arms of the chair as he became tense.

"I'll come back to that question. Are you married?"

"No."

"Do you want to be married?"

"It wasn't a high priority of mine. If I met the right person."

"Why didn't you meet the right person? Were you looking for the right person?"

Mozes lowered his head. He placed his hands together and interlocked his fingers. He started to rock back and forth on the chair. Dr. Polanski gave him time.

After several minutes, which seemed much longer, Mozes slowly raised his head. He looked directly at Dr. Polanski.

"It was always difficult for me. With girls when young. With ladies. All my life. Except."

He abruptly stopped talking.

Dr. Polanski injected, "It is okay Mozes. I want to help you. Take your time. When you're ready, please continue."

"Except for Viktorija. With her, I relax. I'm comfortable."

"Who is Viktorija?"

"Apartment 3C. She lives on the same floor of my apartment building."

"Do you have a relationship with her?"

"A relationship. We know each other about a year. We talk at the elevator. Recently a few dates. Three dates."

"How many other relationships have you been in?"

"If we call it a relationship, she's the only one. A few other dates, single dates, never a second."

"I see. Do you have any family? Your mother and father."

"My father was killed in a coal mining accident. My mother was committed to a state mental hospital, and I had not seen her since. I assume she was dead. There was only my Aunt Llona. That was all. That was all I knew."

"How old were you when your father was killed?

"I was about seven or eight when my father died."

And your mother. How old were you when you mother was committed?"

"About fourteen when my mother was committed."

"Do you know the details of those events?"

"No. My mother never told me about my father's accident. I never asked Aunt Llona about my mother. Aunt Llona is my Godmother, and she took me in when my mother was committed."

"Took you in?"

"Yes. Aunt Llona brought me to Pittsburgh to live with her. I always assumed there was no one else."

"Oh."

"Sorry about the lack of detail about myself. I just don't know."

"I understand Mozes."

Dr. Polanski paused a moment.

"At this point, do you have any questions for me?"

"No. Nothing. I just need the signed certificate so I can go back to work."

Dr. Polanski spoke slowly.

"Mozes, I can't give it to you today. I need a few more sessions at least."

"A few more sessions. Is there something wrong with me? Something I should know about?"

"What a loaded question, Mozes."

"Well, is there something wrong with me?"

"I can't answer that question. In my field of work, I need more time to explore things. That's what I do. That's how I help people."

"So, you're saying I need help. Something's wrong with me."

"Okay. The candor of the matter is you suffer from Posttraumatic Stress Disorder."

"What. PTSD. I didn't shoot anyone."

"The Assistant Chief's suicide was not the event that created your illness. I'm puzzled as to what brought on your illness, the PTSD. The event or events."

"Illness. No. No. How's this going to affect my job?"

"Again, Mozes, there is no consequence to your job. It's a matter of time to get us to the point where you are fit for duty. Please keep this in mind, we work together to ensure you are fit for duty."

"I don't feel like there is anything wrong with me."

"As is typical, PTSD affects your mental health. It shows itself differently to people. Your pain in the head, dreams of murders, and visions of three, faceless, hallowed, figures dressed in the vestments of a Roman Catholic priest are caused by something. There's a stimulus for the pain, dreams, and visions. To be crass, your pain, dreams, and visions are not caused by something you eat."

"I didn't think this could happen to me."

"You took the first and most important step, Mozes. You talked to me today. You didn't lie just to get the certificate."

"I can't lie."

"Mozes, you're a complicated person. The explanation is in your past. Which brings me to ask, how do you feel about having your Aunt Llona at a session?"

"I don't know? She's seventy."

"I can't force you to do anything. I think she has the answers you need. Do you talk to her about your past?"

"No. I didn't want to trouble her. She gave me everything I have."

"All right. If you think of any questions, you would like to ask me, write them down and bring them to the next session."

Dr. Polanski wrote the day, date, and time on an appointment card and handed it to Mozes.

"Here's your next appointment."

Mozes took the card.

"Thank you, sir."

"Your welcome. Relax. We'll work through this. Trust me. Your homework, go on a date with Viktorija."

"What?"

"Go on a date with Viktorija. If she relaxes you. That's what you need to do. Just relax."

"I can do that. I can go on a date with Viktorija."

Dr. Polanski rose from his chair as did Mozes from his. They shook hands and Mozes left his office.

On the drive to his apartment, the hallowed figures appeared. The *Teacher* spoke.

"It won't help *Mo*. Joe won't help."

Mozes ignored them, and they went away. He pushed a button on the steering wheel and announced.

"Call Viktorija."

35   The lower back tattoo

"Hello, Mozes."

"Hello, Viktorija. How are you today?"

"Just fine. How did your visit go?"

"Great. Much better than I thought. The doctor was adept and sincere."

"Good."

"Yeah. I'm comfortable with him."

"I think the doctor's help will be good for you."

"Me too. And you know what else will be good for me?"

"What?"

"Spending time with you tonight."

"Oh. Okay. What do you have in mind?"

"Do you want to go out or stay in?"

"Would you mind staying in?"

"No. I'll take care of it. You come over to my place."

"Okay. What time?"

"Seven o'clock? Will that work for you?"

"Sure will. Are you going to wear a t-shirt and jeans?"

"I don't know," replied Mozes.

"Yes, you are *Hot Mozes*. You're going to relax. And I'll dress casual too."

"Okay. Then I'm going to order in."

"Great. I must go; Sofiya is calling in."

"Oh, boy. See you tonight."

"I can't wait."

Mozes pushed the end call button on the leather-wrapped steering wheel. He continued to operate the Porsche along the Boulevard of the Allies.

At the apartment, Mozes laid down on his bed. He wanted to rest before he started to prepare for his date. He quickly fell asleep.

A knock came from the door, and Mozes sat up in bed. Groggy, he sat there for a minute, and a louder knock came. Mozes rose from the bed and walked to the door. He looked through the one-way peephole and saw Viktorija. Mozes looked at his Rolex; it was four-thirty. Viktorija was early. He smiled and opened the door.

"Hello, Viktorija."

"Hello Mozes. I hope you don't mind I'm early."

"No. Not at all. Come in."

Viktorija looked up to Mozes with seduction in her eyes. Mozes closed the door behind her and did not notice. Viktorija reached to the dead bolt knob and locked the door. She reached over and took Mozes by his hand and led him through the foyer to the hallway. She continued to hold his hand with a firm, controlling, grip as they moved down the hall and into the bedroom. She guided him to the bed, sat on the edge, and again looked up to Mozes, seduction still in her dazzling blue eyes. She locked her seductive eyes to his innocence. Her voice was hushed and sexy.

"Sit down by me Mozes."

Spellbound, Mozes immediately sat down at her command.

Viktorija reached her right hand up and caressed the nape of Mozes' neck. She pulled herself in and softly pressed her lips to his. Once. Twice. Mozes drew back.

Viktorija pulled harder at the nape of his neck. She kissed him again. He relaxed. He closed his eyes and began to kiss her back. They locked in passion.

Viktorija reached with her left hand and started to rub Mozes' chest. Mozes relaxed more. Viktorija sensed this and pushed him back. Mozes melted down onto the bed. She climbed atop him and straddled him. She pressed herself hard against him.

Locked in passion for her, Mozes, with his right hand, caressed her left shoulder. He felt the roughness to the tattoo. With his left hand, he caressed the middle of her lower back. There too he felt the roughness to the tattoo. They continued to kiss. The passionate episode built Mozes' confidence. He began to kiss her harder and caressed her with more force.

266

The episode was abruptly interrupted by a roar of laughter from a male's voice that came from Viktorija. Mozes left and right hands filled with a thick warm liquid. In defiance of gravity, Viktorija rose off Mozes. Mozes opened his eyes and saw Viktorija morph to the *All-Seeing*. As the *All-Seeing* hung in the air above Mozes, his vestments drooped loosely. He extended his hand, pointed his index finger at Mozes and roared with laughter again. The *All-Seeing* spoke.

"See Mozes. You can't escape us. Just like in the nave, the passion with you there as here. Now, like then, we control you."

Mozes looked down to his large, strong, hands. They were covered in a dark, red, liquid. He drifted toward shock. His eyes were closed. He forced them opened and looked up. The *All-Seeing* still hung in the air above him. He watched as the *All-Seeing* threw his vestments off. His naked body rolled over. With his bare back exposed, Mozes saw two areas of flesh removed. The gaping holes bleed profusely, one on the upper left shoulder and the other in the middle of the lower back. The blood flowed onto Mozes and Mozes passed out.

Mozes awoke from the sound of his cellular phone announcing the receipt of a text message. He just laid with his eyes wide open. He continued to breathe heavy as his chest labored the breaths. He raised his hands in the air and inspected them. They were clean. He felt about his body in a slow, deliberate fashion. Everything was dry. He slowly looked down for a visual inspection. Nothing. There was no blood on his clothing. He rested back and forced his eyes to stay open; he feared to close them. He stared at the ceiling fan as it rotated with a beat.

Again, his phone announced the receipt of a text message. He did nothing. He laid in fear and implored out loud.

"God. Help me."

He slowly raised his right hand and looked at his Rolex. It was six-thirty. His arm fell to the bed.

"I didn't even prepare for tonight."

He reached for his phone with his left hand and removed it from the holster. He swiped the screen, enter the security code, and flicked the *Messages* app with a red dot with a white number two. He read the first message.

"HELLO. RUNNING A LITTLE LATE. JUST LEAVING THE STRIP NOW. SORRY. SEE YOU SOON."

He read the second message.

"I WANT TO FRESHEN UP WHEN I GET HOME. WILL SEVEN-THIRTY BE OKAY?"

He flicked the third and final unread message which came in while he read the other two.

"MOZES WHERE ARE YOU?"

Mozes' arm fell to the bed, and he didn't move. He forced his eyes to stay open. He feared even to think, but gave in and wondered.

"Should I cancel? No. I must beat this thing. She makes me happy. Comfortable. I want to see her. To be with her. I have to beat this thing."

Mozes slowly rose from the bed, slid to the edge, and sat. He collected himself, took a deep breath and replied to Viktorija's text.

"GREAT. TAKE YOUR TIME. SEE YOU AT SEVEN-THIRTY."

He rose from the bed and quickly prepared himself to receive Viktorija. He bathed, groomed his hair and finished with a liberal spray of cologne. He dressed in a t-shirt and jeans as Viktorija requested.

A light knock came from the door. Mozes set the bottle of Chinese wine on the table. He walked to the door and looked through the one-way peephole. Viktorija stood there. Mozes stared at a strikingly beautiful woman, even in casual clothes. Her supple brown hair rested on her shoulders. Her plump lips displayed just a touch of red lipstick. She used only enough makeup to accent her natural beauty. Her voluptuous body showed through the untucked light blue t-shirt and faded blue jeans. The low, v-cut, t-shirt directed to the deep groove created by her breast. Through the peephole, he saw a seductress. He smiled.

Mozes placed his hand on the doorknob and took a deep breath. He reflected on the earlier dream.

"I will beat this," he mumbled to himself.

He exhaled and opened the door.

"Hello, Viktorija. You look ravishing tonight."

"Thank you, Mozes. You're in a t-shirt. You look relaxed."

"Yeah. The best I can."

Mozes closed the door and locked it.

"Come in. Would you like a glass of wine?"

"Yes, please."

"It's a Chinese wine. I thought it was the best for our Chinese food."

"Interesting. I'll try it."

Mozes poured two glasses of the wine. He took the glasses with him to the couch and handed one to Viktorija.

"Try it. See what you think."

Viktorija sipped her wine as Mozes stood there. She approved.

"Good. Thank you."

"If you don't like it I have something else."

"No this is fine. Sit down."

She expected him to go over to the armchair again, so she did not move over.

Mozes paused and waited for Viktorija to slide over. When she didn't, he walked around the back of the couch to her other side and sat. He looked at her and smiled. She smiled back. He sipped his wine.

"The food should be here soon."

"Good. I'm hungry."

She moved to the edge of the couch and reached her hand out to set her glass on the coffee table. As she did, her untucked t-shirt slowly rode up.

Mozes stared as the t-shirt rose and revealed Viktorija's bare back. Suddenly, with surprise, he pressed back into the couch.

The bare skin gave way to a tattoo. The t-shirt slowly rose over a tattoo that was in the same position and the same size as the fleshed removed from the murder victims. He looked hard to decipher the tattoo. He was cautious not to get caught as he stared at the tattoo for a clue. He thought.

"My hunch may be way out there, but I know I have to follow it."

Throughout the evening Mozes fought to stay focused on Viktorija. His curious thoughts were directed to the tattoos, thoughts of his earlier dream of Viktorija when he felt the lower back tattoo, and the flesh removed from the lower back of the *All-Seeing*. He wanted to get another look, a longer look.

He wondered thoughts within.

"Was it just coincidental? Were her tattoos the same as the murder victims? If they were this was a huge break in the investigation. I had to ask."

He paused briefly. Then he wondered more thoughts.

"I'm not working the investigation. I'm still on administrative leave with this PTSD. And how will my questions to her impact our relationship? This is not going to be simple?"

Mozes awoke and found Viktorija cuddled on the couch with her head perched on his lap faced away from him. They had fallen asleep. He looked at his Rolex, it was two-thirty in the morning.

Mozes did not want to wake her. He tried to slide out from under her, and she started to move. He stopped and let her adjust herself to a different position. When she did, her t-shirt rode up and exposed the tattoo in the middle of her lower back.

271

Again, he tried to study the tattoo for clues. The light was dim. He saw no details, not even the coloring. He started to fidget with his phone as he thought what to do.

"I'll take a picture. What if she wakes?"

He continued to think how to resolve his dilemma.

"I'll tell her I wanted a picture of her and she looked so peaceful sleeping."

Mozes positioned his phone to use the camera. He watched the screen as he adjusted the position to capture the whole tattoo and to be as close as possible to capture the detail. He tapped the button. It made noise as it cycled to hold the image, to flash, and to take a photograph. He did not move as he looked to see if the noise roused Viktorija. It did not. He reviewed the picture, tapped the camera icon, and thought.

"I need it closer. I'll have to take two pictures to get it all."

Mozes positioned the phone again and looked at the screen. He pinched the screen to operate the zoom. He took a picture and quickly repositioned the phone, checked the screen, and took the second picture. He reviewed them. He was comfortable he had what he needed.

Viktorija continued to sleep.

Mozes thought, "I need a photograph of the other one. How can I do this?"

After he studied the situation, he ever so slowly pulled back Viktorija's t-shirt at the left shoulder area. There it was, the shoulder tattoo. He continued to tug at the t-shirt to expose the entire tattoo. Viktorija's leg jerked. Mozes froze. He held her t-shirt stretched and slowly moved the bra strap out of the way. The tattoo was fully exposed. He quickly positioned his phone and adjusted it. He snapped a picture, repositioned the camera, and snapped the second picture. He reviewed the photos on the large screen, and they were acceptable as evidence. He lowered his telephone.

He stared at the tattoo in the dim light and wondered Viktorija's story. Apparently, she too had a story. He readjusted the bra strap and released her t-shirt. It sprung back and covered the tattoo.

Mozes had a hunch Viktorija had a painful story. He rested his hand over the tattoo as to comfort her. Just then, without any warning, Viktorija reached her hand up and placed it atop of Mozes' hand. This startled Mozes, but he did not withdraw. They both covered the tattoo and for now, the mystery of it. Mozes adjusted himself and went back to sleep.

36   Session Two – The facts of the past

"Aunt Llona this is Doctor Joseph Polanski. Dr. Polanski, this is my Aunt Llona."

"Good afternoon Llona. How are you today?"

"Very well thank you."

"I'm the Psychiatrist retained by the City of Pittsburgh to help city employees, to help Mozes."

"Yes. Mozes explained it to me."

Dr. Polanski looked at Mozes and then back to Aunt Llona.

"Do you mind if I call you Aunt Llona?

"No, that's kind of cute. May I call you Joe?"

"Yes, you may."

"So, how can I help, Joe? I'll do anything to help Mozes."

"Aunt Llona, I'll get right to it."

Aunt Llona interrupted.

"Direct. I like that."

"Mozes suffers from Posttraumatic Stress Disorder. PTSD. Not from what happened at work. From something that took place when he was a child. Do you know of any traumatic events in his life?"

"Yes. There was the death of Mozes' father's. He was killed in a coal mining accident. His mother…"

There was a short pause by Aunt Llona before she continued.

"…was committed to a state mental hospital when Mozes was fourteen. I uprooted him from his birth town and moved him to Pittsburgh. I think those things were traumatic. Luckily I was able to shield him from any further trauma."

"Aunt Llona, please excuse my boldness, my directness. I want to help Mozes. I think you know much more. It's time Mozes learns about his past. About his mother and father. I sense there is more and he needs to know to move on."

Aunt Llona lowered her head. She stared at the floor. She raised her right hand to her face and wiped her eyes.

There was a long silence in the room. Mozes broke the silence.

"Sir, all due respect, maybe this isn't such a good idea."

Dr. Polanski's was stern.

"Mozes, your Aunt Llona is the one to help you, not me. She knows the secrets of your past. She has to share them with you so you can move on."

Dr. Polanski turned to Aunt Llona,

"Did you hear me Aunt Llona?"

Aunt Llona sniffled and wiped her eyes again. She slowly raised her head and looked to Mozes.

"Oh, my dear child, your innocence. You did nothing wrong. You didn't deserve to suffer. They stole your innocence."

"Aunt Llona what do you mean? I don't follow you. What is there?" Mozes said with concern in his voice.

Aunt Llona looked to Dr. Polanski.

"Are you sure this will help him? You better not be wrong."

"Aunt Llona, it will help. It will help. He needs to know."

Aunt Llona briefly looked to the floor. When she raised her head, she looked to Mozes.

"My dear child the doctor is right. There are secrets. Some would say deep, dark, secrets. You're fifty now. You probably should know. I'm seventy. If I don't tell you, no one will. It may not be the right thing to do, to take it to my grave as your mother and father did. I'm going to listen to the doctor. Joe should know best."

Mozes looked to Aunt Llona. Her facial expression spooked him and caused the past to roll through his mind.

"Aunt Llona looked just like mother. Her facial expression was the same as mother's the day mother picked me up from the school nurse's office the day the gym teacher found me in the high school shower in a fetal position. Like mother that day, bitterness showed in Aunt Llona's eyes welled with tears, which she too failed to hold. Her commonplace, sweet, comforting, smile turned to an expression of grief. Her eyes said she was somewhere else, somewhere far away, a bad place. The same look mother had. I didn't ask mother then. That was an opportunity lost to learn about the visions, the dreams, and my suffering. This must stop. Perhaps what she had to say, the facts of my past, would help me. The doctor also needed to hear to help me. This was an opportunity I needed."

Mozes moved closer to Aunt Llona. He placed his left hand on her right shoulder.

"Aunt Llona, please tell me. I'm older now. I'm old enough to know. I want to know. I agree with the doctor. Help me stop it. I want it to stop. Please."

As Aunt Llona looked up to Mozes, she wiped the tears from her cheeks with her hand. Mozes quickly retrieved the primly folded, ironed, handkerchief from his right, inside, suit jacket, pocket and gave it to Aunt Llona. At this moment, she was the fair Pittsburgh lady in need of his emotional support.

Aunt Llona composed herself.

"Your mother and I just wanted to protect you. We just wanted you to have your innocence back."

Aunt Llona looked down.

"I know," said Mozes.

Aunt Llona looked up and directly into Mozes' eyes.

"You have to promise me one thing. You have to promise me."

"I will. I will promise."

"Promise me you will not judge them. You will not be their jury, their executioner. You will not do what you father did."

"I promise. My character, morals, religious beliefs, and values will not let me do anything. I won't do anything. My child rearing will not allow such actions. The Cloth's teachings will not allow such actions."

"What you're about to hear me say may just drive you the wrong way. Take you to the wrong side of the law. Take you away from the Cloth. Promise me, Mozes."

"Aunt Llona, I promise you. I promise as Dr. Polanski is my witness."

Dr. Polanski adjusted his posture in his large, black, leather, armchair. Aunt Llona's initial comments peaked his interest.

Aunt Llona slowly shook her head up and down signaling yes.

"Okay. Okay then."

Aunt Llona reached for her oversized purse and struggled to pull it up on her lap. She reached in and pulled out a stack of paper, shuffled through them, and divided them in half. She gave one-half to Mozes and the other half to Joe.

Mozes quickly started to thumb through the papers.

Dr. Polanski queried, "What is this?"

Aunt Llona reached over to Mozes and placed her hand on top of his hands to halt his curiosity.

"After Mozes asked me to accompany him to this session and after I reluctantly agreed to come with him, I thought this might be what you were thinking Joe. So, for my credibility, so you both believed me, I brought these documents for you each to read at the same time."

She briefly paused and kept her hand on Mozes' hands to maintain his attention.

"You each have a copy of the same documents. When I tell you the facts of the past, it will seem unbelievable. You have copies of the sealed records before you. Those are bona fide copies. You can see and fill the raised seals from the Somerset County Courthouse. Please read them; then I will talk."

Both Dr. Polanski and Mozes eagerly directed their attention to the documents. As Mozes read, he rubbed and massaged the nape of his neck.

Aunt Llona interrupted.

"Mozes you promised. Remember, you promised me."

Aunt Llona became restless as Mozes and Joe read. She rose from the couch and moved about the room. She ended her nervous pace by the window where she stood and looked out.

After some time, Dr. Polanski was the first to set down the documents. He stared at Aunt Llona. Aunt Llona felt Joe's stare, turned, and looked back at him. Neither said anything. She turned back and continued to look out the windows.

Then Mozes exploded with anger. Immediately Aunt Llona turned in his direction. Dr. Polanski jumped to his feet. Mozes started to pace the room like a caged animal. He was not violent; he just paced, as if to express a desire to be free.

Dr. Polanski used a low, comforting, tone.

"Mozes, would you like to sit?"

Mozes just looked at him with blank emotion.

Aunt Llona's tone was with concern.

"Mozes, you promised me. You promised."

Mozes looked away from the doctor to Aunt Llona and said nothing.

"Mozes, please sit. We can work through this. I can help you. We want to help you. You need to know. You need to deal with this atrocity. I can help you."

Mozes looked to the doctor.

"You think you can help me with this."

Mozes looked to Aunt Llona.

"And you took me to church. You made me go into the nave. Did you have any idea?"

Aunt Llona moved to Mozes and took his hands.

"If I only knew Mozes. If I knew all these years you continued to suffer. I thought uprooting you from your birth town solved the problem. I did the best I knew."

Mozes pulled his hands away from Aunt Llona's grip and turned away from her. He paused and immediately turned back to her, moved in close, and hugged her.

He whispered to her, "Yes, you did. Thank you. You took good care of me."

He released his hug, stepped back from her, and looked lovingly into her eyes.

"I promised you."

Aunt Llona wiped her tears with the white handkerchief monogrammed **MO**.

"We'll work this out," said Aunt Llona.

Not showing his sigh of relief, Dr. Polanski added.

"I'll help too."

Mozes turned to the doctor.

"Okay. If you give me the signed Fit for Duty Certificate, I will be on my way."

Mozes held a serious pose for about a minute before he roared with laughter.

"I just had to inject some humor.

"And your humor will go a long way to help you. Here's your next appointment."

"Yes, sir."

Dr. Polanski handed Aunt Llona a card too.

"Thank you, Aunt Llona. Sharing these documents is huge. Will you please join us for his next session?"

"I will. I'll do anything to help Mozes."

She looked deep into the eyes of Dr. Polanski.

"Anything."

Dr. Polanski was not sure how Mozes would react to the facts in the documents. It was a good sign he was not mad or upset with his Aunt Llona, the longtime holder of the events of the past.

37   The Photographs

Mozes rose from his chair as Murry walked toward him. They both reached out and shook hands.

"Good to see you, Mozes. How are you?"

"I'm fine. Thank you."

"Wasn't that something? The Assistant Chief committed suicide right in the conference room, in front of you."

"Well, it was something."

"I was told you're on administrative leave."

"Yes, per OIG policy."

"You were sent to the city psychiatrist?"

"Yes."

"How's that going?"

"Going well."

"So, you wanted to meet me to tell me you received your signed Fit for Duty Certificate?"

"I wish. No, I don't have it yet."

"You sure everything is all right?"

"Yes. Listen. I have three photographs to give you."

Mozes slid a thumb drive across the table to Murry.

"Pictures. For what? Of what?"

"For the murders."

"You're not working the investigation. You're on admin leave."

"Okay. I'll take the photos somewhere else."

Murry quickly reached out and picked up the thumb drive.

"No, I didn't say that," directed Murry. " What do the pictures show?"

"Tattoos. And don't ask anything else. If your checks are negative, then just forget today. If the checks turn something up, I will explain and provide the originals with a completed *Chain of Evidence* form."

Murry sat up straight in his chair, took a deep breath, and exhaled.

"Mozes. I don't know."

"Hey, it's a hunch. Hunches pay off. Right?"

"Yes, they do. Okay. I'll take care of it. Can you at least explain your hunch to me?"

"Sure. I saw a person with tattoos in the same position of the removed flesh from the victims. These tattoos were the same size as the removed flesh. I took pictures of them. It was a hunch."

"That was it. You saw the tattoos, walked up to the person, and asked to take pictures of them."

"No. It wasn't like that."

"Like what then."

"Like I don't want to tell you unless we get something on the tattoos. Murry please."

"Okay."

"Thank you. Anything else going on back at the office?"

"No. Both the Lieutenant and I wish you were still working the case."

"I give you photographs to run. I reach out to one of my informants. I constantly think about the case. I'm here. I'm still working the case."

"You shouldn't be. City policy."

"I'm not carrying a city gun."

"Are you carrying? No. I don't want to know. It's better if I don't know. You know the policy. You're OIG."

"I didn't have time last Thursday to tell you. People on the *Strip* know you're an undercover cop when you're there in the role of a vagrant."

"How do you know?"

"My informant told me."

"What else did he say?"

"How do you know my informant is a he? Maybe it's the transvestite that always follows you when you're on the *Strip*."

Mozes briefly paused.

"Nothing further from the informant. I'm waiting for a call."

Murry pushed his chair back from the table.

"I have to go. I must figure out how to proceed with this investigation. We have no bodies. We have no suspects, no living suspects. The lone suspect commits suicide. The ME closes their cases at the direct order of the lone suspect who commits suicide. The victims are cremated. You know, I could just close these cases on this information."

"Oh, no you're not! I think that's what other co-conspirators want. Don't you see? One dead co-conspirator and one live co-conspirator. And probably will stay alive if she doesn't say anything. She's only looking at one to two years of jail time. She's an acceptable temporary loss to the corrupt political machine. Another hunch of mine."

"You think?" said Murry.

"Don't close the cases. Run the tattoos. Wait to see what we get. And let's wait for my informant. We owe it to the victims."

"Your right. Thanks for your help."

"And we will continue to meet and talk about the case."

"Okay."

"There's no policy to prohibit two friends from sitting around and talking. I'm still a city employee with active security clearances."

Murry rose from his chair and reached for the check. Mozes snatched it from him.

"I'll get this."

"Thank you."

"Your welcome. I'll be talking with you."

Murry turned to leave. He stopped and looked back to Mozes.

"I understand why they call you *Hotshot MO.'* Thanks for your patience with me."

"Get out of here before you hug me."

38   Message from Interpol

After the breakfast meeting on the *Strip*, Murry went directly to the Homicide Squad. Mozes peaked his interest about the missing flesh from the victims. Everyone involved in the murder investigations believed the victims had tattoos carved off their bodies.

Murry opened the thumb drive and looked at the photographs. He did not recognize the tattoos or anything about them.

He created a request and sent it to the Interpol Washington D.C. National Central Bureau (NCB). He requested a Modus Operandi Notice for global circulation to all NCBs. Through them, to all the law enforcement agencies throughout their countries. The notice contained the details of the flesh removal for all twelve victims. It requested any information or related investigations about the tattoos or similar crimes of similar manner or methods.

He immediately received a confirmation email from the Interpol Washington. It stated the request was received, logged, assigned a case number, and circulated worldwide.

With the task completed, Murry began to review other emails. His computer chirped, a signal he received a new email. He saw it was a second email from Interpol Washington and he clicked on it. When it opened, it displayed the word ALERT in red capital letters. The short message was in capital letters and larger than the standard font. It read:

THE REPUBLIC OF BULGARIA, MINISTRY OF INTERNAL AFFAIRS, NATIONAL POLICE SERVICE, NATIONAL ORGANIZED CRIME SERVICE, WILL CONTACT YOU DIRECTLY.

Murry sat back in his chair. A puzzled look came over his face as he thought.

"This was the first time this happened to me with an Interpol request."

He scrolled down to see if there was more to the message. There wasn't. Murry thought again.

"Does he have some type of supernatural ability with investigative work? How good is Mozes? *Hotshot MO.*"

39   Session Three – Aunt Llona tells all

As he entered the room, Dr. Polanski announced, "Good morning."

Aunt Llona and Mozes were seated on the couch. Dr. Polanski took his usual seat, the large, overstuffed, black, leather, chair.

"How are we all doing today?"

As a gentleman, Mozes looked to Aunt Llona and allowed her to answer first.

"Very well thank you, Joe."

"Very well, sir," followed Mozes.

"Good. Shall we start? Do either of you have any questions for me?"

Both Aunt Llona and Mozes moved only their heads to indicate no.

"There is a lot of information in the documents. Aunt Llona, please tell Mozes everything."

Aunt Llona looked to Mozes and then back to Dr. Polanski. She began.

"Mozes you were about five or six. A year or two before your confirmation. Your mother and father thought it would be good for you to be an altar server. Shortly after you started, they observed you experienced pain when church bells rang, only when outside of the church. They took you to a doctor at the company hospital. They thought the pitch of the sounds caused the pain. Some type of ailment with your ears. The doctor found nothing and said it was a figment of your imagination.

Then you started to have dreams or nightmares. Your parents weren't sure. With no pattern, you woke up at night. You cried and rocked back and forth. They comforted you, and you fell back to sleep. They took you to the same doctor at the company hospital to be examined. Again, the doctor said there was nothing wrong and noted to them that small children had bad dreams. The doctor advised your parents to just let you cry, not to baby you over the dreams.

For about a year or two, your mother and father observed your pain continued. They believed the dreams continued with the same frequency and intensity. So, they made an appointment with a doctor in Pittsburgh. It had to be two years."

Aunt Llona stopped talking. She looked to the floor.

Dr. Polanski encouraged, "Aunt Llona, are you okay?"

There was silence.

Mozes slid to the edge of the couch out of concern for Aunt Llona.

"Are you okay? Can I get you something?" asked Dr. Polanski.

The silence continued for a minute or so longer before Aunt Llona looked up.

"Water, may I have some water please?"

Dr. Polanski rose from his chair and walked to the corner of the room. He retrieved a bottle of water from a small refrigerator, opened it, and poured it into a tall crystal glass. He walked over to Aunt Llona and handed it to her with a napkin.

"Thank you."

"Mozes anything for you?"

"No, thank you."

Aunt Llona sipped the water. She cleared her throat and looked to Mozes.

"This part isn't nice. I don't know how else to say it."

Mozes slid back into the couch. He cocked his left arm on the arm of the couch and rested his fist against his left cheek.

"Please, continue. I'm prepared. I must know," Mozes said.

Aunt Llona cleared her throat again and continued.

"It was summertime. You were off school. The priest requested you to be the altar server for the eight o'clock daily morning masses. One day your mother and father had to pick you up right after mass to go to Pittsburgh for a midafternoon doctor's appointment. You were instructed to wait on the sidewalk in front of the church. When they didn't find you there, they parked the car on the side of the church and entered through the side door."

Aunt Llona abruptly stopped. She looked to the floor. She sipped the water. Her voice cracked as she continued.

"Then. Then your mother and father saw the shocking, disgusting, act. The priest. Right in the center of the church. The disgusting act the priest was committing on you in the nave of the church."

Aunt Llona stopped and cried.

Dr. Polanski looked to Mozes and saw Mozes tensed up. There was a distant look in his eyes, and his face was white. He started to recoil in anticipation of Aunt Llona's next words.

Dr. Polanski thought, "I hope Mozes cries. Though the seasoned law enforcement officer is probably too callous to pity such revolting actions, even when the acts are committed against him. The stoic. The impassive. Those are the ones that concern me. And Mozes is a concern to me."

Aunt Llona looked to Dr. Polanski. Her eyes were puffy, and her cheeks were wet with tears.

Mozes retrieved his primly folded, ironed, monogrammed, handkerchief from his right, inside, suit jacket, pocket and presented it to Aunt Llona.

"Thank you, Mozes."

She dabbed her eyes and wet cheeks.

"I don't know if I can continue."

Mozes encouraged, "Rest a minute."

Aunt Llona took a moment to compose herself. Mozes just sat in silence. Dr. Polanski continued to monitor them both.

Aunt Llona sniffed and dabbed her cheeks with the white, monogrammed, handkerchief as she raised her head from the floor.

"Okay. Your mother and father witnessed the priest as he fondled your gentiles. They heard him plead with you to touch him. Then he raised the Sanctus bells in his left hand and rang them. At this point, recomposed from shock, both your mother and father ran toward you. Your father shoved the priest away from you, and the priest's feet became tangled in his vestment and his underwear, which were down around his ankles. He fell to the floor. All the while the priest stumbled about to get his balance, to stand up, your father beat him. Your mother described it to me as a 'savage beating.' Your mother called to your father to stop, but your father's s rage continued. As the priest laid face up on the floor, your father beat the priest unconscious. The priest just laid there with his vestments opened."

Aunt Llona paused. After a minute or two, she composed herself and began again.

"Then your father, with his foot, repeatedly stomped the priest's right hand. With every stomp, he repeated, 'You will never give communion again.' He continued to stomp on the priest's right hand."

Aunt Llona paused again.

Dr. Polanski looked to Mozes. Mozes was pushed back into the couch. His right hand clenched into a fist, knuckles turned white and raised to his mouth.

Aunt Llona took a drink of water. She continued.

"As your father beat the priest, your mother quickly dressed you. With one hand on your shoulder, your mother used her other hand to pull your father away from the priest. In the chaos, your mother pleaded with your father to go and just leave the priest. Finally, your father gave in to your mother's request and slowly walked away from the priest. They rushed you out of the church, to the car, and drove off.

Of course, your mother and father were infuriated. They were beside themselves.

The next day they sat at the kitchen table and talked about the event. They consoled each other. Then there was a knock at the side door to their company home. It was the lawyer for the diocese and one of the Bishop's assistants. They immediately acknowledged the priest suffered from pedophilia and the diocese removed him from the church. The lawyer presented papers to your mother and father as the Bishop's assistant laid $100,000 cash on the kitchen table. All your parents had to do was sign the papers, a legally binding agreement that required them not to discuss the event with anyone and not to bring charges against the priest or litigate the diocese. Your father scooped the papers and the money from the table. He crushed it together and shoved them down the black cassock of the Bishop's assistant and threw them out of the house. Physically, threw them out of the house. Your father didn't even open the screen door. They had to put up a new screen door. The Bishop's assistant, more persistent of the two, from the side porch, asked your parents what it would take to keep them quiet. Your father slammed the door closed on them.

The diocese's impudent approach to resolving the traumatic, revolting, crime the priest committed against you further infuriated your parents. They sought legal counsel which was difficult for them. Very difficult. The local attorneys wanted nothing to do with the matter. They all declined to take the case. Some of the attorneys warned you parents against trying to fight the diocese with its vast resources. Even lawyers in Pittsburgh refused to take the case. Finally, they came upon a young, assertive, Pittsburgh lawyer who took the case. His name was in the court documents."

Aunt Llona quickly looked at Mozes.

"He's your boss now, the IG."

Mozes cocked his head but was not distracted from the past.

Aunt Llona continued.

"As the case progressed your father was murdered."

Mozes exclaimed.

"Murdered!"

"Yes murdered. I referred to it as a coal mining accident, but it wasn't. Your father was murdered."

Aunt Llona extended her arm and placed her hand on Mozes' shoulder to comfort him. She brought her hand back to her glass and continued.

"Yes. And some witnesses came forward to your mother. They told her your father's murder was ordered by the dioceses, by the Bishop. They told her she should have taken the $100,000 dollars. She went to the police. The Chief of Police listened but did nothing. No investigation was opened. The Chief told her he wasn't going to investigate the coal company, the economic lifeline of the community. And he certainly wasn't going to inquire into the Bishop. He too told her should have taken the money. She did not know how the Chief or the others knew about the money.

Time was not on the side of your mother.

You were about six or seven when you were sexually abused by the priest. Though your mother never determined how long it had gone on. You were about eight years old when your father was murder. The civil ligation of the priest and the diocese lingered. You were still having visions and dreams caused by the sexual abuse of the priest. Your mother, my sister, became an outcast from her ethnic church and the coal town. People just refused to believe a priest committed such crimes. The stress of isolation was too much for your mother. She finally went to a doctor for help, the same doctor that examined you, a coal company doctor. Two days after her visit, the Pennsylvania State Police came to her house and executed an Involuntary Mental Health Commitment Order signed by a Somerset County Judge. The doctor at the company hospital initiated the process, and she was committed to the Somerset State Hospital.

I was notified by one of your neighbors in '*40*' that your mother was taken away. Another neighbor took you to the *40 Hotel*. The owner of the hotel hid you from the social service workers and watched you until I came late in the evening to get you to bring you to Pittsburgh.

I visited your mother all those years, and I tried to get her out. All my legal efforts were denied. I tried to get your mother, my sister, out of the mental hospital, but she died there."

Aunt Llona paused. She sniffled and dabbed the tears from her cheeks.

"She shouldn't have been there. She shouldn't have died in there."

She paused again and dabbed more tears from her cheeks.

"They called themselves disciples of God. They preached Jesus' words. I stopped going to church with you because of their hypocrisy."

Aunt Llona stopped talking. She sat and cried. Mozes and Dr. Polanski said nothing; they let her cry.

Mozes sat there and wondered thoughts within.

"It was evident Aunt Llona cried because she couldn't help her sister. She knew her sister didn't have any mental problems all those years she visited her sister in the psychiatric hospital. She failed to help her sister, and my mother died in there, at the hands of the church. It was quite apparent the church was feared and was in control of the legal system, the police, the county courts, the coal company, and the doctors. They were cold blooded killers. The town's people who knew didn't come forward, all devoted to the church out of fear. They all sacrificed my innocence. How many other victims? How many other children had their innocence sacrificed? How many still lived with the pain?"

Mozes fought to hold back his intense sorrow from the loss of a loved one. The big tough guy, a law enforcement officer, tried to remain in control. It eventually seeped out through his tears. He joined his Aunt Llona and healed a little more.

Mozes' past tugged at Dr. Polanski too. His emotional control slipped, something that rarely happened to him. He quickly regained his professional poise, looked to Mozes and, saw he cried too, a visible sign Mozes healed a little in this session as well as the last. He knew the sessions were helping. Still, Dr. Polanski remained troubled. Was he able to sign the Fit for Duty Certificate with a clear conscience? He understood a career rested in the balance. He knew the events were not work related that caused Mozes' PTSD.

"Will Mozes ever be fit for duty again?" Dr. Polanski asked to himself. "Was he ever fit for duty?"

Both Mozes and Dr. Polanski were surprised when Aunt Llona continued. They focused on her words.

"With the attorney, I pursued the ligation against the diocese. The attorney's private investigator had a hound dog persistence, and his investigation disclosed valuable facts. Undisputed evidence that brought the Bishop himself to the negotiation table and forced an out of court settlement. The Bishop agreed to pay you $100,000 dollars a month for life. Even if they stopped paying you tomorrow, you have no financial worries. The agreement included a nondisclosure clause. It was one of the reasons I never talked to you about it. I didn't want to risk the payments stopping. The continuous, outrageous, monthly, payment was the only justice we got, Mozes. Of course, no amount of money replaced your parents. No amount of money brought back your innocence. I saw how you struggled with the females, with the ladies. Your stolen innocence was a huge loss for you. Select members of the Roman Catholic Cloth stole your innocence. They stole from you the very thing for which they stood – marriage, two to become one, family, the blessing of children."

Aunt Llona paused a moment.

"As your mother's sister, your Aunt, your Godmother, I tried to do my best for you. At seventy years, I hope I helped you."

Mozes slid closer to his Aunt Llona, put his arm around her, and they both wept.

Mozes said, "There are no regrets. Certainly, not from me. You're fantastic. Thank you for everything. Thank you, Aunt, Llona. You helped me. Yes, you helped me, Aunt Llona."

Embraced, they rocked back and forth as they comforted each other. The usual method Mozes' used to comfort himself.

40   The driveway meeting

Detective Stewart stayed at his desk the rest of his shift. He even ate his lunch at his desk. He wanted to be there to take the telephone call from the Bulgaria National Police Service. He was still excited that a hunch created an immediate, international contact. He wondered, for the rest of the day, what they had to share.

Murry checked his cellphone for the time. It was five-thirty. He stayed an extra hour and a half then decided to go home, disappointed he did not receive a call.

As Murry eased down the narrow street with cars parked on both sides, he observed a black Suburban, with blacked out windows, parked in front of his driveway.

Murry mumbled to himself, "Great, blocked again."

He quickly looked around for a curb space. He spotted one and parked.

As he walked up to his driveway, the driver's door to the Suburban opened. A female appeared, and her authoritative voice sounded.

"Murry Stewart?"

Surprised, Murry eased his right hand to his duty weapon and bladed his body to the unknown female.

"Yes."

"I represent the Republic of Bulgaria, Ministry of Internal Affairs. National Police Service. National Organized Crime Service."

She presented her credentials. Murry took them, examined them, and handed them back.

"Okay."

"I'm here because of your Interpol Modus Operandi Notice."

"Yes."

"Please get in the Suburban."

"What. I'm not getting into the Suburban. If you have something to share, we can talk right here."

Murray thought, "How would I know if her credentials are real."

In front of his house, as his mind transitioned from family time to defensive tactics, the front passenger window lowered. In a steady, authoritative voice, the passenger spoke.

"Murry, get in."

Murry looked to the window. The city's IG was seated in the front passenger seat.

"Come on. My dinner's waiting."

"Please," said the female Bulgarian police officer, in a cooperative tone.

Murry walked to the rear, passenger side, door and slid in. He closed the door and adjusted his position. He looked to the IG.

"What is it? What do they have?"

The female agent who greeted Murry turned in the driver seat and faced Murry.

"My name is Anna Nikolov. I am an Agent of the Government of Bulgaria. For the past two years, I've been investigating an international prostitution organization. Not just any prostitution."

She stopped and turned slightly to the IG.

"You're sure about this. You're certain he's okay?"

"Yes. I personally vetted Murray," replied the IG

The IG turned to Murry.

"With Mozes on administrative leave, I needed someone else to assist with this. I selected you."

Agent Nikolov turned back to Murry and continued.

"Not just any prostitution organization. This one is an organized adult and child prostitution ring that caters to the Roman Catholic Cloth – the Bishops, cardinalate, priests, and others who pursue such perversion. We have information that alleges this is occurring throughout the local diocese and dioceses throughout western Pennsylvania. Witnesses further suspect it occurs throughout the entire United States, at all diocese in the United States and worldwide."

"How is the City of Pittsburgh involved?" Murry asked.

Agent Nikolov went on.

"The Zlatkov family. The Boris Zlatkov crime family is suspect of running the organized adult and child prostitution ring. We believe Boris Zlatkov uses his daughter's business as a front. They kidnap a mother and her child in Bulgaria. It doesn't matter if the child is a girl or boy. Boris Zlatkov brings the kidnapped victims into the country with the help of a New York City charitable foundation working in collusion with The Zlatkov Global Opportunity Foundation which his daughter, Sofiya Zlatkov, runs. The victims, mothers and their children, all have the proper documents from the appropriate government agencies, both Bulgaria and the United States governments. On paper, Sofiya Zlatkov places the victims with wealthy families in the Pittsburgh area. Some of the members of the wealthy families are employees of the city. One of those families is the Mayor of Pittsburgh. When their clients request prostitution services from the adult, the child or as a mother/child team, they are dispatched. That is what we know to date."

"Okay. How can I help? What could I possibly do for the government of Bulgaria? Me, a City of Pittsburgh Homicide Detective." Murry looked to the IG. "This seems to be way out of my scope."

Agent Nikolov continued.

"The photographs of the tattoos you sent with the Interpol request, where did you get them? Who did you photograph?"

There was silence in the Suburban.

Agent Nikolov politely demanded.

"Murry, where did you get the photographs? How did you get the photos? It obviously wasn't any of the twelve victims. Their tattoos were removed."

Murry said nothing.

The IG injected.

"Did you get them from Mozes?"

The IG paused to let Murry answer. Again, Murry said nothing.

"We need to know," said the IG. "Just because he's on administrative leave, I know he's still working the case."

Agent Nikolov explained.

"Murry, the tattoos mark the victims. It's a sophisticated code. The mother and child tattoos are coded to match, so the clients know they are mother and child. That's for the clients who want that type of sick, sexual, perversion. The clients receive a number. The number is in the tattoo. The client knows which tattoo to look at, the upper left shoulder or the middle of the lower back. The victim doesn't know which one the client will look at. They just know the client will examine their tattoos. If the number is there, the client knows everything is cool."

"I got them from Mozes. I was excited about a lead. We hoped the photographs provided a lead. I worked with him like he was not on administrative leave."

"He didn't tell you where he got the photographs?" asked Agent Nikolov.

"No. From our conversation, I assumed Mozes took them himself."

"Did you ask him who he photographed?"

"No."

Agent Nikolov looked to the IG.

"She's one of them. She's a victim. Whoever it is, if they have the tattoos, they are a part of the prostitution ring."

"I know. I agree with you. Whoever is tattooed, they are involved. Mozes isn't. I know Mozes isn't involved with anything criminal."

"I have surveillance photographs of him talking to Sofiya Zlatkov."

"One time. Mozes spoke with Sofiya one time. With all the surveillance you conducted, he showed up one time."

Murry said, "Outside Gheorghi's Joe when he was with her at the table."

Both Agent Nikolov and the IG turned to Murry and said at the same time, "Yeah. How do you know?"

"I questioned him about it when we started to work together. I saw him there with Sofiya Zlatkov when I conducted undercover surveillance on the *Strip*. He told me how she came on to him. He wanted to see where it would go. It ended with an open invitation to go to lunch; if she was serious. What I found strange about the encounter, she was naked."

Together Agent Nikolov and the IG looked at Murry, and simultaneously said, "Naked."

"Yeah. Naked. No security detail."

"You're right. Sofiya didn't have her security detail with her that day," said Agent Nikolov.

"I agree with the IG. Mozes is straight. He's not involved with the Zlatkov crime family. No way." Murry said. "So, what do we do now?"

Agent Nikolov said, "The person who has the tattoos could help us get on the inside. Get us close to who's running the prostitution ring. They may have information about the murders. Information about the operation."

"Okay. I'll get back with Mozes." Murry said. "I'll update him with all this information and ask him about the origin of the photographs. I'll take care of it tomorrow."

"Murry, let me take care of it," said the IG. I'll talk to him. I'm his boss. The three of us will speak to him tomorrow. We'll meet tomorrow morning at my office. Nine o'clock. We'll go to Mozes' residence to talk with him."

"Good," replied Murry.

"Very well," replied Agent Nikolov.

Murry slid out of the Suburban and walked up the driveway as the black Suburban moved off.

41 Visit with Mozes

Mozes looked at his Rolex. It was ten o'clock in the morning. He thought, "I know my past. Chilling as it is. I know all there is to my past except the whereabouts of my mother's and father's remains. I wonder if Tommy could help me with that. Maybe he knows someone in Windber who could help."

There was a knock on Mozes' door. He set his coffee cup on the saucer on the coffee table. He slowly rose out of the armchair and moved to answer the door. He looked through the one-way peephole. He immediately unlocked the door and opened it.

"Good morning sir. Murry. Madam. What's going on?"

The IG said, "Good morning Mozes. May we come in?"

"Sure."

Mozes moved out of the doorway and back into the apartment. The IG stepped aside and motioned for Agent Nikolov to go first. Then motioned to Murry to enter. The IG followed. The threesome entered as Mozes held the door open.

Mozes closed the door and locked it. He followed the threesome.

"Would you like to sit in the living room or at the table?"

"The table please," said the IG.

"Would anyone like some coffee?"

Murry replied, "Yes. Please."

"Anyone else?"

At the same time, the IG and Agent Nikolov replied, "No thank you."

The IG and Agent Nikolov sat on one side of the table. Murry sat opposite them. It was a large dining table with seating for eight. The satin stained, oak top was adorned with a single, large, twelve candle, crystal, candelabra. The chairs were oversized. Beautiful linen covered the extra thick memory foam cushions. The threesome gaped at the lavishly decorated and furnished apartment.

Mozes returned from the kitchen and handed Murry his coffee. He sat at the end of the table.

"What's up?"

The IG said, "Mozes this is Agent Anna Nikolov. Agent Nikolov is with the Government of Bulgaria. National Police Service. National Organized Crime Service. Agent Nikolov this is Mozes."

They talked over each other as they exchanged greetings and shook hands.

"You know Murry."

"Yes."

The IG continued.

"Mozes, I'm just going to get to it. You know me and my directness."

"Yes. Sure."

The pictures you gave Murry, you came by them how?"

There was an awkward silence. Then Mozes spoke.

"Sir I had a hunch. Apparently, it materialized into something. Perhaps something out of Bulgaria. Agent Nikolov. Bulgaria National Police Service."

Agent Nikolov remained silent and continued to look at Mozes. It appeared she was sizing him up. She maintained a stoic law enforcement pose.

To stall for time to compose an answer to the IG's question, Mozes continued.

"Nice. I'll take that as a yes. Agent Nikolov, why does the Bulgaria government need to know?"

Still nothing. Agent Nikolov continued her silence and just looked at Mozes.

Murry made a nervous adjustment to his posture. The IG composed a smirk on his face as he watched two experienced investigators face-off.

The IG injected "Anna do you want me to explain this or would you like to?"

Agent Nikolov replied, "I don't like his attitude."

"You don't have to like my attitude," countered Mozes.

Murry again made a nervous adjustment to his posture.

Mozes broke his stare with Agent Nikolov and looked to the IG.

"I'm on administrative leave. Do you want me to get a doctor's note?"

"Come on Mozes. You and I both know you're still working the murder investigations. That's who you are. Just tell Agent Nikolov about the photographs. Come on, already."

"Sir. I'm indebted to you for the help you gave me with my career. Not to mention the help you gave to my mother. To my Aunt Llona. I learned all about that a few days ago, thank you."

The IG said nothing. He did not even present a noticeable nonverbal replied to Mozes comment. He knew to what Mozes referred; he remembered too.

Agent Nikolov jerked her head and glared at the IG. Her blatant nonverbal display was a puzzled look. She did not know to what Mozes referred.

Murry looked to the IG and then to Mozes. He too did not know the relevance of that verbal bandy.

"But. While on administrative leave, as I reflect on my life, on myself, over the last few days. Sir, you know my financial situation. So, you know work and the earnings aren't necessary for me."

The IG interrupted Mozes.

"Come on Mozes you don't want to go there. You enjoy the work. Perhaps it's your past that drives your present. Makes you do what you do. And you do it so well. You don't want to quit *Hotshot MO*."

"Sir, all due respect, I think I do. I think I do."

"Well you know there are three or four ways we can compel your cooperation."

"Sir."

The IG cut Mozes off.

"Stop it with the sir. Call me Roger."

The IG adjusted himself in the plush chair and continued.

"Please consider what you're doing. You're going to walk away and leave the murders unsolved. Are you able to forget they're victims? Victims of the same atrocity of which you are a victim. You can do that? I don't think so."

"What. What did you say? Victims like me?"

"You say you know all your past secrets. Then you know you are a victim."

"They are victims like me? Victims of the same atrocities?"

"Yes," replied Roger.

Murry made a nervous adjustment to his posture which caught the attention of Mozes.

"Murry, do you need my help?" asked Mozes.

"Yes, I do. But who needs your help more are the victims and potential victims. Mozes, the victims, need your help. You need to hear from Agent Nikolov. You need to listen to the results of her two-year investigation."

"You think so, Murry?"

"Yes, Mozes. I didn't eat last night after she told me. This was the first time my job troubled me to the point I didn't eat. I just sat around all night and pondered the sick, sexual, perversion."

Murry abruptly stopped talking. He stared past Mozes and shook his head from side to side.

"Murry's right, Mozes," said Roger. "The victims need your help. They too are young and they're victims of the same predator. The predator who steals innocence. They need the full weight of the investigative prowess of *Hotshot MO*."

"Roger, I'm indebted to you. I'm going to work off some of my debt. I'll stay on until the murder investigations are closed. And I will close them without the bodies."

Mozes looked to Agent Nikolov.

"Until we close your investigation if you can stand to work with my attitude?"

Mozes rose from his chair.

"Would anyone like a cup of coffee?"

"I'll have another, partner," replied Murry.

"Me too," replied Roger.

"Please. I better have a cup too, partner. We may be here awhile," replied Agent Nikolov.

Mozes walked to the kitchen to get the coffees. He served Roger last and asked, "How do we work the administrative leave? The doctor is not ready to sign the Fit for Duty Certification."

Roger sipped his coffee then lowered his cup.

"Yeah, I know. I'll take care of it."

"And my weapon?"

Roger set his cup down on the saucer.

I'll get it to you."

"And my raise?"

Roger jerked his head to look at Mozes. Everyone laughed.

Composed from the laughter, Mozes looked to Agent Nikolov.

"Will you brief me on your investigation, please?"

Murry shifted in his chair to prepare himself to hear the details of the sick, sexual, perversion again.

For Mozes' in brief, Agent Nikolov repeated what she told Murry last night.

When she finished, Murry asked, "How do you know this. These facts. How do you know some of the details of the criminal operation?"

"I had an informant."

"Had!" Murry and Mozes exclaimed at the same time.

"Yes. She just disappeared. She stopped her contact with me. I even risked going to her place of employment on the *Strip*, Gheorghi's Joe. No one said anything there."

"Was your informant a female?" asked Murry.

"Yes."

"Was her name Rhonda Popa?"

"Yes. Do you know her?"

Murry replied, "She was murdered. She was Vic 12. The only one we had a name for. I recognized her from going into Gheorghi's Joe."

"How many murder victims do you have?" Agent Nikolov inquired.

"Twelve. Eight adults and four children."

"All white, Caucasian?" asked Agent Nikolov.

"Yes," replied Murry. "Would you like me to in brief you?"

"No. Roger has kept me up to date with the murder investigations."

"Okay, Mozes. You had enough time to decide to give us your source for the photographs," said Roger.

"It's complicated Roger. I need time to work this out. I can't give up my source just yet. If ever."

"No," Agent Nikolov replied. "We already lost one informant, a potential witness. If there's someone out there, we need to protect her. She should be in protective custody."

"I need more time with this. I may not give the name up. And Roger you can do what you want to me. I won't risk what I have."

"Are you in a relationship with this person?" asked Agent Nikolov. "You are. Holy shit, you're in a relationship with one of Zlatkov's people."

Mozes went stoic; he did not say anything.

Murry adjusted himself in his chair. He was becoming overwhelmed by the intricacies of the investigation. He investigated many cases over his years with PBP, none as dimensional as this one.

Mozes broke his silence and said, "I'm finished here for today. I have work to do. And just so there are no secrets, I have an informant working on getting information about the Zlatkovs. When I have something to report from the informant I will."

Mozes rose to his feet, stepped behind his chair, and slid it under the table. This was his sign to the threesome the meeting was over. They slowly rose from their seats and pushed their chairs back under the table. Murry started to clear the table.

"I'll get that Murry. Just leave it," said Mozes.

"Okay. Thanks for the coffee."

"You're welcome."

Mozes walked to the door, unlocked it, opened it, and held the door as the threesome walked out of his apartment. He shook each of their hands as they passed him. He closed and locked the door after their exit.

He walked to the living room and sat in the armchair. He stared at the painting across the room as he thought how he was going to talk with Viktorija. Now there were four things to discuss with her. His past. Their relationship. Her tattoos. And her past.

His investigative mind wondered thoughts.

"Was it possible Viktorija worked for the Zlatkov crime family? Nefariously involved in the conspiracy. At the *La Belle Vue*, she said she worked for Sofiya Zlatkov. Just when I started to understand myself and I thought I had a serious relationship. She seemed to care for me. The dreams and the visions subsided a lot since we spent time with each other. Was I now faced with the possibility I fell for someone entwined with the criminal class?"

Mozes rubbed and massaged the nape of his neck in an attempt to ease the tension brought on by the sharp pain that moved through his head.

He continued to wonder thoughts within.

"This is it. I'm done after this investigation. But could this investigation provide the ultimate healing I need? Is this my exorcism from the dreams? The visions? The images? The pain? Am I under the control of a higher power?"

He continued to stare at the painting across the room.

42   Yet another dream

There was a knock at the door, and Mozes rose from the armchair to answer it. He looked out the one-way peephole and nearly fainted. He took his eye away from the peephole and thought it was a dream. He quickly looked back. The older lady stood there and adjusted her clothing. The facial features were the same. An older person now, but the distinct cheek bone. The nose. Those blue eyes. The thick hair that was once a dark reddish-brown, now gray. Void of makeup.

Nervous, Mozes fidgeted with the door lock and finally got it unlocked. He took a deep breath as he reached for the door knob. He turned it and pulled the door open. When he looked, no one was there. He walked into the hallway and quickly looked left, then right. No one was there.

The elevator arrival bell sounded. Mozes ran to the elevator alcove and saw the doors close tight. The bell sounded to signal the elevator's descent.

Mozes rushed back down the hallway to the stairwell door. He pushed through it and kept running down the flights of stairs. He pushed through the stairwell door on the first floor and frantically looked around the lobby. No one was there. Out of the corner of his eye, he saw a yellow cab pull away from the front door, crescent, driveway.

He leaned against the wall and slid down to the cold marble floor. He drew his legs into his chest and held them with his arms. He sat and rocked back and forth.

Mozes thought, "My mother. Was that my mother? Why did she leave me again?"

As he continued to rock back and forth, he slowly opened his eyes. Seated in front of him, with their legs crossed, were the three, faceless, hallowed, figures. They mimicked Mozes as they too rocked back and forth. When they started to laugh at him, he closed his eyes tight. So tight, his teeth made a grinding sound.

After some time, a faint voice called out.

"Mozes. Mozes."

Mozes heard his name and listened to a soft, soothing, coddling voice, the same voice that woke him for school. There was no mistaking, it was his mother's voice. He cocked his head up but feared to open his eyes only to be disappointed again.

The voice persisted.

"Mozes. Mozes."

Mozes coiled back when a soft, gentle, hand touched him. He began to shake and mumble meaningless words. He breathed in deeply to calm himself. He breathed in again, and there was a scent he recognized. He breathed in a third time to use the sweet scent as smelling salts to pull himself conscious. He slowly opened his eyes and saw a figure in front of him. With his eyes opened wide, he saw it was Viktorija. Embarrassed, he turned away.

Viktorija did not know what to do. She had knelt before Mozes and stayed in front of him, leaned back on her calves. She said softly but direct, "Mozes, let me take you upstairs. Let me take you to your apartment."

Viktorija sensed something when Mozes looked at her. She saw a look she only saw one other time in her life. She started to back away to get up. Mozes reached out and forced her to him. He kissed her hard. His hands forcefully explored every inch of her body.

Viktorija cried, "No. Not here. Not like this, Mozes."

Viktorija pushed Mozes away with force. His head whiplashed into the hard, white, plaster wall, and the impact created a small blood splatter. His head involuntarily sprung forward and then hung lifeless.

Viktorija sprang back with shock. She composed herself with speed gained only by tortured, life experiences. She cautiously moved back toward Mozes. She knelt in front of him and softly cried out, "No. No. Mozes."

She shook him. His head bobbed freely, and there was no response from him.

"What have I done? No. Not my Mozes," cried Viktorija.

43   A few days later

Mozes stood by his dining room windows with a cup of coffee in his right hand and the saucer in his left. He stared out to the streets of the old city and sipped his coffee. He was deep in thought. Thoughts that were interrupted by a sound that announced a text message from his cellphone. Mozes' natural reaction caused his head to jerk in the direction of the phone.

He thought, "What if it's Viktorija? I don't know if I can ever face her again."

He turned back to the window and the city. The phone announced another text and then started to ring. He walked to the dining table, set the cup and saucer down, and picked up the phone as it continued to ring. The screen displayed Viktorija as the caller.

Mozes swiped the screen to answer the call. In a sheepish tone, he said, "Hello."

"Hello, Mozes. How are you?"

"I'm fine. Thank you," replied Mozes still with a sheepish tone.

"What are you doing?"

"Nothing."

"Would you like to have lunch today?"

"I don't know."

"Well, you can't just stay in your apartment forever."

"Maybe."

"Come on, let's have lunch."

"I don't know."

"You know I'm not going to beg you. You need to get out."

"Okay."

In a spirited tone, Viktorija said, "Great. Would you like to meet me at the sandwich shop on the *Strip*?"

"Okay."

Viktorija cut Mozes off, "I know you need thirty minutes to get dressed."

"To get presentable to the public," Mozes emphasized.

"There you go. Now you sound better," Viktorija encouraged.

"It's you Viktorija. You're like my guardian angel. You're always here for me. Thank you."

"If you let me I'll be here for you Mozes. I'll see you for lunch. Don't keep a lady waiting. Okay, *Hot Mozes*."

His spirit uplifted, Mozes replied, "No, I won't. I'll see you there."

44   Session Four – A call to duty interrupts

Aunt Llona and Mozes entered the room and took their seats on the couch.

Dr. Polanski was seated in his large, leather, chair. He raised his head from his notepad.

"Good morning. How are we all doing today?"

When he saw Mozes, he continued.

"Oh, my. Mozes, what happened to you? Did it hurt?"

"What this little cut?"

"A little cut, but a big bandage."

"I'm okay. It just looks worse than it is."

"Tell Joe how it happened," said Aunt Llona.

"Aunt Llona, that's not necessary," replied Mozes.

"I think it is. It's a result of one of your dreams?"

"Is that correct Mozes?" said Dr. Polanski.

"Yes. It's a result of a dream."

"What happened? Please explain what happened."

Mozes felt his left side.

"Please excuse me."

He released his cellphone from its cradle and looked at the screen. It displayed Mr. C. This was Mozes' code for his informant, Cipő.

"Please excuse me. I have to take this call."

Mozes stepped outside the room.

"Hello. How are you?"

"Fine Mozes. We must meet. We have to meet today." There was anxiety in the voice.

"Okay. Where?"

"Same place as last time."

"Okay. What time?"

"As soon as you can get here. I'll be waiting for you."

"I'm on my way. It'll be about thirty minutes."

"See you when you get here. Hurry."

Mozes hung up from the call, placed his telephone back into the cradle, and went back into the room.

"I'm sorry. I must go. I have an urgent matter to handle."

"Mozes are you working?" inquired Dr. Polanski.

"Let's just say I have an urgent matter to handle."

"*Hotshot MO*. Come on. You're not cleared for duty."

"Did the IG talk to you?" asked Mozes.

"No," replied Dr. Polanski.

"You need to call him."

Mozes waited for Aunt Llona to gather her things. He held the door open for her and they walked through an alternate door to leave.

As they left, Dr. Polanski said, "I'll send you an email with your next appointment."

At their cars, Mozes opened the driver door for Aunt Llona to get into her car. Mozes moved to Aunt Llona and gave her a hug and a kiss on her cheek.

"Sorry, Aunt Llona. I need to go."

"Okay Mozes. We'll talk later. Love you, honey."

"Love you, Aunt Llona."

Mozes closed her door and rushed off to his car.

45 Informant debrief

It was slow going through the *'Burgh* traffic. It seemed midday had all the crazies out. The business sales people moved about for lunch and to their next prospect. The office workers moved from building to building in search of their favorite luncheonette. The crowded streets also contained suburbanites in the *'Burgh* to enjoy the amenities. Vehicular traffic was slow and inattentive. The pedestrian traffic crossed the streets everywhere but at the cross walks.

Mozes was stopped for a red light at Stanwix Street and Boulevard of the Allies, and a drove of pedestrians crossed in front of his car. An older lady vigorously waved as Mozes gazed at the crowd. The lady looked familiar to Mozes. He cautiously waved back and looked harder.

Mozes mumbled to himself, "It can't be. Is that? No way."

The older lady kept waving as she left the drove of pedestrians and walked in the direction of Mozes. As she came closer, Mozes exclaimed out loud, "Oh my God! Is it!"

At that moment, the three, faceless, hallowed, figures appeared by the older lady. The older lady made no sign she knew they were there.

Mozes rubbed and massaged the nape of his neck in an attempt to ease the tension brought on by the sharp pain that moved through his head.

Mozes refocused his eyes on the older lady. When he did, the hallowed figures began to levitate. They rose off the black asphalt roadway, and the older lady rose with them. Mozes watched the four as they all rose into the sky and disappeared.

Mozes rubbed and massaged the nape of his neck again. He sat and thought to himself, "Was that mother? She looked so much like mother."

The blare of the car horns from behind brought Mozes back. The traffic light was red when he looked up. He knew he held traffic up by sitting through a cycle of the traffic light.

When the light changed from red to green, Mozes accelerated through the intersection onto the Boulevard of the Allies. He continued his way to and through the Liberty Tunnels, and onto Dormont to meet Cipő.

Mozes entered the Potomac Avenue Grill and surveyed the area for Cipő. Cipő raised his hand and signaled to Mozes from a rear corner booth as Mozes made his way through the restaurant. When he reached the table, Cipő rose. They both extended hands and greeted each other, then sat.

Cipő said, "Oh, my. Mozes, what happened to you? Did it hurt?"

Mozes replied, "What this little cut? Why does everyone ask me about this?"

"That's a big bandage for a little cut."

"I'm okay. It just looks worse than it is."

"Your friend is here today. Wait until she sees this."

"Hm."

"She asked about you."

"What did you say?"

"I told her she needed to try harder. That you play hard to get."

"Come on Cipő. You didn't."

Cipő looked at Mozes and smiled.

"Here she comes."

"Hello stranger," announced the bullish waitress. "What the hell happen to you?"

"Hello," replied Mozes in a bashful tone. "Nothing. I'm okay."

Cipő said to the waitress, "See. What did I tell you? He's shy."

"I see," said the waitress. "I can help him with that. I'm not changing the bandage, though."

Mozes blushed.

The waitress said, "You blushed. How sweet. You're cute. A real looker. And a fancy dresser too. What will you have?"

"Just coffee please."

"Okay."

The waitress scurried off.

Mozes looked to Cipő.

"What have you found? You sounded anxious on the phone."

"First thing. Are you sure you want to go after these people?"

"Yes, I am. I'm sure. It's part of my self-prescription to heal. And before you ask, I don't want to talk about it. What do you have for me?"

"These are some very, very, very bad people. You must understand."

"Okay. Got it. That's why I must go after them. I must get them. They have to be brought to justice."

"Yeah. Yeah. Save it for the press release. Don't say I didn't warn you."

"Okay. Just tell me what you know? Please."

The waitress appeared at the table. She placed a cup of coffee atop a saucer on the table in front of Mozes.

"There you are Mozes."

She also placed a napkin on the table next to Mozes. She reached her hand to Mozes' shoulder and lightly massaged it. She said with glee, "Just in case."

Mozes looked up to the waitress and said, "Thank you."

The waitress dramatically turned and in a deliberate, slow, gait walked off.

Mozes' eyes glanced at the napkin. There was a heart drawing on it. The name Suzie was written in the middle of the heart. Below the heart was a seven-digit telephone number. At the end of the phone number, a smiley face was drawn. Mozes eased his hand to the napkin to cover the drawings and writings.

"Are you trying to cover it up?" said Cipő "I see the writing and drawings. Suzie wants you."

Cipő sat there with a big smile on his face. He held back laughter but kept the smile on his face. Mozes blushed.

"Okay. Tell me what you found out," said Mozes.

"So, your hunch that the political machine is covering up murders in the *'Burgh*. You're right. I don't know how you do it, Mozes. It's like you have some supernatural power to fight crime. A supernatural crimefighter."

Cipő paused, looked past Mozes, then continued.

"Yeah. There's something big going on in the city. A lot of politicians and influential people are involved. What's disgusting to me, the local diocese is involved."

"It is."

"What I know so far, there's a club they call *In the Nave*. You become a member. You buy into the club with an initial membership fee. Then there's a monthly fee. Both the original membership and monthly fees the members pay by placing the money into a plain white envelope and marking it 'For the Charitable Appeal Fund.' They put the plain white envelopes into the offering collections during mass. Since it's in a plain white envelope with the markings, the church, without opening the envelopes, sends them to the diocese office. From there I don't know what happens with the envelopes, the payments.

Apparently, once you are in you are never out. If a member tries to get out, tries to stop paying, the member is reminded their encounters with the sex slaves are recorded, both video and audio. All their encounters, starting with the first one. The club membership is an extortion scheme."

"Interesting," Mozes injected.

"And of course, the Zlatkovs operate the extortion scheme. The club. Not a surprise to me."

"How do the members get in touch with the sex slaves?" asked Mozes.

"Everything is done on a schedule. The members go to the church and whoever is there is who they get. There's no picking or choosing. They do it that way to eliminate or to minimize the contact. The diocese distributes the schedule by mail to the members. The schedule is the dates and time the sex slaves will be at the church. Some sort of code or something. They do the mailings under the guise of the Charitable Appeal Fund."

"What assures them law enforcement will not infiltrate the club?" Mozes asked. "Can I join?"

"They record all the encounters beginning with the first one. Do you want to go undercover, so they record your sexual acts with a child? Is the IG going to sanction that? As sick as it is, it's a brilliant plan. A brilliant scheme."

"So how is law enforcement going to break this up?"

"I'm sure *Hotshot MO* will figure it out."

"What else?"

"Isn't that enough?"

"Well is that all you got. You probably have more."

"I do. The sex slaves, they are a mother and her child. The child is a male or female. They kidnap them from Bulgaria and bring them into the country through the Zlatkov Global Opportunity Foundation in collaboration with a prominent charitable foundation out of Little Rock, Arkansas or New York City. I was not able to get the name of that organization yet or exact location. Then they place the sex slaves with families here in Pittsburgh.

The murders. The Mayor is covering up crimes. The victims are sex slaves who try to escape, both adults and children. Pieces of the flesh are missing from the bodies, whether adult or child. Tattoos are removed from the upper left shoulder and lower middle back. The significance of the tattoos, I do not know. There's a little work for you."

"A little work for me? Cipő, I must work to find the evidence to prove what you say. A little work."

Cipő continued.

"Here's more sickening information. The members commit sick, sexual, perverse acts against children. Statutory rape at least. Against the mothers too, the unwilling, nonconsenting adults. Rape. Sometimes with both the mother and her child or in the presence of one or the other, they force them to watch each other. Corruption of a minor. And these acts, these sick, sexual, perverse acts, some are committed at the center of the churches. Right in the nave of the church."

Mozes remained silent.

332

Cipő looked hard at Mozes. He raised his right hand, extended his index finger, and shook it at Mozes.

"You better be careful. You better be careful here Mozes. These are very, very, very bad people. They're killers. I know the Zlatkov family will kill anyone who is in their way. Anyone. It doesn't matter if they're a law enforcement officer. Their killers. The people out of Little Rock or New York City, they too are quick to eliminate their threats with death. I like you, Mozes. I want you to stay safe."

"Thanks, Cipő. Who is your source? I need to talk to that person. I need to make them a confidential informant."

"Mozes. Mozes. What a pathetic attempt to get her name. I can't tell you her name. If she shows up today, you'll know who she is. If she doesn't show up, you won't know her name. You know that's the way I work."

"I had to try."

"I guess. I gave you useful information, work with the information *Hotshot MO*."

"Yes, you did, as always. Thank you, Cipő."

"This is big Mozes. Bigger than the priest pedophilia, the priest child molesters that the Pennsylvania Attorney General in looking into with an Investigative Grand Jury. This might be too big to take down," said Cipő. "I mean with the involvement of the Roman Catholic Cloth. Are you going to place handcuffs on the Bishop? Are you going to do a perp walk with the Bishop in his cassock? Would you arrest all the priests? Who would give mass? Arrest the Mayor too? The Zlatkovs?"

"Yes, to all of it. I would personally handcuff and walk the Bishop out of the diocese. I would go into the nave and walk the priests out. Oh, yes, I would perp walk them. Cipő, no one is above the law. If what you say is true. If I can prove it, they all should be prosecuted to the fullest extent the laws provide. I need to protect the victims. How well I know how the victims suffer from the sick, sexual, perverse acts. How they suffer for years. How well I know."

"What does that mean Mozes?" asked Cipő.

There was a long pause then Mozes broke the silence.

"Nothing, I don't want to talk about it."

With his left hand, Mozes reached into his right, inside, suit jacket, pocket. He retrieved a primly folded, ironed, white handkerchief monogrammed **MO**. He dabbed his eyes. The information he gathered pushed on his emotions. He found himself in need of emotional support. He wanted Viktorija.

Cipő said, "Mozes there's one other thing. Someone I want to introduce to you. Apparently, my source wants you to know who she is."

A sweet scent moved into the area of Mozes and Cipő. Mozes recognized it. Before he turned around to investigate the origin, a gentle touch was laid on his shoulder, and a sexy, Bulgarian voice sounded.

"Hello, Mozes."

Mozes recognized the voice. He was startled by it and turned to look.

"Viktorija. Hello. What are you doing here?"

He immediately rose from his chair in a show of respect for a lady in his presence.

Cipő rose too. He said, "Mozes this is my source for the information. I understand you know each other."

Mozes turned to Cipő.

"Yes, we do."

Cipő turned to Viktorija and said, "I see you decided to come."

"Yes. I must help. Mozes must also know everything there is to know about me."

"Then I shall go. You two have a lot to talk about." Cipő looked to Mozes. "And again, I helped you, Mozes. You owe me."

"Yes. Thank you Cipő. I'll be in touch."

"Don't let her get away Mozes. She's an angel. She's a sweet lady. They don't come any better."

Cipő stepped to Viktorija, and they cheek kissed.

"You'll do fine. Everything will be okay. If you need me, call me."

Viktorija's voice cracked as she replied, "I hope, Cipő. Thank you, for everything."

Cipő, in a distinct Pittsburgh gait, walked to the entrance door and left the Potomac Avenue Grill. He did not look back.

Viktorija took his seat at the table.

Mozes said, "Hello, Viktorija. Thank you for coming."

Mozes reached his hand out, held Viktorija's hand, and cast his blue eyes on hers.

"I hope you still want me after what I tell you," replied Viktorija. "After I tell you about me."

She lost her emotional restraint and softly cried.

Mozes reached his left hand into his right, inside, suit jacket, pocket. Again, he retrieved the handkerchief monogrammed **MO**. He offered it to Viktorija. She took it and dabbed her eyes. Today, he found himself in the company of a fair Pittsburgh lady in need of his emotional support. His desire was no longer awkward.

They sat in the busy restaurant and Viktorija willingly shared her personal experiences of horrid, criminal acts of which she was a victim. She risked embarrassment as she disclosed facts to put the atrocity into perspective. Viktorija willingly wanted to help Mozes.

46   Ten months later

"Good morning. Thank you all for coming today," said Roger V. Deri. "I am the Inspector General for the City of Pittsburgh. I want to report the culmination of a three-year long joint investigation into an international human trafficking and smuggling conspiracy, the cover up of a murder spree in the City of Pittsburgh, and a global child and adult sex slavery conspiracy.

These criminal activities were organized and carried out by the Zlatkov crime family which operated their global criminal enterprise from the Strip District. For years, their criminal enterprise was aided and abetted by the corrupt officials and employees of the City of Pittsburgh, the Roman Catholic Cloth, and an international charitable foundation.

I want to caution you all before I state the details. I must report some very appalling facts to have transparency. Those weak of mind or stomach may have trouble with these facts. If you need to leave, at any time, please do so.

I want to begin by recognizing the law enforcement officers and law enforcement organizations. All were instrumental and indispensable to the pursuit of hideous criminals, for the past three years.

The Interpol Washington National Central Bureau as well as the vast network of National Central Bureaus worldwide. The extensive network of law enforcement brothers and sisters from around the world. A lengthy roll call. Thank you all."

Behind me and to my right, Agent Anna Nikolov. She is an Agent of the Government of Bulgaria. National Police Service. National Organized Crime Service.

Behind me and to my left, Detective Murry Stewart of the Homicide Squad, Pittsburgh Bureau of Police.

The vast network of state, county, city, and borough law enforcement organizations throughout Pennsylvania and the country. A lengthy roll call. Thank you all.

Roger reached for a bottle of water. He unscrewed the lid and sipped the water in his no-nonsense Brooklyn character. He paused in what appeared to be deep thought. He sipped the water again. He replaced the cap and returned the bottle to a shelf in the podium.

"I also want to recognize two other individuals. They are unable to be with us today."

Anna and Murry, from behind Roger, looked at each other and smiled.

"Mozes Olah, Criminal Investigator II, Office of Inspector General, the City of Pittsburgh, Retired and a Confidential Informant for the Bulgaria National Police Service. National Organized Crime Service. They willingly shared their personal experiences of horrid criminal acts of which they were victims. They risked embarrassment and disclosed facts to put this atrocity into perspective. The sheer investigative prowess of Mozes Olah, *Hotshot MO* as he was known on the streets of Pittsburgh, was indispensable to ferret out the vast number of wretched humans, disgusting criminals, to arrest. Indeed, their assistance, their willingness to share lifted Operation Atrocity in the Nave to success. Victims themselves, they helped the many, many other victims."

338

Rodger became emotional. He reached his left hand into his right, inside, suit jacket, pocket. He retrieved a primly folded, ironed, white, handkerchief monogrammed **MO**.

Simultaneously Anna and Murry mimicked Rodger. They too retrieved a primly folded, ironed, white, handkerchief monogrammed the same. Together, Anna and Murry shook their handkerchiefs and fashioned it in the outer breast pocket of their suit jackets. **MO** was prominently displayed.

This unheralded to Rodger placed a puzzled look on his face when the press corps blinded him with their multiple camera flashes. The press corps started to chant *MO. MO. Hotshot MO* and the spectators joined.

Rodger looked around the stage and realized what was going on. He too fashioned his white monogrammed handkerchief into the outer breast pocket of his suit jacket to prominently displayed **MO**.

After the crowd had settled back, Rodger continued.

"Today, we on this stage announce the arrest of four hundred and sixty-six individuals for a host of crimes. Those crimes include murder, conspiracy to commit murder, bribery, malfeasance in office, extortion, kidnapping, rape, sex with a minor child, child exploitation, child pornography, human trafficking, prostitution of minors, and conspiracy. On open warrants are another two hundred and fifty fugitives from justice on the same or similar charges.

Operation Atrocity in the Nave is what we dubbed this law enforcement operation.

For me personally, this horror story began when I was a young private lawyer here in Pittsburgh. I represented a client from a small western Pennsylvania coal mining town. The client was a victim of sexual abuse by a Roman Catholic priest who committed sexual acts on a child in the nave of the child's, the victim's, church. Back then I thought it was an isolated incident, as all professions have their bad ones. Over the years, I continued to hear stories. About two years ago, Agent Nikolov presented cold hard facts that disclosed information alleging these horrid, criminal acts continued. Continued through a global web of conspiracy and organized crime. Facts alleged the hideous sexual acts were carried out in modern day Pittsburgh and throughout the world. Allegedly, the horrid acts never stopped. Forty years later the heinous crimes are alleged to continue locally and around the world."

Roger paused. His emotions stirred again. Once under control, he continued.

"Agent Nikolov's case started with missing people. Her investigation quickly disclosed over two thousand six hundred citizens of Bulgaria disappeared. All of them were women and their children. There was no trace of them nor was there an explanation for their disappearance. Two years ago, her investigation tracked down one of the missing persons here in Pittsburgh. Agent Nikolov was assigned to Pittsburgh to pursue the lead. That victim turned informant, revealed the horror of marked humans. Humans marked by tattoos. One on their left shoulder and another on the middle of their lower back. Elaborately designed tattoos that included a numbering system. Yes, reminiscent of the marked Jewish during World War II.

The victim turned informant, disclosed mothers and their children were marked with tattoos to facilitate the perverted, lustful, desires of the sexually perverted subculture around the world. Subscribers to the organized sex slavery included the corrupt clergy of the Roman Catholic Cloth and prominent and influential people in our midst."

340

Rodger's eyes filled with tears. He retrieved the white monogrammed handkerchief to comfort his emotions. When he returned it to his breast pocket, he was ever so careful to ensure **MO** was prominently displayed.

"That informant was murdered and her bodied carved of tangible evidence. Her lifeless body still marked. She was the only one of the twelve murder victims we identified. She was cremated like the other eleven. Among many, Shepherds conspired to kill her, to stop her from helping law enforcement.

Make no mistake, Operation Atrocity in the Nave brought down the institution of the Roman Catholic Cloth in the two dioceses mentioned. Facts alleged the conspirators, of the atrocity I'm about to describe to you, reached to the Holy Sea. There was an elaborate conspiracy to cover up this crime..."

Rodger slammed his fist on the podium.

"... and Popes knew of the cover-up and conspired to perpetuate the cover-up of criminal activity. This included the current Pope and his predecessors back to the mid-1940s.

The two dioceses I mentioned are being dismantled as I speak. Their physical assets are being padlocked, and their monetary funds and accounts are frozen.

Shortly, we will work with prosecutors to gather the money and turn tangible assets into money. A fund will be established to disperse the money to the victims, for them to use to recover their stolen innocence. If that is even possible.

These law enforcement actions stripped the assets from the dioceses and precluded the dioceses from taking in money. We coordinated with the proper state and Federal government agencies. They reviewed the evidence we provided and concluded the alleged criminal activity warranted the tax-exempt status of the two dioceses be stripped until the allegations were proved or disproved. The institution of the Roman Catholic Cloth ceased to exist in the eyes of Government at these two dioceses.

The law enforcement and administrative actions are the results of criminal investigations that disclosed sick, sexual, perverse acts committed against children. Against unwilling, nonconsenting adults, the children's mothers. Sometimes with both the mother and her child or in the presence of one or the other. Forced to watch. And these acts, these sick, sexual, perverse acts, some were committed in the center of the churches – atrocity in the nave. The service of search warrants, at various locations, discovered digital recordings of the sex acts. Further, the criminal investigation disclosed information that alleged a worldwide conspiracy by the clergy of the Roman Catholic Cloth to cover up the sex crimes."

Rodger slammed his fist on the podium again.

"People, that precipitated the seizure of the property from the two dioceses. The property was used to facilitate the crime. Just like an automobile used in drug trafficking."

He raised his right hand and shook his right index finger and exclaimed, "No difference!"

"This brought the operation to the murder spree in the City of Pittsburgh. Victims surfaced in the three rivers, for a year. The murder victims were adults and children. All the victims had flesh removed. Their tattoos were crudely removed from their left shoulder and the middle of their lower back. Their naked bodies, with their folded hands in front, left over right, were placed in the rivers.

The investigation disclosed people were murdered to stop them from coming forward, potential victims and/or witnesses. Others died at the hands of their predators, from the predator's aggressive sexual acts they committed against the victims.

The operation moved to investigate political corruption by Pittsburgh city officials. Corruption which started at the top. The Mayor was the ringleader in the conspiracy to cover up the murders. The investigation disclosed the Mayor was intimidated to give orders to cover up the killings. That was extortion. The extortion was not reported to the Office of Inspector General per the Mayor's signed policy. My office was not solicited for counsel or requested to investigate the extortion. Again, both required by the Mayor's approved policy. The Mayor did neither. Instead, he capitulated to the extortionists through his political position. He used his official capacity to order his high-level subordinates to carry out his order to close the Medical Examiners Cases on the murder victims. The Mayor ordered, and the Medical Examiner carried out the illegal order to cremate the bodies. This criminal act voided any possible prosecution of alleged perpetrators of the murders, the victim's killer. It destroyed evidence. This was obstruction of justice and conspiracy to obstruct justice. Government employees, who we trusted, committed malfeasance."

Roger paused. He took the white monogrammed handkerchief and dabbed his eyes. Then adjusted it back to continue to prominently display **MO**.

"They also denied the loved ones and the family of the victims to properly bury the victims. Perhaps for some, a proper Roman Catholic burial. Because of the cremations, the identity of eleven of the twelve victims was not ascertained. An atrocity."

The IG briefly paused, then continued.

"The operation moved in pursuit of the Zlatkov Crime Family. Many of you in the press corps have covered them during their philanthropy events. You called them Philanthropists. The investigation disclosed the family members, the ring leader Boris Zlatkov and his oldest daughter Sofiya Zlatkov, ran their criminal enterprise from the hills of western Pennsylvania and in Bulgaria.

The investigation disclosed they were corrupt and conspired to control an organized, international, human trafficking and smuggling ring to supply children and adults for their sex slavery business.

The investigation disclosed the Zlatkov crime family provided kidnapped women and children for the corrupt cloth. Their actions coerced mothers and their children into sexual servitude. They coerced them with the constant threat of murdering their family members, most often their mothers and fathers. Many times, underlings carried out the murders simply as a show of force. Sometimes it was for noncompliance of the women and children forced into sexual slavery.

Law enforcement continued their investigative efforts to determine how widespread was the Zlatkov sexual slavery business. Operation Atrocity in the Nave disclosed the Zlatkov criminal enterprise was national and international in scope. It worked in collusion and was aided by a prominent charitable foundation located in Little Rock, Arkansas and New York City. The name of that charity will not be disclosed today because of ongoing investigations.

I will not take questions today. Please take an information packet with you when you leave. They are with the people at the doors. I invite you back tomorrow with your questions.

One last point. There were times I had a heavy heart when I directed and participated in this massive investigation. Yes, the investigative results saddened me. I am Catholic, and I too find myself in a quandary. What will I do for a place to worship?

Committed to fighting crime, like Lady Justice, I kept the blindfold in place. When I used the scales of justice, no one was above or below the law. I didn't see an institution too big to fail. I saw a criminal enterprise. I saw the predators and the prey. I saw victims. I saw innocence stolen.

From my years of experience with our criminal justice system, I know there are victims. Sadly, the victims are punished too. The faithful are the victims today. They are punished with the loss of their religious institution.

From my years with the faith and the faithful, I know those whose faith is not shaken will rebuild those whose faith is shattered. They will restore the monetary assets. They will reconstruct the brick and mortar houses of worship. The faithful, proud people comprised of generations of European descendants with strong minds and stronger backs.

God's will be done, there will be peace in the nave."

47   Somerset County records disclosed

Tommy rose from his chair and extended his hand as did
Mozes as they approached each other and greeted. Tommy
turned to Viktorija, and they greeted with a cheek kiss.

Tommy turned to the table and said, "Mozes. Viktorija. This is
Gino."

Standing, Gino extended his hand and greeted Mozes and
Viktorija.

This evening, Gino did not display his broad smile he inherited
from his father. Wisdom guided Gino tonight. He sensed a
feeling of melancholic apprehension about the group of five
gathered for dinner and more.

Gino turned to the table and said, "Mozes. Viktorija. This is
Joe. Joe. Mozes and Viktorija.

Standing, Joe extended his hand and greeted Mozes and
Viktorija.

"Welcome. It's a pleasure to meet you both."

"Please sit and enjoy the delicious pizza," said Tommy.

The waitress came to the table and looked to Viktorija.

"May I get you something to drink?"

"Water please."

"And you sir?" The waitress looked to Mozes.

"The darkest beer you have on tap. Please."

"Yes, sir."

The waitress moved on to retrieve the beverages.

"How was your trip in Mozes?" asked Tommy.

"Good. A little foggy coming up the mountain on the turnpike."

"Mozes, after we are done eating, we are going to the *40 Hotel*. Gino will introduce you to Estella. If anyone can help you with information about your mother, Estella can."

"I appreciate your help, Gino," said Mozes.

"Not a problem. Tommy told me you needed help; it was done."

"So, you have MJ's telephone number then?" Tommy asked Gino.

"Whose?"

"MJ's."

"Were you serious?"

"Did the fumes from your car go to your brain? Yes, I was serious."

"Well, I…"

Tommy cut Gino off.

"Think I'm too old? I should embarrass you right here. I should take you down to the floor. You're lucky I don't want to mess up my hair."

The five laughed.

Tommy abruptly stopped laughing.

"I'm serious. I don't want to mess up my hair. He fights like a girl. He'll pull my hair."

Everyone continued to laugh.

Tommy too sensed a feeling of melancholic apprehension about the group and tried to lighten the moment.

The waitress said, "Here you go. Water. A dark beer."

"Thank you," replied Viktorija and Mozes.

The waitress turned to Gino.

"Can you keep it down? The other customers are complaining about the noise from this table."

The waitress laughed as Gino started to compose himself.

"Yeah, Gino. Keep it down. Come on." Tommy injected. "You're the Vice President of the Borough Council. Show some leadership here."

The waitress said, "I'm just kidding."

Gino responded with his large, inherited smile as conditioned.

The waitress continued, "Is everything all right?"

"Yes. Excellent," replied everyone.

At an opportune time, Tommy looked to Joe and said, "Joe, please explain to Mozes what you found."

"Mozes, I was involved with Somerset County law enforcement for many years. Tommy asked Gino if he knew anyone who could assist to find your mother. Gino brought Tommy to me, and Tommy briefed me on the situation. I searched all the records I could find. Some of the files I knew about, others I discovered as I searched. All the documents disclosed your mother passed away while she was in the Somerset State Hospital."

There was silence at the table.

Tommy looked to Mozes. He reached his hand out and placed it on Mozes' shoulder.

"I'm sorry Mozes. My condolences."

Gino said, "Sorry Mozes. My condolences for your loss."

Under the table, Viktorija reached to Mozes and placed her hand on his thigh to comfort him. Her gentle touch told Mozes she was there for him.

Gino noticed the waitress coming toward them. He waved her off to give Mozes time to process the unequivocal news of his mother's demise.

After a few minutes, Tommy said, "Joe, tell Mozes the rest. Tell him what your inquiry disclosed."

"Is there more?" asked Mozes. "What do you know? Please tell me."

"From my law enforcement experience, I believe there was foul play in the death of your mother," said Joe.

Joe retrieved a document from his briefcase. He slid it to Mozes and explained.

"This is the Death Certificate from the Somerset County Coroner's Office. The Coroner lists the cause of death as asphyxiation from hanging."

Joe retrieved a second document from his briefcase. He slid it to Mozes and explained.

"There was only a one-page Investigation Report (IR) from the Pennsylvania State Police (PSP) that reported the homicide investigation for your mother. Notice mid-way down, the box for notes. The Trooper wrote.

"SUSPICION SURROUNDED THE CAUSE OF DEATH OF KRISZTINA OLAH."

Joe pointed with his index finger.

"Right there."

"Yes," acknowledged Mozes.

"This is the only IR for your mother's death. I personally know the Trooper whose name is at the top of the IR. He's retired from the PSP. Has been for many years. In fact, he is up in the age, eighty-nine years old. He lives in Somerset."

Mozes, Viktorija, Gino, and Tommy sat on the edge of their chairs with interest.

"I went to visit him. When I showed him the documents, he started to tremble. After a few minutes, he calmed down. He agreed to talk to me under one condition, I told no one he gave me information. I agreed and assumed he meant no one outside of the five of us."

"The retired Trooper explained the Barrack Commander, at the time, directed him to close the homicide investigation based on the cause of death listed on the Death Certificate. He followed the command, but he put the note on the IR as you read. And these were the retired Trooper's exact words, 'The Catholic Barrack Commander directed me to close the case. The Catholic Barrack Commander didn't want the PSP to embarrass the Roman Catholic Cloth because, throughout Pennsylvania, it contributed too much money to the PSP Trooper's Benevolent Fund for that to happen.'

The retired Trooper then produced a leather-bound notebook, with numbered pages. He showed me his entry on page 150. He wrote, 'Homicide Investigation. Deceased Krisztina Olah. Suspicious death. Custodian Joseph Marks discovered the deceased hanged in her room immediately after visited by the Bishop and his three-person entourage from the diocese. The Barrack Commander ordered me to take that fact out of my report.'

That was all I found."

Mozes sat back in his chair. He took a deep breath, held it, and then slowly exhaled. Gino and Tommy also sat back in their chairs.

Tommy looked at Gino, then Joe, and finally to Mozes. "Are you okay, Mozes? This is a lot."

"Mozes, there was no other way to tell you," said Joe. "Sorry, you heard this from me."

"Joe, can you open an investigation on this?" asked Gino.

Showing himself as a grandmaster of police work, Joe gave the victim his due respect. He looked to Mozes and said, "Mozes, is it okay if I continue?"

"Yes, Joe. Please. I'm good. I want to hear it all."

Joe looked around the table and stopped at Gino.

"Well, I thought the same, Gino. My research disclosed the then PSP Barrack Commander, the custodian, and the then Bishop were dead. The diocese refused to give the names of the then Bishop's assistants because of the current litigation from the Pennsylvania Attorney General's office.

The only reason I have the hard facts is the retired Trooper is still alive. The notebook is the retired Trooper's CYA, his Cover Your Ass notebook. From his tremble, he will protect it until he dies. Even in retirement, he protects himself from the past corruption of some in the PSP command. I remember those days myself. No, Gino, there is nothing to do at this point. There are no criminal actions to file. The Roman Catholic Cloth gets away with murder. Sorry, Mozes. Sorry."

"Joe, I understand. I know how it goes for the investigators and the victims," replied Mozes. " Do you know where my mother's remains are?"

"No. That is something I just could not find. I agree with Gino, Estella may help. She just may know or may be able to direct us to someone else."

"Okay," said Mozes. "I think it's time to visit Estella. Let me pay the check, and we'll go."

"I took care of the check," said Tommy.

48   Intoxicated truth for repose

Mozes flicked his right turn signaled, eased the Porsche to the right, and started down the hill into *Mine 40*.

"I remember this hill," said Mozes.

Mozes operated the Porsche through the downhill S-turn to the straightaway into *'40'*.

"I think I'll take a cruise around before we go to the *Hotel*."

Mozes reminisced as he drove and said aloud.

"There's the tipple. The mine opening. These two large buildings. I never did know what they did in those buildings."

He slowed as he approached the site of the company store. When he saw only the concrete steps and sidewalk remained, he exclaimed, "The store is not here! What a shame."

He brought the Porsche to a stop as he came to the playground. He stared out to a macadam-paved lot overgrown with weeds. Some of the metal poles for the swings still stood. He felt a chill. His mind flashed back to his childhood, to the day the faceless, hallowed, figures first appeared to him.

Mozes thought to himself, "They don't appear now. Here. I'm here where they first appeared to me. They don't appear now."

Mozes looked about the interior of the Porsche; it was absent the figures.

He continued his thoughts, "I'm in control. I'm healing."

Mozes realized then and there, forty-three years after the first vision, he was healing. He renounced the hallowed figures. He renounced his past. Then, the aroma of Viktorija came over him. The sweet scent brought a huge smile to Mozes' face. He reached to Viktorija and took her hand and squeezed it tight. He held it for its healing power. Viktorija looked his way and smiled. She too knew he was healing.

Tommy, Gino, and Joe said nothing. They weren't three guys savvy to the ways of Psychiatry. They were just three gentlemen whose sound judgment told them Mozes was deep in thought. Therapeutic thought.

Still holding Viktorija's hand, Mozes eased the Porsche off. He turned left onto Third Street and slowly drove along the narrow street with cars lined on each side. Mozes steered through the intersection and continued to the top. There he slowed the Porsche as it moved by his childhood home on the left-hand side. He vaguely remembered the home, but he recognized the door and the front porch to the lower half of a coal company house that was his first home.

He eased the Porsche to a stop. Today he was not startled when he saw his mother and father seated on the old metal glider on the front porch. It was a childhood image, apparently still in his memory and resurrected today. Both parents displayed a pure contentment. His father sipped coffee from his favorite cup. Mother sat with her smile on her face; the smile that comforted Mozes so many times. They waved to Mozes and Mozes waved back as they slowly disappeared from the porch.

Viktorija watched Mozes wave in the direction of the empty porch. She looked to Mozes to offer her blue eyes for comfort if he wished.

Tommy, Gino, and Joe also watched Mozes wave in the direction of the empty porch. All three lowered their heads in respect and sympathy for Mozes. The three gentlemen said nothing; they let Mozes have his time.

Mozes eased away. He turned left at the alley and followed it to the top of Second Street, turned left again, and moved down Second Street to the intersection. He turned right, proceeded to the second intersection, and turned left.

As they passed house 934 on the left, with pride, Tommy reminisced to himself about his happy homestead. He wanted to tell Mozes that was where he lived and grew up. He did not. He did not want to distract Mozes from his healing. Tommy just stared and smiled to himself.

Mozes continued to the *40 Hotel*. He eased into the parking lot, parked the Porsche, turned it off, and everyone slowly slid out.

Gino broke the meditative silence.

"Mozes, if you don't want to go in, we understand. This is a lot of information for you today."

"Thank you, Gino. I need to go in. You all don't know how helpful this is for me. I want to go in."

"Okay. This way Mozes."

Mozes reached back and took Viktorija by her hand and ushered her close to him. He followed Gino up the steps and through the front door to the bar area. Tommy and Joe followed.

Gino looked around and found Estella seated on a stool deep in the bar. As he started to walk to the far end, Gino looked back to Mozes and said, "Come on."

Still holding Viktorija's hand, Mozes followed Gino. Tommy and Joe followed Mozes.

A gruff voice sounded, "What the hell you doing here?

Gino continued to move forward.

"Estella," he said. "This is Mozes. He's the gentleman who needs your help."

"Yes," said Estella

Gino looked back to Mozes and extended his right hand to guide Mozes to Estella. Mozes moved closer.

"Estella, this is Mozes. Mozes Olah. Mozes, this is Estella."

Estella quickly rose from her bar stool, moved to Mozes, and gave him a big hug. She pushed back from Mozes.

"Do you remember me?" asked Estella. "No. No way. You were young. That was so long ago."

Mozes replied, "No madam. I don't remember you. Sorry. These gentlemen say you may be able to help me with my family history. My mother."

"I can do that. What do you want to know?"

"Where is my mother buried?"

"The Hungarian cemetery up on the hill in Windber."

"Thank you."

"How did you know my mother?"

"She and your father came in here, from time to time. Sit down Mozes."

Estella looked to the entourage and announced.

"You all sit-down. Let me get you all a beer."

Estella moved behind the bar and drew five drafts. She placed one in front of each. Estella noticed Tommy and exclaimed, "Hey there! Tommy! How are you?"

"Fine, thank you."

"I haven't seen you for years. What are you doing hanging out with Gino? You two. Now that's trouble waiting to happen. Is the FBI interested in this too? A little late for that, I think."

Estella turned and retrieved a bottle of whiskey from the display shelf on the back bar. She reached out with her other hand and snatched six shot glasses, turned back and set them up on the bar. With the ease of a long time, experienced, bartender, Estella poured each shot glass full and did not lose a drop. She set the whiskey bottle down and slid a shot glass of whiskey to each. She picked up her whiskey shot and raised it in the air.

"To Krisztina and Mozes. May they rest in peace."

She threw the shot back and slammed her empty glass on the bar. Mozes, Viktorija, Tommy, Gino, and Joe did the same.

"Mozes was your father. Yes, Krisztina and Mozes, good people. The best. What happened to your mother wasn't right. It just wasn't right. And you father. Murdered. Those bastards just didn't talk. They didn't come forward. They didn't want to oppose the church. The diocese. They feared the diocese would close their ethnic churches. They're all dead now. In hell, I hope. Bastards."

"Where was my father buried?"

"Mozes, his body never came out of the mine. There was no body to bury. A few of my patrons told me the murderers threw his body into one of the abandon-mined shafts as the Bishop ordered. The Bishop wanted the body to rot. He wanted the smell of death to be a warning to anyone who thought about coming forward to the police. And the Bishop didn't want your father to have a church burial. That was so painful for your mother. So, painful."

Estella paused to control her emotions.

Shocked by the truth, Mozes slowly lowered his beer to the bar. He lowered his head and tears started to roll down his cheeks. Mozes reached his left hand inside his suit jacket and retrieved a handkerchief monogrammed **MO.** He dabbed his eyes and wiped his checks.

Tommy, Gino, and Joe did not move; the three mesmerized by the tale of murder. Viktorija gently rubbed the nape of Mozes' neck. They all let Mozes have his time.

Estella finally broke the silence.

"No one should have suffered a wretched youth as you did, Mozes. They stole your innocence. The Roman Catholic Cloth stole your innocence. It was painful for me to tell you all this. Even your Aunt Llona didn't know everything."

Mozes jerked his head up and looked to Estella, "You know my Aunt Llona.?"

"Yes. You were lucky you had Aunt Llona. I met her when she visited your mother. They would all come in here. And she came to get you. Your neighbors on Third Street brought you here when your mother heard the State Police were coming to take her away. The police had a commitment order. Your mother feared for your safety, and she didn't want you in a foster home. I hid you out in the hotel until Llona came to pick you up late that night. And that commitment order was bullshit. Someone coerced the doctor at the company hospital to sign it. There wasn't anything wrong with your mother. You heard me, Mozes; there was nothing wrong with your mother.

Estella paused, sipped her beer, and continued.

"Mozes, your parents loved you. They loved you. What happened to you was wrong. The abuse right in the center of the church was an atrocity. The diocese wanted to get all three of you, to kill all three of you. They feared your mother and father would go to the newspaper with the information. The diocese controlled everything in this area except the owner of the local newspaper, a Jewish guy. The diocese thought since he was not Catholic he would write an article or direct an investigative news story about the diocese, about the atrocities perpetuated by the Roman Catholic Cloth. The Bishop didn't want that exposure."

"Estella, what about my father. Did he have family here? In the area, somewhere?" asked Mozes

"No, Mozes. He came to Windber from Hungry to work in the mine. Rumor was, he was running from the law in Hungry. He was wanted for murder. Allegedly, he killed the savage that raped and murdered his sister. Again, that was all rumor. But he had no family here."

Tommy, Gino, and Joe shook their heads when they heard the rumor of Mozes' father's past. The three looked at each other. They did not have to say what they thought – How much more calamity was in this family?

Everyone sat in the eerie silence within the walls of the *40 Hotel*. Walls that held over a hundred years of intoxicated truth. Some of the intoxicated reality now passed to Mozes for his repose.

49   "Most pihenünk, béke Anya."

With Viktorija at his side, Mozes stood in silence. He stared down at a simple, flat, grave marker flushed with the earth. It was bronze colored with lighter gold like raised trim and lettering. The severely, simple inscription read:

Krisztina Olah
Born 1948
Died 1984

Mozes and Viktorija knelt, genuflected and said a short prayer in silence. They genuflected again. Mozes leaned forward, placed his right hand on the grave marker, and softly said, **"Now we rest in peace, Mother."**

He leaned back and slowly rose. He assisted Viktorija as she rose.

Mozes reached his left hand into his right, inside, suit jacket, pocket. He retrieved a primly folded, ironed, white, handkerchief monogrammed **MO**. He dabbed his eyes and dried his checks. He offered it to Viktorija. She took it and dabbed her eyes too then handed the handkerchief back to Mozes.

With the handkerchief in his left hand, Mozes knelt back down and laid the now tear damp, handkerchief atop the simple, flat, grave marker. He strategically placed his right hand on the marker. Today, Mozes found himself in the company of a fair Windber lady in need of his emotional support. He put a small stone on the handkerchief, which left **MO** prominently displayed in the secrecy.

A gentle breeze swayed the trees as Mozes stood up. His body palpitated and he felt a warm, gentle hug. He was not spooked; he knew who it was.

Mozes also felt a release of pressure at the nape of his neck. He was aware it announced his mind was void of mental stress. It mediated the end to the pain in his head. It announced the visions were renounced and his faith in himself professed. It announced a new-found belief in himself and the end of the dreams of murders. Freed to the comfort of the lady he desired and who coveted him. Freed to dote Viktorija, Mozes smiled largely.

Mozes stepped to Viktorija's left side. He reached out his right-hand and strategically placed it in the middle of Viktorija's lower back atop the mark. With a soft, gentle touch, Mozes sauntered away from the past with Viktorija at his side. Today, the graveside visit ushered the two into all their tomorrows.

Finally, today, Mozes did not pull away. Today, he leaned into Viktorija and whispered, "The awkwardness is gone. I'm ready."

Viktorija looked to Mozes and smiled gleeful content. She leaned into Mozes and hugged tighter. She received the response she desired, Mozes did not pull away.

The Beginning.